I HEARD FOOTSTEPS OUTSIDE. I COULD SEE SOMEONE'S outline through the translucent fiberglass. I heard the clank of metal against metal. Then nothing but receding steps.

I smashed my shoulder into the door. The greenhouse shook, but the latch held. "Who's out there?" I said. No one was. Not anymore.

I turned and surveyed the greenhouse. Wasps filled the airspace—yellow jackets, golden polistes, mud daubers. And somewhere off at the edge of my vision I caught a glimpse of something bigger, something that was black and orange and altogether too frightening to focus on.

Buzzing came from overhead. My right hand tickled. I looked down. A golden polistes rested atop my knuckle. I flailed my arms. As the wasp flew off I dove under the bench. Up above I could see the big black and orange thing, could hear the hum of its wings as it searched for a fat, tasty mammal to sting.

Suddenly, as if at a signal from the barely seen giant, half a dozen winged creatures surrounded me. . . .

The Cactus Club KILLINGS

A Joe Portugal Mystery

NATHAN WALPOW

A DELL BOOK

Published by
Dell Publishing
a division of
Random House, Inc.
1540 Broadway
New York, New York 10036

ISBN: 0-440-23491-3

Printed in the United States of America

Published simultaneously in Canada

May 1999

10   9   8   7   6   5   4   3   2   1

OPM

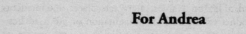

For Andrea

Acknowledgments

Thanks to Bill Relling for his advice on the manuscript, and for convincing me I knew more about writing mysteries than I thought I did.

Thanks to Paul Bishop for help with the cop stuff. If I got it wrong, it's my fault.

Thanks to the members of the Cacti_etc Internet mailing list for sharing their expertise on euphorbia toxicity. And to the members of the Sunset Succulent Society for inspiration. And to Kathy Lord for the ace copyediting.

Finally, thanks to my agent, Janet Manus, for selling this book; to my editor, Jacquie Miller, for buying it; and to both, for their excellent guidance.

1

Ultimately, it was the wasp's fault that I plunged Gina into the pool of insecticide. But maybe I shared the responsibility. I could have waited a couple of days, until it was time to go over to Brenda's anyway to feed the canaries, to find out just which variety of *Euphorbia viguieri* I had. Gina would have been at work, helping people with too much disposable income decide which overpriced furniture to dispose of it on. The Cygon would have soaked into the ground, rendered relatively harmless.

I could have waited, but I didn't.

The sequence of events culminating in Gina's toxic bath began Memorial Day afternoon, around four-thirty, the end of the beginning of another sunshiny Los Angeles summer. An out-of-season deluge the night before had rendered the air smog-free and the ground swampy. I was out back, nosing around my collection of cacti and other succulent plants, killing time until Gina arrived with the Jackie Chan videos essential to our planned evening of comedic mayhem and take-out Thai.

I cruised by the winter-growers on the bench outside the greenhouse. Old Sam Oliver kept telling me that, since

I lived on the relatively cool Westside, if I kept watering the pelargoniums and sarcocaulons—the so-called succulent geraniums—they'd stay green all year round. But they weren't having any of it, dropping waves of leaves between the slats of the bench and onto the redwood bark below. As if to mock both Sam and me, the rain had accelerated the defoliation rate.

I entered the greenhouse and noticed my *Euphorbia viguieri* was loaded with spiderwebs. I had no problem with a living room that hadn't been vacuumed in weeks, and my pickup truck resembled the aftermath of a hurricane, but anything in the greenhouse was a different story. I started at the crown of big oval leaves and worked my way down the two-foot stem, removing webs and sucked-dry insects from the profusion of gray spines that would make you think the plant was a cactus if you didn't know better. When I got down to soil level, I realized the label was missing. A quick search failed to turn it up.

One might wonder why I couldn't just make another, since I knew which species it was. But I didn't remember the variety. There were four, all impossible to spell or pronounce, and for the life of me I couldn't recall which one I had. I could look in Rauh's Madagascar book, but experience had shown me no matter how many photos they put in the books, none of them would match my plant. No, this would require a trip to Brenda's. My viguieri was originally a piece she'd accidentally knocked off her gigantic specimen; I just had to bring it over and match it up.

"Joe? You in there?" I poked my head out of the greenhouse. Gina stood just outside the back door with tapes in hand. She'd let herself into the house, just like she always did. She had on a sleeveless yellow blouse and denim shorts and sandals, and her hair was carelessly pinned up. She looked gorgeous—just like she always did—and, just like always, I wouldn't tell her so unless she needed to hear it, which was typically about once a month.

"What'd you get?" I asked.

"Crime Story and *Rumble in the Bronx."*

"Crime Story?" I shut the greenhouse door and headed for the house. "Didn't we hate that one?"

"Yeah. The one with no comedy and all the gratuitous violence."

"As opposed to the essential violence in the others. Remind me, why did we want to see it again?"

"I thought we'd give it another chance. Maybe we're missing something. Maybe there's some inscrutable Oriental way of viewing it we haven't figured out yet. If we still hate it we can skip right to *Rumble."* A slight pause. "When was the last time you shaved?"

I rubbed my hand along my chin. It did feel a little furry. "Last Thursday, I think. For the Subaru audition. I planned on doing it again Wednesday, for the Olsen's shoot. Why? Are you ashamed to be seen with me?"

"I wonder how you'd look with a beard."

"Just like I did sixteen years ago. You hated it, remember? Among other things, you said it tickled your—"

"Of course I remember. But tickling me isn't an issue anymore, and with the way your face has filled out I think you'd look good with one now."

"I think I'd look like a rabbi with one now. Besides, people with beards don't get commercials."

We went inside and into the living room. Gina slid *Crime Story* into the VCR and moved toward the couch. "Don't sit down yet," I said.

She gave me a dirty look. She has this sixth sense about when I'm about to propose something stupid. "Why not?"

"We have to go over to Brenda's first."

"What for?"

"To check on the canaries."

The look got dirtier. "She just left for Madagascar, what, a couple of hours ago?"

"Actually, I'm not sure her flight's even taken off yet."

"So why would the canaries need checking on?"

"Maybe she forgot to feed them before she left."

"She loves those damned birds. We can assume they've been fed." She pointedly sat down on the couch. "Therefore, there's no reason to go over there now." She cocked her head. "This has something to do with plants, doesn't it?"

"No. I'm just worried the birds might be freaking out because she's not there and—"

She jumped up and wagged a finger at me. "You want to wander around her greenhouse, don't you? You want to prowl around in there without her breathing down your neck. She's not gone an hour and—"

"It's the canaries, I swear."

"Your nose is growing."

"Okay, it's not the canaries."

"It's the plants, isn't it?"

"Yeah. But it's not some prurient wandering mania. I have a very specific need." I told her about the missing label.

"And this can't wait a day or two?"

"If I don't figure it out now, it'll bug me constantly and I won't fully enjoy Jackie. I'll sit and sulk and make you miserable too."

"I will never understand plant freaks."

"No one else does either. Come on, she's only ten minutes away; we'll be back in half an hour."

She gave in. She always does, like I always do when she wants to go for ice cream at one in the morning. We piled into my Datsun pickup and drove over to Brenda's. We walked around back and carefully picked our way over the soggy ground toward the greenhouse.

This brings us to the wasp. It came out of nowhere and dive-bombed my head. I reacted like I usually do when a wasp shows up. I took a flying leap.

If one were to list the adjectives most often applied to me over the preceding ten years, since I gave up the theater world, *lazy* would probably rank number one. *Lacking direction* would be way up there. But one that I'd never heard, in all my forty-four years, was *well-coordinated*. Which helps explain why the space I took my flying leap into was the one Gina already occupied, why my feet slipped on the muddy turf, and why, when I grabbed for whatever was handy, it was Gina's arm. Three death-defying seconds later she toppled backward and dropped hind-end-first into a big puddle reeking of Cygon.

She unleashed a stream of Spanish invective. I knew it was invective because Gina speaks the tongue of her forebears only when she's cursing.

"Don't let it get in your eyes," I said, trying to help her up without getting the smelly liquid on myself.

"Goddamn it, Joe, that's about the only orifice it isn't in." She managed to get to her feet. Her eyes swept down, surveying the damage. "My shorts are ruined."

"I'll buy you some new ones."

She wrinkled her nose. "This stuff really stinks. What is it?"

"Cygon. Brenda must have done a drench right before she left."

"Sounds deadly."

"To mealybugs, scale, and the dreaded red spider mite."

"How about humans?"

"It's a systemic. It has to get inside you to do any damage."

"Have I mentioned my orifices?"

"Good point. You'd better use Brenda's shower. Come on."

We hustled around to the front door. I had some trouble with the lock. Gina jabbed me in the small of the back. "I'm dying of insecticide here."

We passed through Brenda's jumbled living room. She'd left one of the barred windows open and a fan going for the birds, but it was still stuffy. Scores of botanical texts, dozens of books on Madagascar, and an assortment of erotica competed for space on the mismatched bookshelves. Native artifacts, heavy on the zebu horn, filled the gaps. The curtains were a colorful print she'd brought back on one of her forays.

Canary cage number one stood on a brass stand in the corner. Muck and Mire chirped a greeting. "Hi, guys," I replied.

"Can you talk to the birds later?" Gina said. "This stuff is eating away at my skin."

We went down the hallway and into the bedroom. A brass bed with a gauzy blue canopy dominated it. In the far corner, next to the computer table, a vertical metal framework lined with chicken wire divided off the three-by-three area that was home to the rest of Brenda's canaries: Groucho, Chico, Harpo, Zeppo, Gummo, and Brillo. "Go on into the bathroom," I said. "I'll find you a robe or something."

"Okay."

I turned to the walk-in closet and pulled the door open. A hint of Brenda's perfume wafted out. Memories of evenings spent under that blue canopy flickered through my mind and brought a smile to my lips. I stepped in and searched for a bathrobe, but none turned up. "Hey, Gi," I said. "No robe. Is there one in there?"

She didn't answer. I exited the closet and yelled at the closed bathroom door. "Gi? Is her bathrobe in there?"

Still no response. I got concerned. Maybe she'd slipped and cracked her skull open. "Gina?"

Nothing. I rushed toward the bathroom. I'd nearly

reached it when the door opened. Gina stood there wearing a stricken expression. She seemed smaller somehow. Shrunken.

"What?" I said.

She didn't reply, merely stared back over her shoulder toward the tub. For some reason I thought there was a dead animal in there. A squirrel had gotten in and starved to death, or a wild bird had come to visit its domestic buddies and bashed its head in on the sliding shower door. But then I, too, looked over Gina's shoulder, and that was when I saw my friend Brenda Belinski.

She wore one of the loose tank tops she favored, a green and purple stripe. Whatever else she had on lay hidden behind the sliding door's frosted glass. Her skin was waxy and her lips pale. Her auburn hair hung limply against the white fiberglass of the tub. Her eyes were closed tight, as if squeezing away some awful sight.

But it was her mouth that grabbed my attention. Rather, what was in her mouth. It might have been weirdly erotic under other circumstances, some Lewis Carroll rendition of fellatio, if she'd exhibited even the slightest hint of life. But she was deathly still. And the four inches of *Euphorbia abdelkuri* jutting out between her lips was merely obscene.

2

Gina finally found her voice. "I thought, why not start the water first, because you never know how long it'll take to get warm, so I slid the door open and there she was. Is she dead?"

"I think so," I said. "I've never seen a dead person before."

I squeezed past Gina, knelt on the tile floor, slowly reached my hand into the tub. I carefully touched the euphorbia, avoiding the congealing yellow sap on the stem and on Brenda's face. Euphorbia sap's not to be trifled with. Depending on the species, it can be anything from a mild irritant to fish poison.

The plant, an inch or so in diameter, resembled a melting candle as much as it did a member of the vegetable kingdom. Its skin was gray, mottled with hints of white and dull green. No leaves, spines, or branches broke its knobby surface.

I hesitated, then lay my fingers on Brenda's arm. It felt like an arm. A little cool, maybe. I don't know what I expected.

I pressed the back of my hand across her cheek. Then my fingertips between her breasts, feeling for a heartbeat I knew I wouldn't find. "She's dead," I said.

Gina whipped her head around. "I heard a noise out there."

"One of the birds, probably."

"It could be the killer."

"What makes you think there's a killer?"

"You think she choked herself with that thing?"

"Good point. We'd better call 911." I stood, took one more look at Brenda, and pulled the shower door shut. Pushed Gina out of the bathroom and closed the door behind us.

"You're touching things," she said. "On cop shows they always say you shouldn't touch things."

I nudged her through the bedroom and into the kitchen. I took the phone down off the wall, sniffed the air, put the phone back. "You still need to wash that Cygon off."

"Oh, fine," she said. "Why don't I just march back in there, nudge Brenda out of the way, and take a nice relaxing shower?" She dropped into a wooden chair. "I don't think so. Not with that cactus sticking out of her mouth."

"It's not a cactus. It's a euphorbia. Different family entirely."

"Spare me the lecture and call the police."

"Right." I grabbed the phone again, hit 9, caught another whiff, hung up. "You *have* to get that stuff off you."

"I don't want to leave the scene of the crime."

"And I don't want to be dealing with *two* dead bodies. Go next door. This old lady lives there, Mrs. Kwiatkowski. I gave her a sansevieria once. You know, a mother-in-law's tongue. She loves me. Tell her you have to use her shower. Tell her Joey the Cactus Boy sent you. Wait a sec, I'll get you some clothes."

I lurched back into the bedroom and found some sweats. Picked the underwear drawer on my second try and pulled out a flowery blue one that seemed like it ought to work. But Brenda's bras would be far too big; Gina'd have to go without. I tossed a look at the bathroom door before escaping back to the kitchen.

I pushed Gina out the front door, dialed 911, and immediately got put on hold. "Jeez," I told any canaries within earshot. "What if the victim weren't dead yet? They would be by the time these bozos answered."

"I heard that, sir," said a female voice at the other end.

"Excuse me. Just venting. I'd like to report a dead body."

"Are you sure it's dead, sir?"

"Just about. I'm not an authority. Can you get the police out here?"

"I'll have to send the paramedics as well."

"It's probably not necessary."

"We have to send the paramedics, sir. It's policy."

"Whatever you say. You know best." I gave her my name and a bunch of other information and sat down in the living room with the canaries to await the LAPD's arrival.

🌵

The first policeman to arrive was an African-American man about as big as Darth Vader. Before I could embarrass myself by spewing something about basketball he identified himself as Officer Benton, determined who I was, and came in. His partner followed. Her uniform was too tight and her hair too blond and her name tag identified her as Jones.

The paramedics showed up right on the cops' heels and piled into the bathroom. One came back out a minute later. "She's dead, all right."

"We'll have to call Homicide," said Officer Jones.

"Sure," I said. "I'm sure Brenda won't mind if you use the phone."

But Jones, after tossing me a dirty look, went out to call from their patrol car, returning a minute or two later to announce, "Casillas and Burns are on their way."

Benton nodded. "You didn't touch anything, did you?" he asked me.

"The body, to see if she was dead."

"Shouldn't have touched the body."

"How the hell else was I supposed to tell if she was dead?"

The front door swung open. There stood Gina, carrying what I assumed were her clothes in a plastic garbage bag and looking terribly uncomfortable in a pink polyester jogging suit. Brenda's sweats lay over her arm. "Mrs. Kwiatkowski made me," she said, plucking at a sleeve. "Said she'd grown tired of the color and that it suited me perfectly."

I went over and checked her out. "You still smell a little."

"I stood under the shower for fifteen minutes," she said. "Mrs. K. kvetched about me using all the hot water, so I got out."

"Who's this?" asked Officer Jones. I explained. We all stood around staring at each other. I picked up a magazine. "Don't touch that," Benton said. I put it down and went to sit. He gave me a look. I stayed on my feet.

Ten minutes later a short Hispanic man in a navy blue suit strode through the front door. A solid-looking African-American woman followed immediately behind. They quizzed Benton and Jones before heading for the bathroom. When they came back fifteen minutes later, the woman returned to the patrol officers, and the man came over to Gina and me. He looked to be about fifty, with a complexion a shade darker olive than Gina's. Most of the hair was gone from the top of his head; what remained was near black. His deep brown eyes wore half-glasses and had that seen-everything look, and the bags under them were grayish.

He silently inspected me, with that look I get a lot where

somebody thinks they've seen me before. He caught me staring at his tie, a maroon one patterned with little cannons. I caught him catching me, and we played eye games until I looked away. He'd obviously played before.

The woman walked up. "I'm Detective Burns; this is Detective Casillas. I'll be the primary investigator on this case." Like she was telling us she going to be our waitress at California Pizza Kitchen. She was in her late thirties, I guessed, and wore a tan linen pantsuit over a white blouse, and from the way it fit and the way she moved, you could tell she took care of herself. She had superlative posture, and that made her seem taller than her height, which was no more than five-four. Eyes nearly black in a long face. A strong mouth. Her black hair was medium length, her earrings small gold hoops.

Casillas stood poised with a pocket-size leather-bound notepad and one of those pens you buy for $9.95 at the mall, the ones with a wood inlay that look like a great deal until you examine them closely. Burns had a more utilitarian pad but an identical pen. Maybe they'd gotten the quantity discount.

Burns consulted her notes. "You're Joseph Portugal?"

"Uh-huh."

"Tell me about the dead woman."

"Can't we call her something besides 'the dead woman'?"

"Yeah," Gina said. "It gives me the creeps."

Casillas butted in. His voice was high and reedy. "Homicide gives everybody the creeps, Miss—" He checked his book. "Miss Vela."

Two men and a woman popped through the door, carrying cases and cameras and other items I assumed were crime-scene paraphernalia. Burns directed them to the bathroom. Casillas said, "Okay, talk to us."

"What about?" I asked. Stupid, but I was nervous.

"Jesus," Casillas said. "Are we going to have an attitude? Look, we can do this here or we can do it at the station. Most people'd rather not go to the station."

"Joe, be nice to the nice detectives," Gina said.

"If you insist, dear."

"Detective Casillas," Burns said. "Why don't you interview Ms. Vela in the kitchen?"

He threw her a slightly dirty look and led Gina off. Burns turned back to me. "Go ahead, please."

"Brenda taught at UCLA. Professor of botany. Been there over twenty years."

"Seems young for that."

"She was older than she looked. She'll be—she would have been—fifty next month."

Burns made notes in her little book. When she wrote, her tongue stuck out the corner of her mouth like a three-year-old's. "Go on."

"She was supposed to be on her way to Madagascar," I said. "I was taking care of her birds."

"What's in Madagascar?"

"Brenda had a thing for everything Madagascan. Or Malagasy, to use the right adjective, which few people do. I'm babbling, aren't I?"

"You're doing fine. Please don't be nervous, Mr. Portugal."

"Sorry. I've never known anyone who was murdered before." I took a deep breath, let it out. "She first went to Madagascar twenty years or so ago and has been there maybe a dozen times since. Recently it's been yearly. She loves the people, the culture . . . and the plants. She was real active in the succulent world."

"The succulent world?"

"Succulent-plant collectors. You know, like cacti."

"Like the one in her mouth."

I shook my head. "That's not a cactus. It's *Euphorbia*

abdelkuri. Different family entirely. That plant's more closely related to a poinsettia than to a cactus."

"Where's it from?"

"Africa, probably. Euphorbs grow all over the world, but most of the tall succulent ones are from Africa." I told her a little about the plants and their nasty sap. Then I said, "Wait a minute."

"What is it, Mr. Portugal?"

"Brenda has the biggest abdelkuri I've ever seen. Six or seven branches, over three feet tall. I wonder if that's a piece of it."

"Where is this plant?"

"Should be in her greenhouse."

"Show me."

I led her out back and into the greenhouse, which was jammed with euphorbias of every shape, size, and origin. I spotted the parent of my *E. viguieri* but didn't think taking the time to check the label would sit well with Detective Burns. A bit later I tracked down the abdelkuri. None of it was missing. "That's funny," I said.

"What is?"

"That Brenda would have another abdelkuri around. She was always complaining how she didn't have enough space in the greenhouse. So whenever she got a plant that was better than one she already had of the same species, she would get rid of the old one. She'd bring them into club meetings sometimes and auction them off and give the money to the club. So maybe—nah, it seems too stupid."

"Let me be the judge of that, Mr. Portugal."

"Maybe the killer brought the plant with him. Or her."

"Why would he or she do that?"

"How do I know?" I laughed weakly. "I'm not the killer."

"No one said you were." She jotted something down. "You mentioned a club. Which club would that be?"

"The Culver City Cactus Club. She was the president."

"And you're a member of this club."

"I'm the secretary."

"And Miss Vela?"

"No. She's thinks plant people are crazy."

We went back inside. A skinny Asian guy walked by, carrying what looked like a giant meat thermometer. "What's that?" I asked.

Burns glanced over. "Liver thermometer. To determine time of death."

"They're going to stick that in . . . in . . ."

She nodded. "Anything else you can tell me about the victim?"

"Huh? Oh, sorry. Let me see. She was in charge of the Kawamura Conservatory, up at UCLA. Second-biggest succulent collection in southern California, after the Huntington."

"What was the purpose of the victim's current trip to Madagascar?"

"She was looking for new plants. A lot of the species there don't grow anywhere else, and there's still lots of new ones to be discovered. Lots of euphorbias there. She was also going to check up on habitat destruction. They're really tearing up the place there, and lots of plants—and animals—are endangered. And she was going to look into plant smuggling. Brenda was active in trying to enforce CITES."

"What's that?"

It took me a few seconds. "Convention on something, something in Endangered Species. International Trade, that's it. It's a treaty concerning commerce in endangered plants. Animals too."

"People smuggle plants?"

"I hear it's big business, Detective. There's people out there making a lot of money smuggling plants. Brenda could have stepped on some toes. Maybe they came after her. You might want to follow up on that."

She let me have a little smile. I was glad I was amusing her. "We'll be following up on everything you tell us. Do you have the names of any of these people?"

I shook my head. "I think they're mostly Europeans. Germans. Czechs, maybe."

"Can you think of anybody else who might have had a reason to kill Ms. Belinski?"

"No one comes to mind." I shrugged. "But Brenda could be abrasive. She would get really irritated when people didn't know stuff she thought they should, or when she thought they were wasting her time. Maybe she pissed somebody off enough to . . ." I let it trail off.

She wrote another few words. "What do you do for a living, Mr. Portugal?"

"I'm an actor."

Her expression grew dubious. I knew what she was thinking. Everyone in Los Angeles claimed to be an actor. Unless they said they were a screenwriter. Or both. I waited for her to ask what she might have seen me in, but she refrained. "How well did you know the victim?"

"She was a friend. Probably my second-best."

"A lover?"

I looked in her eyes. No prurient interest there, just a cop doing her job. "A long time ago."

"How long?"

"Four years."

"Who ended it?"

"She did, more or less. Look, Detective, that was four years ago. You think I waited around four years for the perfect opportunity to stick a plant down her throat?"

"Any other relationships you know of?"

"A few."

"Names?"

A gave her a couple. She wrote them down. "Any family?"

"My dad. He lives in the Fairfax district."

"I meant the victim. Does she have any family to be informed?"

"Oh. Sorry. Her parents are dead. She's got a sister, but they weren't close. She lives in Wisconsin, I think, some university town."

After a few more questions she said, "That's all for now. We'll probably be looking you up, but in the meantime . . ." She gave me a pair of business cards. I checked them over. Her first name was Alberta; his was Hector.

Casillas was done with Gina too. We headed for the door. I stopped and got Officer Jones's attention. "What about the birds?" I asked.

"What about them?"

"Who's going to feed them?"

"I don't know. Hey, Detective Casillas, what about the birds?"

He regarded her balefully over the top of his glasses. "What about 'em?"

"They'll need to be fed," I said. "I could take Muck and Mire with me, of course, but the ones in the bedroom—"

Casillas rushed up and waggled a surprisingly well-manicured finger under my nose. "You're not taking anything out of here. They could be evidence."

"How can birds be evidence?"

"Maybe they saw something. Maybe we should take them down to the station and show them mug shots. Hey, Benton."

"Yeah?"

"Round up all the birds and bring them—"

"Come on," I said.

"You got a problem?"

"You'll traumatize them."

"So what? They're only birds."

"But—"

"You eat chicken, don't you?"

"That's different. That's—"

"Keep your pants on. Someone will take care of the birds."

"You sure?"

"Sure I'm sure. Tell you what. Because you've been so cooperative, when we get the guy you can take them home."

"Me? What am I going to do with eight canaries?"

"How the hell do I know? That's your problem."

Outside, yellow crime-scene tape roped off a portion of the front yard. Beyond it a crowd of onlookers gaped, Mrs. Kwiatkowski among them, in a chartreuse outfit identical to Gina's but for the color. We waved at her, made our way to my pickup, and drove away from the scene of the crime.

3

THE JACARANDA HAD BLOOMED LATE. EVEN ON MEMORIAL Day a purple haze billowed over every block. Off to the west, ruffled clouds reflected shades of violet and pink. The air, stripped of pollutants by the previous night's rain, smelled strangely clean. Kids played ball, while their parents watched them with half an eye. All was right with the world, except someone I knew was dead.

We stopped at Hurry Curry to pick up a couple of combination plates and got back to my place around eight-thirty. The motion-detector light in the driveway didn't go on. Whoever'd offed Brenda had disconnected it. He was lying in wait for me. He had a master plan to kill off all the succulent-plant collectors in Los Angeles in order to win all the trophies at the Intercity show.

I made it through that fantasy and we went inside, where I jumped in the shower while Gina dished out the food. I was rinsing off when I heard her say, "Anybody dead in here?"

I poked my head around the shower curtain. She'd ditched Mrs. Kwiatkowski's polyester and had on my Procol

Harum T-shirt and my purple sweatpants, all bunched around her calves. "Very funny," I said.

"What do you want to drink?"

"A beer," I said. "Beer goes good with Indian food."

She nodded. "I'll have one too."

"You don't drink beer."

"I'll make an exception." She disappeared back into the kitchen.

Five minutes later we were arrayed on the couch. I sniffed. Either the Cygon smell had worn off or I'd gotten used to it.

Gina's method of distributing our food had been to place each Styrofoam container on a plate and cut off the tops. While we ate we exchanged summaries of our interviews, after which she said, "Do you really think she was murdered?"

I downed a forkful of lentil curry, took a sip of my beer. It was the only thing I could taste. "Even given Brenda's fondness for cylindrical objects in her mouth, I don't think she put this one in."

"Whoever did picked a particularly weird one."

"It is more bizarre than most, isn't it?" I got up, took *Succulents: The Illustrated Dictionary* down from the bookcase, and leafed through until I found *E. abdelkuri*. "Uh-oh."

"What?"

"It says here it's from Socotra."

"Why is that an uh-oh?"

"I told that lady detective it was probably from Africa."

"I don't think being wrong about that is a felony. You did say 'probably.' Where is Socotra, by the way?"

"The Middle East somewhere, I think." I grabbed an atlas and riffled pages. "It's an island off the coast of Somalia, although it looks like officially it's part of Yemen."

"That's more or less Africa."

I was already back in the succulent book. "This also points out that the latex is yellow, which I noticed when we found Brenda."

"Latex?"

"Sap."

"So what if it's yellow?"

"Most euphorbia sap is white."

"Is this significant?"

"How the hell do I know? I'm just making observations."

"You're supposed to know these things. I'll give you another chance. Do you think she was poisoned to death, or did she strangle on that thing? Or what?"

I shrugged. "We succulent people are always talking about how euphorbias are poisonous. How you shouldn't get the sap—"

"Latex."

"—in your eyes or in an open cut. This book makes a point of saying abdelkuri's is poisonous." I scanned some other euphorbia entries. "It doesn't point that out on any of the others. So maybe abdelkuri's is especially bad. I wonder if the killer knew that." I put the book away and returned to the couch. "Gi, I don't have any idea how it killed her. Maybe it got in her stomach and was digested and poisoned her blood, or maybe it just closed up her breathing passages, or—"

"Enough already," she said. "The whole thing gives me the creeps."

"To quote our friend Casillas, 'Homicide gives everybody the creeps.'"

I ripped off some *nan*, wadded it into my mouth. A little burned piece tumbled from my lips and fell in my lap. I brushed it off, pursued it into the crack between the cushions, pushed it out of sight. "You know, it's hard for me to deal with the fact that somebody's dead."

Gina nodded.

"Somebody I knew."

Another nod.

"Somebody I slept with."

"I know exactly what you mean."

"You do? How could you?" I went to the kitchen and returned with a container of Cherry Garcia and a couple of spoons. Gina'd taken her shoes off and propped her feet on the coffee table. She'd turned on the TV; Jean-Claude Van Damme was doing the splits to avoid some menace or other.

I flopped down next to her, handed her a spoon, dug in with my own. My taste buds were back on duty. I took another bite and turned over the container. "So who do you think did it?" I asked.

She ran the spoon around the inside of the container, removing little overlooked driblets. Ever precise, my Gina. "My bet's on those CITES people. I don't trust those Germans."

"Bigot."

"Okay, I'm kidding about the Germans. But not the rest. Plant smugglers makes sense to me."

"Plant smugglers makes more sense to you than one of Brenda's boyfriends?"

"Call me a romantic."

"You think an angry plant smuggler is more romantic than an angry boyfriend?"

"Romance ain't what it used to be."

I grabbed back the ice cream, dug out a couple of chunks of chocolate, let them roll around my tongue. "Tomorrow night's the CCCC meeting," I said. "I'm going to have to tell all those people about Brenda."

"Won't they read about it in the paper?"

"Will it be in the paper?"

"She was pretty well-known in her field, wasn't she? It

seems like the kind of thing you see on page one of the *Times* Metro section. PLANT KILLS UCLA PROFESSOR, something like that."

She shoved me toward the end of the couch. Wouldn't give up until I was squashed up against the arm. She lay her head in my lap, fixed her gaze on the TV. "Maybe one of the club people offed Brenda."

"Yeah, right."

She sprang back to a sitting position and looked me in the eye. "No, really. God knows there are enough weird characters in that club. Maybe one of them got a bug up their ass about something Brenda did and euphorbiated her."

"Come on, Gi. They're harmless."

"That's what all murderers want you to think. I'll bet it was one of them."

"Nah. It was plant smugglers or a spurned lover or some nonaffiliated euphorbia fetishist."

"You're no fun." She gestured with her spoon. "Is there any more?"

I peered into the ice cream container. Three spoonfuls remained. "Here, finish it."

A little later she roused herself and got her stuff together to go home. I walked her out to her Volvo, gave her a hug, and slammed the car door behind her. She jammed the transmission into drive and blasted off into the night. I went back in and to bed.

🌵

I woke at seven to the sound of theremin music next door. The people there had moved in three years before, although which of the never-ending stream of slightly seedy characters actually lived there was something I'd never quite figured out. For a while I'd thought they were drug dealers. Then I decided it was a whorehouse. My current theory was that they were running a bookie joint. There was always some racket or other emanating from over the fence, wailing babies or barking dogs or chain saws. Now it was electronic music. Maybe they were auditioning for the remake of *Plan 9 From Outer Space*.

I made some tea and went outside. The June gloom continued. It had shown up in May, just like every other year. Sometimes I enjoyed the succession of cloudy mornings, the result of some weather phenomenon I chose not to understand. Doves would coo and mockingbirds would mock, and baby possums would dash by inches from my toes.

But sometimes the June gloom was a depressing thing, and this particular Tuesday morning, a perfect marriage of gray sky and chill air, was a prime example. I'd expected a night's sleep would buffer me from the mortality I'd suddenly been getting in touch with. It hadn't.

I pulled my robe tighter and went into the greenhouse. It's about twelve by eighteen feet, with benches all along the inner walls and another one down the middle. The ground is covered with gravel, and the walls and roof are corrugated fiberglass panels that have turned translucent from exposure to the sun. There's a series of so-called automatic vents around the top of the walls, which work when they feel like it, as well as a temperature-activated fan at the far end. Five hundred or so plants live there in relative harmony, grudgingly sharing space with an assortment of seed and rooting trays.

I started my rounds. Each morning I would meander through the greenhouse, dressed in a bathrobe and karate slippers, sipping a cup of tea. I'd note who'd put on a little growth spurt, who had buds or bugs, who needed a bit of extra water. Fortified with a reassurance that life went on, I'd be ready to face the day.

Two minutes along I realized it was silly to think I could just carry on my ritual like nothing had happened. Every time I saw a euphorbia, I thought of the previous evening's events. New buds struck me as inconsequential. Mealybugs seemed a really stupid thing to worry about. All the growth spurts in the world weren't going to bring Brenda back.

I abandoned my rounds and retreated to the house. I took a shower, ate some toast, and went out front to the Jungle. That's what I call the patio at the southeast corner of my house, right by the front door. A gigantic elm on my oddball neighbors' property blocks most of the direct sun, so I've filled it up with plants that don't need a whole lot of light. It's jammed with viny hoyas and ceropegias, rattail cactus and epiphyllums, jungle cacti with big showy flowers. I'll sit in one of the wicker chairs and let the plants droop down around me and imagine I'm in Africa or Costa Rica or someplace. At dusk I'll relax out there, pretend the trees lining Madison Avenue don't exist, and imagine I'm watching the sun go down.

I put my feet up on the railing and thought about the meeting that evening. Brenda's presidency of the CCCC had been a good thing, in that her quirky energy brought some life to a lackadaisical crowd. The flip side was that she would get snide with people she thought were stupid or ignorant, occasionally embarrassing them in front of the whole club.

Now the duty of keeping things going fell on Dick McAfee, the vice president, who was as far from Mr. Excitement as a saguaro is from a petunia. He would ramble on and on about the most inane little thing, be it botanical or whatever, worrying a subject to death even after it had expired. Not only that: He mumbled. He'd start a sentence and you'd think you were following, and then you'd realize that you hadn't the foggiest idea what he was talking about.

I pictured them all sitting in their folding chairs at the

Odd Fellows Hall. Dick would be up there saying, "Brenda is dead; somebody killed her; they stuck a *Euphorbia abdelkuri* down her throat. An interesting thing about *E. abdelkuri*: In its native habitat the goats make it into canoes." Or at least that's what it would sound like. But with Marblemouth Dick you couldn't tell; that might really be what he was saying.

I was going to have to take charge. I was, after all, now next in line for the presidency. I'd taken the secretary's job because no one else would, which was basically how anybody got any job in the club. Except Brenda; she'd actively campaigned to be president—against no opposition—because she thought she could then get the members interested in volunteering at the conservatory. She'd had the post for almost five months, and in that time the most notable foray by CCCC members up to UCLA had been by an elderly couple who got lost and ended up trimming bamboo at the Mildred E. Mathias Botanical Garden.

I got together a few sentences that didn't sound too maudlin and began strolling around, practicing my delivery. I was on my third run-through, declaiming on what a wonderful person Brenda was, when Detective Hector Casillas, who'd stealthily insinuated himself halfway up the front walk, said, "Very impressive," and frightened me half to death.

"Jesus," I said, after returning from the stratosphere. "Do you always go sneaking up on people like that?"

"Sure. They give a course at the academy, Sneaking Up 101. I got an A. Seen today's paper?"

He waggled a piece of the *Times* in the air. The Metro section. When I shook my head he came the rest of the way up the walk, handed me the paper, and sat down in one of the wicker chairs. He sat idly fingering the dangling, pencil-thick branches of a rhipsalis while I scanned the front page. I skipped over PROBE POINTS TO HIGH-LEVEL INVOLVEMENT and LOTTERY WINNER GIVES TICKET TO DIOCESE, and then there it was. UCLA PROFESSOR KILLED WITH PLANT.

"Nice picture of the victim, huh?" Casillas said.

It showed Brenda a couple of hairstyles ago, displaying plenty of cleavage. The photo was probably from some fundraising thing. She was always hobnobbing with the semi-rich and almost-famous, digging up cash for her botanical activities.

I read a few paragraphs. They got the plant's name right, but capitalized *abdelkuri*. Not proper nomenclatural practice. I handed the paper back.

He looked down and said, "I like this part. *The body was discovered by actor Joe Portugal, forty-four, best known for his role in a breakfast cereal commercial.* I thought you looked familiar."

I made a little bow.

"You make a living off that stuff?"

I shrugged. "More or less. I do about a half dozen commercials a year. Shoot one tomorrow, as a matter of fact."

"What for?"

"Olsen's Natural Garden Solutions."

"Half a dozen gives you enough to live on?"

"My expenses are limited. My dad owns the house." I sat in the other chair. "Mind telling me the purpose of this visit, Detective?"

He plucked one of last year's fruits off the rhipsalis. White, about the size of a BB, the reason they call rhipsalis "mistletoe cactus." He squeezed it between his fingers. Pulp and seeds spurted out. "Jeez," he said. "What a stupid thing to do." He pulled out a pocket pack of tissues and wiped his fingers. "I'm a cop; I like to investigate things. Sometimes I get into things I shouldn't." He was trying to ingratiate himself with me, and not doing a bad job of it. "But to answer your question, information gathering is what we call it. This succulent-plant stuff. Burns and me don't know anything about it. I called the guys at Scientific Investigation Division. They don't know anything about it either. I thought maybe you could fill me in." He began fingering the plant again.

"Could you not diddle my rhipsalis?" I said.

He let go of the plant, absentmindedly swabbed his fingers with the remains of the tissue. "See, I need some help here. And I thought, here's this smart guy, he knows all about this plant stuff, and he's probably interested in seeing justice done, am I right? On account of he knew the victim. So I put two and two together and came on out here."

"Do you always drop by without calling first?"

"See, I'm still confused about cacti and euphorbias and stuff. You got some you can show me? Maybe I can learn the difference."

I couldn't see a good reason not to, so I got down off the patio and led him down the driveway and into the backyard. The June gloom had mostly burned off, and the yard was bathed in pearly sunlight.

"Watch for the wet spots," I said. "It's still kind of mushy from the rain Sunday night. Did you check Brenda's yard for footprints? With the rain they would have shown up nicely, I would think."

"Sure we checked."

"What about fingerprints, stuff like that?"

"We checked all that. You're not dealing with a bunch of amateurs here."

"No, sorry, I—"

"Who'd you think all those other people were, hanging around the crime scene? The *National Enquirer*?"

"No, of course not. Any idea who did it?"

"We figure someone she knew. No sign of forced entry.

Where were you yesterday afternoon, by the way? Around three o'clock?"

"That when she died?"

"That's what the coroner's office says."

"I was at home. Watching the hockey playoffs, working in the greenhouse. Uh—"

"Yeah?"

"What was the actual cause of death?"

"Evidently, that sap's pretty bad stuff. Her windpipe closed up, shock, tissue damage, all sorts of things. Girl who did the autopsy said she saw things she never saw before. Oh, there was some blunt-force trauma around the back of the head too, but she probably would have gotten over that."

"She wasn't, uh . . ."

"Sexually assaulted? Uh-uh."

We went into the greenhouse. Casillas spotted the gallon of water and stack of paper cups by the door and raised his eyebrows. I said, "Sure."

While he was pouring himself a cup, the fan kicked in. Six years I'd had that greenhouse, and still every time the fan went on it gave me a start. It was a big fan. "Kind of jumpy," Casillas said.

"I guess I'm a little scared. There might be a serial succulent killer around."

" 'Serial succulent killer.' I like that." He pointed at a plant with inch-thick branches growing from a swollen main stem. Foot-long flower stalks were tipped with yellow bell-shape flowers. "That a euphorbia?"

"No. *Pachypodium horombense*. Related to the oleander." I led him over to some euphorbias, and I picked up one with a spindle-shape stem about eight inches tall and a nice head of elliptical leaves. "This is *Euphorbia pachypodioides*," I said.

"Which is it?"

"What do you mean?"

"Is it a euphorbia or a pachy-whatever?"

"It's a euphorbia. Its specific name comes from it looking like a pachypodium."

"It's like that one you showed me a minute ago, except thinner."

"To the untrained eye, yes, but—" It probably wasn't too clever telling a detective about his untrained eye. "It's all in the flowers."

"What is?"

"How you classify plants. A euphorbia's a euphorbia because of the flower. All the euphorbias in the world, from the tiniest spurge up to the biggest tree species, have flowers with the same basic parts in the same basic arrangement." I grabbed an *E. flanaganii*, one of the medusa-head species, and pointed out the little yellow cyathia, which is what you call euphorbia flowers, unless there's only one, in which case it's a cyathium. "Like this. And that pachypodium I showed you has flowers like an oleander, which it's related to."

"You said something about spurge. My wife's always complaining about that. She shows me this weed."

I nodded. "A euphorbia. In fact, they call the family the spurge family. The flowers are tiny, but the structure's the same."

"So they're not all what you call succulent."

"No. Poinsettias, for instance. They're euphorbias too. Like I told your partner, they all have sap you want to stay away from, although I read somewhere that poinsettia sap's not so bad, that you'd have to eat five hundred leaves or so to kill yourself."

I kept spouting succulent lore, and he kept lapping it up. We'd just covered what made a cactus a cactus when he said, "You got one like was in the victim's mouth?"

"No."

"Any of your friends have one?"

"A couple."

"If you saw the one we pulled out of the victim, could you recognize it?"

I shook my head. "Abdelkuri just grows straight up. They look pretty much alike until they get big and get some character."

"Sort of like dicks, huh?"

The only thing I could do was stare at him.

He held up a hand. "Sorry about that. A lousy try at a guy thing. They got all this sensitivity bullshit going on in the department; sometimes I just have to do a guy thing. Jeez, it's hot in here." He downed the rest of his water, walked back down the aisle, and exited the greenhouse. I followed. When I got outside he was mopping his substantial forehead with another tissue. He crumpled his cup and I took it from him.

He asked how I'd gotten interested in succulents. I told him how I'd stumbled into CCCC's annual show at the Veterans' Auditorium seven or eight years back and fell in love with a cyphostemma, a grape relative with leathery leaves and white, peeling bark. That's how a lot of people get into succulents. They'll see one plant that turns them on, and before they know it they're up to their eyeballs in them.

He got ready to leave. "Thanks," he said. "This has been real helpful. If you think of anything, give us a call." He started to go, then pointed at the little lean-to where I keep my dwarf Madagascar euphorbias. "What's in there?"

"Stuff that doesn't need much sunlight."

"Really? I thought all this shit grew out in the desert." He wandered over and poked his head in. "Hey," he said. "There's one plant in here that's real interesting. Come on over and tell me about it."

Like I said, I'd seen it before. Somebody would think

succulents were an utter waste of time, and then one particular plant would fascinate the hell out of them, and they were hooked.

I was *so* wrong.

Sitting there among all the Madagascar plants in my shade house was one plant that didn't belong. It was from a different island, the island of Socotra. A *Euphorbia abdelkuri* in a four-inch green plastic pot. Or rather, the remains of one, a couple of inches of stem with the tip snapped cleanly off.

4

For at least the sixth time I said, "it's not my plant."

I was in an interrogation room at the LAPD's Pacific Division. I'd driven past the building hundreds of times, at the broad, dusty intersection of Centinela and Culver boulevards, a site that's always lonely no matter how many day workers are congregated there looking for a few hours' pay. I'd even been in the lobby once to borrow an electric engraver to carve my social-security number into my so-called valuables. But never past the front desk. Never into the bowels of the place.

It had been an hour since Casillas brought me there in his Chevrolet sedan. I wasn't in custody, but it had been abundantly clear that if I hadn't come with him voluntarily I would have been.

The room was utilitarian and too hot. Urine-colored perforated sound-insulation panels lined the walls. I sat at a Formica table decorated with gouges and stains, on a hard metal chair with one short leg. Across from me Casillas looked up from his notebook. Burns stood in a corner with her arms crossed over her chest.

Casillas slapped the book shut and tucked it and his cheesy pen into his pocket.

"Look," he said. "There's an easy way and a hard way."

"Please, Detective, spare me the clichés. No matter which way you cut it, it's not my plant and I don't know how it got there. Somebody else obviously does though. Whoever called and told you where to find it. Any idiot could guess that."

His eyes narrowed.

"Not that I'm implying you're an idiot."

He didn't say anything. He just regarded me like I was a particularly ugly crime-scene artifact.

I couldn't stand the silence. I knew he was playing some sort of cop head trip on me, yet I couldn't keep my mouth shut. "I can't believe I told you all that stuff about succulents while all the time you were intending to bust me. What kind of crap is that?"

He pulled out one of those damned tissues and blew his nose. He took out the pen again and tapped it on the table.

I realized they were stalling. They knew even if I'd killed Brenda, I wasn't dumb enough to leave the plant sitting around. "I'm not under arrest or anything, am I? And since you've run out of new questions and are asking the same ones over and over, I can probably go, right?"

Burns sighed, came and leaned over the table, put her hands flat down on it. "Yes, you can go."

Casillas said, "But I'm going to be keeping—"

"An eye on me. I know, I know."

I went out into what had turned into a glorious spring day, wondering if I should be looking into getting a lawyer. I rejected Burns's offer of a ride home and walked east along Culver, past block after block of run-down two-story apartment buildings. Past the five-for-$10 T-shirt place, past the mamas and the babies and the preteen boys in their pregang outfits. I walked straight out of Los Angeles and back into Culver City, my hometown.

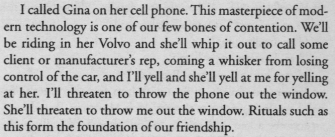

I called Gina on her cell phone. This masterpiece of modern technology is one of our few bones of contention. We'll be riding in her Volvo and she'll whip it out to call some client or manufacturer's rep, coming a whisker from losing control of the car, and I'll yell and she'll yell at me for yelling at her. I'll threaten to throw the phone out the window. She'll threaten to throw me out the window. Rituals such as this form the foundation of our friendship.

I found her locked in traffic on the Hollywood Freeway. "How are you holding up?" she asked.

"I had a visit from Casillas this morning."

"Are you a suspect?"

"Evidently. He took me down to the station."

"No way."

"He thought it an appropriate course of action." I filled her in on my visit to Pacific Division.

"Sounds like someone's trying to frame you," she said when I finished.

"Or just throw the scent off themselves."

"We might want to poke into things a little."

"Could be an idea. I don't feel like just sitting around waiting for Casillas to come up with something else he thinks incriminates me. Or finding out about Dad."

"There is the Dad thing." She was quiet for a moment. "I better get off."

A couple of minutes later Frank Balter, Brenda's lawyer, called. I'd met him a few months before when he gave CCCC's officers some advice on nonprofit status. He told me Brenda had left an envelope to be opened in the event of her death. Just like in the movies, I thought. She'd known someone was after her and identified the killer.

No such luck. The envelope gave instructions for her burial. She had a plot picked out at Final Haven up in Pacific Palisades, L.A.'s premier multicultural burial ground. A friend of hers was to handle the details. "This friend has quite an unusual last name," Balter said.

"Razafindratsira?"

"Yes. Do you know him?"

"I met him at a party at Brenda's."

Balter had already spoken with him and told me the funeral was going to be at three o'clock Thursday. Brenda's instructions asked for me to be in charge of calling the succulent crowd. The family, what there was of it, had been informed, and her sister, Amanda, was flying in from Wisconsin that evening.

I almost asked Balter to recommend a good criminal lawyer, just in case, but I didn't. I was innocent, damn it, and I wasn't going to give the cops the pleasure of making me spend money on an attorney.

After we hung up I slouched on the couch, trying to identify what I was feeling. Presently I identified it as anger. I'd basically had two friends, and now someone had taken one of them away. I still had all the cactus people, but I wasn't really close to any except Brenda. And I'd long since lost touch with all my acting cronies. So it had been Gina and Brenda, and now it was just Gina. A good thing no one had offed her; she was more than a friend. She was my alter ego. If anyone had hurt her I would have done anything to bring them to justice.

But I cared about Brenda too. Sure, she could be strident and pushy. But after our romance ended and our friendship began, she'd learned how much bullshit I would put up with and acted accordingly. I was getting pissed off that someone had had the nerve to kill her and cut my stack of friends in half. I needed to do something about it. For her. And, since people were starting to think I did it, for me too.

❦

Around one I went out to my pickup. It's a '72 Datsun that I bought back in '79, when I began managing the Altair Theater. It's been faithful to me ever since, and I to it. I stuck Blind Faith in the eight-track. Stevie Winwood complained that he couldn't find his way home. I pushed the button to switch tracks. Squeaks, then silence. I popped the cartridge. Out it came, except for the long strand of tape that was jumbled in the works. Perhaps it was time for one of those new-fangled cassette players.

I backed out of the driveway, went up to the corner, and followed Braddock Drive through the amoeba-shape enclave called Culver City. Braddock runs east and west a couple of blocks south of the studio, which used to be MGM and now belongs to the Japanese. I followed the tree-lined streets until I came out on the stretch of Jefferson Boulevard where there's a tire store on every block. I passed Sorrento Italian deli, where a million kinds of olives occupy the claustrophobic aisles. Then on past the Western-wear shop with the huge cactus out front. They used the place in a movie called *Eight Million Ways to Die*. Everywhere in L.A. you saw stuff from TV or the movies. Sometimes it was fun. This afternoon it was old.

I took the San Diego Freeway north to Sunset and headed west. Soon I was winding uphill along a narrow Pacific Palisades road. I turned right onto a long snaky driveway. Halfway up it the native plants gave way to exotic ones. Tree aloes on the left; giant Bosch-esque philodendrons to the right. The puyas, huge terrestrial bromeliads, were all in bloom; turquoise and violet-blue flowers reflected the broken light with the sheen of carved wax. Under a huge buttress-rooted ficus, dozens of epiphyllum hybrids dangled, bearing a multicolored profusion of flowers, some as big as dinner plates.

The jungle parted and I reached the clearing at the top of the hill. A log cabin and a greenhouse, larger than the cabin, occupied it. Sam Oliver knelt out front, tending to a bed of pale green thick-leafed rosettes. *Dudleya*, his favorite genus. He wore dark green shorts and a T-shirt commemorating the Intercity cactus and succulent show from a few years back, the rare variation with "eighth" misspelled as "eigth." A pair of glasses dangled from his neck on a red and green cord.

Sam had been an active member of succulentdom for well over a generation. He'd been president of the Cactus and Succulent Society of America and was a life member of every local cactus club. He spent at least two months a year overseas, in Botswana or the upper Amazon or some godforsaken corner of Borneo, seeking out new plants. Succulents, bromeliads, orchids, aroids—anything rare or weird.

He was about eighty, but you would have thought he was twenty years younger. He had pale blue eyes in a thin face. He hadn't lost a lick of his brown hair, and neither it nor his goatee carried more than a trace of gray. He'd had a couple of minor skin cancers removed but was otherwise healthy as the proverbial horse.

The air was cooler than at my place, and as I exited the truck a bit of breeze tickled my skin. The ground was moist but not mushy; it looked like they'd gotten less rain up there.

"Hey, Joe," Sam said. "Want an omelet? I've got some eggs to use up before I leave."

The fact that he was leaving explained what I was doing there. He was headed for Tucson that night to spearhead one of his succulent symposiums. This would be followed by a week of botanizing in Baja. I'd agreed to come up and check on things a few times while he was away and to do a watering or two. Today he was going to show me what needed special attention. I hoped to have better luck sitting his babies than I'd had with Brenda's.

I said yes to his omelet offer, and we went into the cabin's one big room. "You heard, I suppose?" I asked.

"Yes, yes, terrible thing. Gives euphorbias a bad name. You want mushrooms?"

"Mushrooms would be good. I'm just trying to get my mind around this whole thing. I knew her pretty well."

"As did I, my boy. Cheese?"

"No. Yes. Forgive me for saying this, but you don't seem very upset."

He pointed the skillet at me. "I've seen a lot of people die lately. They're dropping like flies. When you get to be my age—shit, Joe, you don't need to hear this. I spent the morning feeling bad. When you're as old as I am, that's all you can afford." He shook the pan. "Hard or runny?"

"Hard, please. Want to hear something funny? The police suspect me."

"Did you do it?"

"Of course not."

"Didn't think so, though my first thought was one of her boyfriends. Crime of passion sort of thing. Then I thought, no, it's the damned smugglers. I'm probably next."

"You think so? I mean about the smugglers? I keep hearing about them, but I don't really have a grip on how nasty they are."

My omelet was ready. He handed me the plate, told me to grab a drink from the fridge, snatched an apple for himself. "Let's talk outside."

A redwood table and chairs were set out under a giant *Dracaena draco*. A dragon tree, with clouds of dagger-shape leaves. We sat. He crunched his apple, chewed, swallowed. "About those smugglers. I wouldn't underestimate them. Anything you've heard is true, in spades. They're nasty, all right. It's not enough the natives have burned down most of the island for charcoal. No, these people have to come in and take the rest. They'll wipe a new species from the habitat in a day or so and then sell it to the Europeans. The Europeans'll buy anything that's new and different and won't care where it came from. Won't wait until we can get a decent stock from seed. Two times ago when I was in Madagascar, we—Doug Hammer and I, you know who he is?"

"That British guy. The one who writes all the books."

He nodded. "Doug and I found an undescribed species of euphorbia. It grew like milii but had leaves like francoisii. It was the most amazing damned thing I ever saw."

Euphorbia milii is the spiny, leafy plant known as crown of thorns because it resembles what Christ supposedly wore on his head when he was crucified. *E. francoisii*'s a popular dwarf with a fat stem and multicolored leaves. Collectors would eat up a combination like that.

"Next time I went back," Sam said, "—and mind you, this was just a year later—almost all of them were gone. Some had been ripped from the ground and just left to die. We saved a few, maybe enough to perpetuate the species. I have one. You want a cutting?"

"Maybe some other time, Sam. About the smugglers . . ."

"Right, the smugglers. Evidently, a ranger down there came across them while they were doing their dirty work, and they macheted him right across the throat. Then they left him there."

"Do we know who any of these people are?"

"I have some names, not the actual smugglers but the people in Germany who are receiving the plants."

A yellow jacket circled in and alit on my omelet. I watched, unable to move, as it carved out a tiny piece of ham.

Sam saw my reaction and casually brushed the wasp away. "Nothing to worry about, my boy. It's just a yellow jacket."

Embarrassed, I said the first thing that came into my mind. "Did you know I was taking care of Brenda's canaries?"

"A fine thing, young man, a fine thing."

"But all she gave me was her departure and return dates and her bird vet's phone number."

"I have the whole itinerary, and I've already cabled Doug Hammer to tell him what happened."

"I don't follow."

"Sorry. Doug was one of the people she was meeting down there. Him and Willy Schoeppe."

I raised an eyebrow. "A German?"

"Yes, but a good German."

"Could I have a copy of the itinerary?"

"Might I ask why?"

Good question. What was I going to do, press it up against my head like Carnac the Magnificent and divine who had killed Brenda?

I told Sam the truth. "I don't really know. I just have this vague urge to do something about Brenda's death, and this would be something tangible to . . . to . . ."

Sam laughed. "If you want it, young man, you shall have it. Come inside, I'll make you a copy. Another omelet?"

I looked down at my plate. Someone had cleaned it. Chances are it was me, but I hadn't been aware of doing so. "No thanks. I'm watching my cholesterol."

"I'm paying someone to watch mine. I'm glad you want the itinerary; it'll give me a chance to show off my new toy."

He led me inside to a cluttered corner where a plastic

contraption the size of a small TV sat on a desk next to a computer. "It's a combination fax–printer–copier–scanner," Sam said. "Watch."

He pulled open a drawer, riffled through some papers, withdrew one, fed it into the machine. A few seconds later I had a copy of Brenda's itinerary in my hot little hands. I edged toward the door, but he stopped me. "Great things, these computers," he said. "I can do things I wouldn't have dreamed of ten years ago. And, of course, there's the Internet."

Ah, yes. The mighty Internet. I'd managed to ignore it up till then, and I didn't see any reason to stop doing so. "I'm afraid I'm not very computer literate."

"You don't have to be. Let me show you."

He got his computer going. A lot of gobbledygook flashed across the screen. I called upon my acting skills and displayed mild curiosity.

"And of course there's cacti et cetera," Sam said. "It's what they call a mailing list. You can post questions, and well over a thousand members see them and can give you an answer."

"Fascinating."

He studied my face. "You really don't care about this stuff, do you?"

"I'm sorry, Sam, it's just not for me. Maybe some other time."

"No, no, don't worry about it. Here, come outside and I'll show you what needs tending."

Three quarters of an hour later I exited the greenhouse, carrying a list of plants that needed special attention. I also had five new plant fragments to shepherd but managed to turn down the wacky euphorbia on the grounds that I wasn't worthy.

5

WHATEVER GOD DECIDED THE CULVER CITY CACTUS CLUB should hold its monthly meetings at the Odd Fellows Hall had a marvelous sense of humor. The building was on an especially dull stretch of Sepulveda Boulevard, flanked by a Foster's Freeze and a taco stand whose name changed every three months. It was a relic of the fifties, with a fading-wood-and-chipped-stone exterior overlooking a cracked parking lot. Inside, the dominant theme was paneling. The walls were paneled. The ceilings were paneled. The linoleum of the floor was patterned to look like paneling. Even the bathrooms were paneled, in an especially awful faux mahogany.

The walls were lined with plaques, proclamations, and photos documenting the history and good works of the Odd Fellows and their ladies' auxiliary, the Rebekahs. After four years of going to meetings there, I had yet to determine what the purpose of the group was. All I knew was you had to be at least seventy and have no fashion sense to join.

I got there at seven, half an hour before the meeting was scheduled to begin and, most likely, forty-five minutes before it would. I'd brought a flat of cuttings and plants I'd grown tired of to give away, with a book I was returning to the club library tucked in among them. I was about to lift it all out of the truck bed when a familiar Volvo zipped into the next spot.

"I've got a sandwich for you," Gina said out the window. "Turkey breast, from Wild Oats."

"How did you know I would need a sandwich?"

"Because you never take time to eat a proper dinner." She exited the car and beeped the alarm. She was wearing one of those flowery sundresses she looks so good in and some colorful dangly earrings. Her hair was pulled back in a ponytail. She had the brown-paper-wrapped sandwich in one hand and her portable computer in the other. "What would happen to you if you didn't have me to look after you?"

"I'd probably end up in a police interrogation room or something. What are you doing here? You still suspect one of the cactus people did Brenda in?"

"Could be. Also to give you moral support."

"What makes you think I need moral support?"

"Joe." She dumped the sandwich on top of the plants and put her hand on my shoulder. "You were nearly arrested today. You need moral support. Do you need a hug too?"

I considered it. "Not now. Maybe later."

"Okay, just let me know. Anything to report?"

I briefed her on my trip to Sam's, then told her, "Let's get inside before the teeming millions catch me and besiege me with questions."

We found our veep Dick McAfee and his wife, Hope, inside, shoving tables around. They had my vote for couple of the year, that year and every year. They'd been married just short of four decades and were still as affectionate as the day they wed. Always holding hands, exchanging tender little words and gestures.

They saw us and came over. As we said our hellos, some

errant breeze blew Dick's hair awry. It was the finest I'd ever seen, like a baby's, and pale blond. You could barely tell where it ended and his scalp began. Blond hairs grew from his ears as well, but these were coarse and wiry. Dick was tall and angular and reminded me of Ichabod Crane. He had on an ugly shirt he often wore to meetings—a drab green and beige stripe—and some stretchy brown slacks.

I began to introduce them to Gina, but Dick remembered her. "Yes," he said. "I met you the time we had the speaker on the succulents of Saudi Arabia. That was the night the cook's nose fell in the tourniquet." Evidently Dick's mumbling quotient was at its highest that evening. It was odd: When he put stuff down on paper, he communicated better than almost anyone I knew. He'd recently had a letter published in the national journal, taking to task those who illegally took plants out of habitat, and it was a model of clarity and brevity.

He kept rambling, and somewhere in there he switched the conversation over to Brenda. "Zubba-zubba-zubba, and with such a rare plant."

"Apparently," I said.

"And she seemed so young," Hope added, brushing an invisible piece of lint from Dick's sleeve.

I smiled at her. "She was older than me."

"As I said, so young." She smiled back, a charming smile in a charming face. Hope was aging beautifully, and at sixty or so looked ten years younger. I knew she went to the gym regularly, but that didn't explain how she'd avoided wrinkles as well as she had. Her blond hair came from a bottle, but it was the right kind of bottle. Maybe the way she dressed helped with the illusion of youth; this evening she wore jeans and a T-shirt featuring Pongo and Perdita from *101 Dalmatians*. Or maybe never having kids had kept her youthful.

Dick asked my advice on how we should handle "the Brenda thing." I told him what I thought. He agreed, and he and Hope went back to work.

More members arrived. Some were oldies-but-goodies, people like Dick who'd been members practically since cacti evolved, or at least since the club's founding in 1955. There were newbies too, folks who'd wandered into our annual show, bought a couple of weird plants, and soon found they couldn't live without several dozen more.

I dropped off my giveaways and stopped by the library table to return my book. Austin Richman, club librarian and unreconstructed hippie, greeted me. "Hey, man, how's it going?" He'd dressed formally—he had a T-shirt on under his overalls. I gave him the book, and he dutifully signed it in. We exchanged grimaces about Brenda, and I moved on.

A big burly fellow carrying a flat of plants arrived. "Who's that guy?" Gina whispered. "He looks suspicious."

"That's Lyle Tillis. He's a part-time grower. He's been in the club forever. Past president; treasurer now. Nice guy. Always giving away plants to people. He gave the program last month, about his trip to South Africa." A short woman—vaguely eastern European, with sad dark eyes—followed Lyle in. "That's his wife, Magda," I said.

I found seats in the back against the wall. Gina pulled her computer out of its case. She turned it on and began typing. "What are you doing?" I asked.

"Taking notes. I don't want to trust all this to memory."

"Notes on what?"

"Suspects."

"Oy. Don't piss anybody off."

"Maybe I should. We could get them mad, and they'd get confused, and they'd confess."

I patted her hand. "Behave, okay?"

"I will, I promise. Tell me about Lyle."

"He and Dick are old buddies. Best buddies. Jesus, I feel like an idiot doing this."

"Shut up and tell me more."

"Lyle provides a lot of the succulents that Dick sells at the nursery."

"What nursery?"

"McAfee's. Perhaps you've seen it."

She could hardly help having seen it. Dick's nursery was a giant landmark on Washington Boulevard, near the marina. They sold all manner of plants in huge quantities. Indoor, outdoor, everything. In December they added a bunch of Christmas paraphernalia, and the indoor section was awash in more *Euphorbia pulcherrima*—poinsettias—than you'd ever want to see. Dick fancied himself the poinsettia king of Los Angeles.

"He's *that* McAfee? They must be loaded."

"They live modestly."

"What does she do?"

"She doesn't have a job, but she does a ton of volunteer work. Can we stop this cross-examination, please?"

She gave me a look, seemed about to answer. But she got distracted. "Who's that?"

"That" was Rowena Small. A little old lady—very little, like four-six. Her hair was pure white. Stick legs poked out from a pair of cutoffs. She was a fixture at meetings, dispensing advice to all the newcomers. It was an amazing mix, this advice. Sometimes it was perfectly accurate, useful, and succinct. On other occasions it was utter hogwash.

"Don't tell me you think she looks suspicious too."

"She's too hyper. She's hiding something."

"She's always like that."

"Maybe she's been killing people all along."

Over the next fifteen minutes, several people came up and asked about Brenda. I told them I wanted to wait and talk to everyone at the same time. Others stood around the room, sneaking glances at me as if I were a hero for discovering the body.

At seven forty-five, Dick called the meeting to order. He introduced a couple of new members. They each got a round of applause. Members of CCCC were so conditioned. Introduce anyone, they clapped their hands off.

With this nicety complete, Dick managed to turn the meeting over to me before dazing and/or confusing more than a handful of attendees. I stepped up to the front. A table in front of me displayed a variety of plants the members had brought in to brag about, complain over, or give away. To my left, a bust of some great Odd Fellow of the past stared off into infinity. On my right, a moth-eaten American flag hung limply from a once-golden pole. My shirt was already stuck to my back; except in the dead of winter, we had to choose between sweating our asses off or struggling to be heard over the two industrial-strength fans, and this evening whoever was in charge of such things had opted for sweat.

I gazed out over the assembled masses. Three dozen faces stared back. All suspects, to hear Gina tell it. I caught her eye. She gave me a smile, lowered her head, and entered something into the computer.

What to say? They'd all read the paper or spoken to someone who had. They all knew what had happened. I could deliver a lame eulogy. I could describe the death scene.

I could go home.

That was *exactly* the thing to do. Whip off a few quick wasn't-she-greats, turn the meeting back to Marblemouth Dick, and flee.

"Tell us everything!" shrieked Rowena Small.

The dam broke. A thousand questions poured out at me. Did she look like it hurt? Was she naked? Did this mean

Dick was president now? Whose plant was poking out of her mouth?

Wait, I thought. Who was that? That doesn't sound like one of the members. That sounds like . . .

Detective Hector Casillas stood at the back of the room, partially obscuring a photo of two dozen old women in frilly pink dresses. "Hi, Portugal," he said.

"What are you doing here?"

"Just trying to find out whose plant was sticking out of the victim's mouth like a big green—"

"Ladies and gentlemen," I said. "This is Detective Hector Casillas of the Los Angeles Police Department. I'm sure he'll answer all your questions about our president's demise." I clapped my hands together, one-two-three-four, like a rich person telling a servant to hurry up. They all picked up the clapping. I dashed out from behind the table. When the applause began to die down, I said, "Come on, is that how you welcome one of L.A.'s finest?" They started up again, viewing him adoringly, awaiting momentous information. I threw him a smug smile.

Rowena Small, wearing a fiendish expression, shot out, "Did the poor baby suffer before she went?" and before you knew it Casillas was answering a barrage of questions. Gina sat furiously typing the answers into her computer. I stood off to the side, trying not to laugh at my tormentor's predicament, then sidled outside and indulged in a giggling fit. I'd shown him.

I stuck my head back in. I'd shown him nothing. He'd moved from the back of the room to the front, where he leaned against the table, notebook in hand. While I was off having hysterics, he'd turned things around. Now it was him asking the questions. Had there been any suspicious characters at the last meeting? Had Brenda said anything to anyone about her trip to Madagascar? Did anyone recognize the plant in the photograph he just happened to have in his jacket pocket?

I withdrew from the doorway and wandered out to the curb. A breeze was up. A lone jacaranda across the street shed lavender remnants onto a parked car. "You prick," said Casillas.

"That's twice you've snuck up on me."

"You dumb-ass prick. Don't *ever* try to make me look bad."

"I thought you were going to accuse me right in front of everybody."

"I can't do that. Not enough proof. Yet." He smirked. "But I got some good stuff just now. Thanks for getting me in with those people."

"My pleasure. Tell me something. Do you really think I killed Brenda?"

He shrugged. "Don't know. You could have. Any of those people could have. But I got to tell you, the plant matched up. Makes it look kind of bad for you." He pulled out a tissue, removed those damned half-glasses, scrubbed the lenses. "It's nothing personal. You shouldn't take it personal. Sometimes you got to step on a few toes to make an omelet." He replaced his glasses, adjusted his suit collar, glared at me. "Better watch yourself. One false move and pow!" He strode over to his Chevy and drove off into the night.

I watched his taillights until he turned the corner. After that I imagined I was still watching them. Then—

"Here he is," screeched Rowena Small. "Are you a suspect? Vera Berg says you're a suspect." Vera was about a hundred years old and always spent the meetings at the refreshment table, sucking up cookies.

Rowena stood in the doorway, positively shivering with anticipation. Next to her, Dick and Hope McAfee had their arms around each other. The rest of the members pressed up behind them, threatening to burst out the door, but holding back as if afraid to share the out-of-doors with me until I was cleared of all suspicion.

"I don't think I am," I said.

"He most certainly is not," Gina said. She pushed her way into the crowd and popped through to join me outside. She turned, took Rowena firmly by the shoulders, and shoved. The crowd swallowed Rowena up. "Please," Gina said. "Everyone go inside. Show's over." She pushed and prodded and got them all in. She slammed the door behind them and leaned her back against it. "I told you, Joe," she said.

"Told me what?"

"They're wackos, this cactus club. They're wackos, each and every one of them. And I think one of them killed Brenda."

I decided CCCC could manage the rest of the meeting without me. Someone else could take notes. Nobody ever cared about the minutes anyway.

But before I could escape, Dick and Lyle emerged from the hall. Our speaker hadn't shown up. Someone had called him and found out he thought the meeting was the following Tuesday. What were we to do now?

We made an executive decision. We told everyone the funeral arrangements and sent them home. At least I think that's what we did; I didn't stick around to find out. For all I know, no one could understand what Dick was saying and they sat around until the wee hours of the morning discussing my possible guilt.

I drove home, and Gina followed. Somewhere during the fiasco at the Odd Fellows I'd misplaced my sandwich. Gina proposed to throw together some pasta. I wandered outside with a flashlight to see if any of the night-bloomers had done their thing. None had, but I surprised a possum who was poking around the greenhouse door.

A pungent Italian-cooking smell hit me the instant I walked back into the house. I followed my nose to the kitchen. I'd had one tomato, one carrot, one green pepper and one onion, and Gina'd found them all. "Sit," she said.

I meandered into the living room, sat on the couch, flicked on the remote. Must've been Van Damme week on Channel 6. He was punching some Asian baddie senseless.

I turned off the sound and listened to the hissing of the sautéing vegetables, the clink of utensils, the little foot squeaks on the kitchen floor. I turned and watched Gina's activities over the counter between the kitchen and living room. After a bit I directed my attention back to the mute TV. "I'm going to smoke myself a joint," I said.

"You are not."

"Why the hell not? It'll make me feel better."

"Stop acting like a four-year-old, Joe. You can't get loaded just because you have troubles to take your mind off."

"Can too."

"We have to figure out what to do."

"I already figured it out. I'm going to smoke a—"

"Joe." Something about her tone made me look at her. She'd moved into the kitchen doorway. She stood there with an oven mitt on one hand, holding a wooden spoon in the other. "Whoever did this didn't just kill Brenda. They did it by sticking a plant down her throat. Your run-of-the-mill murderer's not going to do that. It takes a plant nerd to catch a plant nerd."

I said nothing.

"You know you want to look into this."

"Do not."

"What harm could a little investigating do? We haven't had an adventure in almost two years."

Our last adventure had been river rafting on the Colorado. I came out of that one with a broken arm and twelve stitches in my temple. I'd told Gina the next time she wanted an adventure, she should go with her boyfriend. Or girlfriend. Whatever she was into at the time. I reminded her as much now.

"Do you have anything better to do?" she asked. "Other than playing with your plants and watching wrestling and waiting for Elaine to come up with your bimonthly commercial?"

"I only watch wrestling once in a while. On weekends."

"You need some mental stimulation. This is a chance to get some and get Casillas off your back too."

"What if I run into the killer and he's moved on to Cygon injections or something?"

She went back to the stove before replying. "Carry a gun."

I stood and walked over to the counter. She was at least half serious.

"Where am I going to get a gun?" I asked.

"I have one."

"Excuse me?"

"What part didn't you understand? I have a gun."

"When did you get a gun?"

"Two years ago, when we had that serial rapist in West Hollywood."

"Where'd you get it?" I asked, certain I knew the answer.

"From your father."

I was right. "How come you never told me?"

"I was embarrassed about it. I took some lessons at the Beverly Hills Gun Club, and then I put it way back on the top shelf of my closet and I never took it out again."

"Why don't we just leave it there? All I need is for Casillas to come talk to me and find out I'm packing."

"Maybe I wasn't serious about the gun. But I'm serious about the rest."

She wasn't going to let it go. What had started as a whim had evidently turned into an obsession. "Just assuming I went along with this insanity," I said, "how would we start?"

She smiled for the first time since I'd come back in the house. She shut off the heat under the skillet and started pulling on cabinet doors. As she tracked down dishes she said, "I have a spreadsheet."

"Fascinating."

"It's not finished yet, but I've been organizing everything we know into an Excel spreadsheet. I have a column for suspects, and one for motives, and one for miscellaneous. So far most of the stuff's under miscellaneous. Go grab us some napkins and drinks and sit."

I did as I was told, wondering what had gotten into my dearest friend. "This is what you've been doing all day."

"When I wasn't with a client." She placed a plate of pasta on the table in front of me.

I had an appetite for the first time since we'd stumbled across Brenda. I took a big forkful. It was perfect. I could taste all four of my vegetables. "So now we have this spreadsheet." I had only the vaguest idea what a spreadsheet was but figured that could come later. "What do we do with it?"

She looked up from her plate, held up a let-me-swallow finger. A drop of sauce lingered on her chin. I reached over the table and dabbed it off with my napkin. "We start questioning people," she said.

"Just like that?"

"We're smart. We'll figure it out. Does this need more red pepper?"

We cleaned our plates, had seconds, washed the dishes.

By the time we were done with ice cream and *Letterman* and the Cary Grant movie we found ourselves watching, it was one-thirty in the morning. Too late for Gina to go home. I pulled out the bed hidden in my couch and brought her the oversize T-shirt she kept at my place. I tucked her in and hied myself off to the bedroom. I stripped, set the clock, memorized my two lines for the commercial shoot in the morning, and went to bed.

But I couldn't sleep. I'd eaten too much and given myself a stomachache. The air in the bedroom was too still, and the fan hadn't made it in yet from the garage, where it liked to spend the winter. I lay there thinking about the fix I found myself in. This led me to Gina's notion of poking into things ourselves. This led me to Gina.

We'd first met in 1981, when I was managing and acting at the Altair. She'd recently moved back to L.A. after ending a four-year affair with another Harvard alumna she'd met in her senior year there. Someone recommended her to design sets for our revival of *Private Lives*. We hit it off and steamed into one of those fast and furious flings theater people are so adept at. It burned out around opening night, and when the run ended we lost touch.

Fast forward eight years to a Passover seder at my cousin—and commercial agent—Elaine's. It was the first seder I'd ever been to. When I was growing up, my father's Judaism and my mother's Catholicism neatly canceled one another out. We had Christmas, and that was about it.

The doorbell rang, I opened it, and there stood Gina. She was doing the interior of Elaine's new office in Westwood, and Elaine had invited her on the pretext of expanding her religious horizons but with the ulterior motive of fixing us up. Gina and I were uncomfortable—for the first thirty seconds or so. By the end of the evening we were the best of friends. She brought me up to date; she'd gotten married and divorced, been through a punk phase, and started her own interior-design business.

We were a couple of jerks that evening, ignoring everyone else except Lauren—Elaine and her husband Wayne's daughter—who was nine and a fine audience for our antics. By the time the last matzo was eaten, Gina and I had arranged four or five activities together.

Being in the entertainment world—however loosely you use that phrase—meant I'd always had female friends. But there was generally an undertone of sexual tension, on my part at least. I'd treat the women as buddies and secretly plot some way to get them into bed. It happened once or twice and ruined the friendship.

But when I ran into Gina again, I felt no chemistry. We'd used it up back in '81. She obviously felt like I did, and besides, her social life was already complicated enough. She'd been juggling two lovers, one male and one female, for several months. Before our reacquaintance was a week old, she'd related all their shortcomings to me—*all* of them. I responded with similar complaints about the woman I'd been seeing on and off. It was great. It was like suddenly having the sister I'd never had, except you couldn't talk to your sister about blow jobs.

Being a guy, I was more interested in what went on with Gina's female lover. She would demand to know why men were so aroused by the thought of two women together. I could never think of anything to say other than, "It's a big turn-on," at which point she would ask how I would respond to the sight of two men together. I would mouth platitudes about how everyone had the right to whatever orientation they chose, then curl my nose and say that actually seeing two men together sounded icky.

I smiled in the dark. "I still think it sounds icky."

"What'd you say?" It was Gina, standing in the doorway to my room, her slim form outlined by the light of the moon.

"Nothing. What are you doing up?"

"I had to pee. You?"

"Couldn't sleep. Casillas and all."

Her silhouette nodded. "Forget him for now. Get yourself some rest, baby."

She slipped off toward the bathroom, and I was asleep before she came back out.

6

ON WEDNESDAY MORNING, WITH GINA STILL ASLEEP IN THE living room, I washed my six days' growth of beard down the drain and left the house at six-thirty. My destination was West Covina, one of a patchwork of small cities to the east of Los Angeles. It's along Interstate 10—which is the Santa Monica Freeway in my part of town but the San Bernardino out there—and out past the 605. The 605 has a name too, but no one can ever remember it.

The whole commercial thing had gotten pretty routine. Every couple of months one of my auditions would work out and I'd find myself on a soundstage or in some rented house. The other actors would be obsessing about pictures and résumés and casting-director workshops, and I'd be daydreaming about pachypodiums. Acting was so important to some of my competition that occasionally I felt guilty for nonchalantly taking some of their jobs. But not often. Especially not when the residual checks came.

I got off the freeway and followed the fluorescent-orange signs with OLSEN's lettered in Magic Marker to an address on a residential street. Equipment trucks lined the block; a covey of crew clustered around the honey wagon. I found a spot half a block away, checked in, and went to my dressing room—a trailer segment—to await my makeup call. I ran into the woman who'd been cast as my wife, played the game where we tried to figure out where we knew each other from, finally realized she'd been in a visiting production at the Altair.

I lay on my tiny bunk thinking about Brenda. My mind must have considered this a huge imposition; next thing I knew a knock on the door startled me awake. The assistant director poked her head in. "Rise and shine, sleepyhead." It was a quarter to nine.

I rose and shone, got made up, and went out to the backyard, where they were shooting. They were getting the kid scenes out of the way first so the dear little tykes wouldn't get overtired and become pains in the ass. My "daughter" explained to my "son" how she felt safe playing in the yard now that Mom and Dad had stopped using those nasty chemical insecticides. "Son" replied that it was fun watching all the ladybugs. They shot the thing a dozen times, took a break, shot a half dozen more. Around eleven they had what they wanted, dismissed the kids, and moved on to my "wife" and me. They set us up by some rosebushes, where I, as the somewhat befuddled husband, held a pack of ladybugs up to my eye, while my wife, the clever one, told me how each one could eat eight gazillion times its weight in aphids. We rehearsed it twice, I developed just the proper look of amazement, and we shot the thing. We were such professionals that we got it right on the seventh take. I left for home at twelve-thirty.

Gina'd left a note saying she had a couple of clients to see and would call me in the late afternoon. I considered a swing through the greenhouse to make up for the one I'd missed in the morning because of my early call. But that special connection I always felt on my early-morning jaunts was never there later in the day. Trips to the greenhouse in the afternoon were for practical purposes, watering and disposing of bugs and removing detritus.

Such tasks seemed most unappealing at the moment, so instead of going out back I entered the Jungle with the itinerary Sam had given me. It said Brenda's flight had been scheduled for five-twenty, Monday evening. She had a three-hour stopover in Paris, then on to Antananarivo, Madagascar's capital. She would have spent a day there before leaving for the bush.

I looked up. Maybe I could have saved her if I'd been more insistent. I'd offered to drive her to the airport, but she preferred the shuttle. It avoided those tearful good-bye scenes, she said. I pointed out we were several years beyond tearful good-byes. She laughed and said, "You never know."

Now I shook my head. "You never do, do you, Brenda?"

The night before, Gina and I had talked about interrogating somebody. It was time to start. But with whom?

Half an hour later I pulled in next to a decrepit lime-green Renault Le Car in the Kawamura Conservatory's tiny parking lot. My spot was marked STAFF ONLY. I silently dared the Parking Gestapo to do something about it.

The conservatory was in the northwest quadrant of the gargantuan UCLA campus, near Pauley Pavilion. A ramshackle wooden sign announced it was only open to the public on Saturdays and alternate Tuesdays. This was because they had no funding. The reason they had no funding, according to the late Professor Belinski, was pure unadulterated asininity on the part of the administration. Brenda'd been fond of pointing out how the football team always had all the money they wanted, even though they sucked a lot of the time. She never did get it about college football.

I found the full-time staff of the conservatory, one Eugene Rand, in front of the entrance, digging up an aloe that had been infested with aloe mite. Not even a tub of Cygon will cure aloe mite.

Rand was in his mid-thirties, a failed graduate student unable to find his place in the world, who'd migrated to the conservatory because he liked plants more than he did people, and who Brenda kept on staff because he would work cheap. He'd lost his hair early and blown large portions of his meager salary on unsuccessful grafts. Something to do with an allergy to his own skin. The result was a red blotch resembling a map of Argentina right above where his hairline would have been if he'd still had one. I knew all this because Brenda had told me, which made me wonder what kind of privileged information about me she'd shared with other people.

Watery blue eyes studied me from beneath Rand's mistreated pate. "Hello," he said, tossing the uprooted aloe into a wheelbarrow. He was no more than five foot five, with skin dark from his hours in the sun. He wore a plain white T-shirt and a pair of threadbare denim shorts.

I told him who I was. He got a funny look on his face. "The article in the paper. You're the one who found her."

"Yes. I'm sorry for your loss." A little trite, but serviceable. "I just came up here to see if there was anything I could do."

"Do? Do? Just look at this place. It's falling to pieces. We have whiteflies and blackflies. I don't have money for fertilizer. My tools are all broken. And now, with Dr. Belinski gone, who's going to raise even the little bit we did get?" He nudged the wheelbarrow with his foot. "You see this? I bought it with my own money."

"I'll bet that hurt," I said.

"What did that mean?"

I smiled charmingly. "Just that universities aren't known for their generosity with their staffs. I'll bet you're not paid half of what you're worth. You could probably get a better job somewhere else. It's only your love for the conservatory that keeps you here."

A weird expression crossed his face, somewhere between puppy dog and sex offender. "That's right. Absolutely right."

I'd gotten on his good side, but now what? This interrogating business was harder than it looked. "Do you have any idea who might have wanted Dr. Belinski dead?"

"I don't think I want to go through this again."

"Again?"

"Yes. That detective was here yesterday afternoon. What was his name? Carillo. Cabrillo."

"Casillas," I said. "I'm kind of working with him."

"Then you should get the information from him. I don't want to talk about Dr. Belinski any more right now."

"You have no idea who might have wanted to kill her?"

"No! She was a wonderful woman. Why would anyone want to do that?"

"She could be nasty on occasion, couldn't she? Was she ever that way to you?"

"If she was ever unpleasant she had her reasons."

"The story goes that she stepped on a lot of toes, what with her pushing for tighter CITES enforcement."

"If toes were stepped on, they deserved to be."

"Yes," I said. "I'm sure that's true, but I hear they're desperate people, these CITES flouters. Did she ever receive any threats?"

"No. I'm sure Bren—Dr. Belinski would have told me if such a thing had happened. We were very close."

"How close?"

"What do you mean?"

"Word on the street is that she got around."

Silence. Lack of understanding. Or refusal to understand.

"That she had a lot of men friends. I was thinking maybe you were one of them."

"Never. I would never even think of such a thing. Dr. Belinski was a fine woman, whose social behavior was none of my business."

"Maybe," I said, "one of her lovers did her in."

Eugene Rand stared at me. Then he remembered his wheelbarrow needed to be somewhere else. He picked up its handles and marched it off toward a metal shack.

"Mr. Rand," I said, "I didn't mean to disturb you. I'd really like to catch Dr. Belinski's killer. They found the death plant at my place, you know."

He stopped and put down the wheelbarrow. He seemed about to say something, but after a few seconds he hoisted the barrow again and disappeared into the shack.

" 'Death plant'?" I said aloud. "What the hell kind of thing is that to say? And what was that about 'CITES flouters'?"

I hung around a few minutes, just in case the killer should show up to restock. He or she didn't. I returned to the truck and got out of there just as the Parking Gestapo showed up.

❦

Some freeways are dependable. For instance, you can pretty much count on the northbound San Diego just above LAX being jammed from seven till seven on any weekday. But the Santa Monica's capricious. It'll give you smooth sailing at rush hour for several days in a row, then entrap you in some ludicrous jam at 1:00 P.M.

So it was this afternoon. Just past the National–Overland exit, traffic squealed to a stop. All lanes were packed for as far ahead as I could see. When a minute's delay stretched into five, I got curious. So did the suit in the Infiniti to my left. He climbed out of his car and craned his neck off to the east, never losing a beat in his cell-phone conversation.

"Get off the damned phone," I told him. He didn't hear me.

I picked up my Earth Opera cartridge and considered whether to chance the player. What the hell. You could always get new copies of your eight-tracks. I shoved the tape in. They were just kicking off "The American Eagle Tragedy," their very sixties allegory of LBJ and Vietnam.

I slumped into the seat. The gods of traffic had dumped me there for a reason, I decided. I was to think about Brenda's murder until I came up with something significant.

But nothing useful percolated up from the recesses of my underused brain. I got thirsty. I dug around under my seat and came up with a bottle of Mango Madness Snapple with an inch of orange liquid remaining. Lord knew when I'd dumped it there. I dropped it on the passenger seat in case I got desperate. I glanced over at Infiniti Man. He was still yakking.

Think, I told myself. What do you know?

It had to be somebody involved with succulents. The chances of some transient or old boyfriend using a *Euphorbia abdelkuri* as a murder weapon? Next to nil. Add dumping the thing at my place and I lost the *next to*.

But what if someone wanted me to believe exactly that? What if someone from another part of Brenda's life had wanted to off her, had known about her involvement with succulent plants, and had learned just enough about them to be dangerous? And what if that person had it in for me and wanted to see me implicated? Was there such a person?

There might be. Four years before, when I'd started dating Brenda, she was seeing a guy named Henry Farber. Another professor, English or history or some social-science thing. He'd lived on a boat down in Long Beach. Brenda had planned to dump him anyway, but when she started seeing me she accelerated the timetable.

He came to my house one night and accused me of alienating her affections. I said I'd done no such thing, that they were alienated well before I came on the scene. He promised revenge. He was still there when Brenda happened to stop by. We had an ugly scene, with much wailing and gnashing of teeth. Brenda banished me to the greenhouse, and when she let me back in, Farber was gone, supposedly convinced I'd had nothing to do with her dumping him.

But what if he hadn't been? Or he had, but four years later, sick with regrets about a wasted life, he thought back to when things went wrong and pinpointed that moment at my house? He joined the Long Beach Cactus Club, borrowed a few volumes of the *Euphorbia Journal*, laid his nefarious plans. And one fine spring afternoon he ambushed her and stuck a plant both toxic and phallic down her throat, then left it at my place to make me the prime suspect.

Given the obvious symbolism of the murder weapon, this new twist on the spurned-lover theory had a certain attractiveness. I'd have to look up Mr. Henry Farber.

I needed to know more. I needed copies of the police reports. Oh, sure. I'd just march into the station. Find Casillas. *Hey, Hector, I need to know what the coroner had to say. If you'd be so kind, could you run me off a copy? Thank you so very much. I really appreciate it.*

When at last I got home, I decided to call Lyle Tillis. He was as active as anybody in the succulent subculture. Maybe he could provide me with a clue. I dialed him at work, and we arranged to meet at his place in the Valley at six.

I took a shower and walked naked into the backyard to air-dry. Gina thinks this practice is barbarous, but she's just jealous because she doesn't have a backyard. I stood in the sun, stretched my arms to my sides, enjoying the cooling effect of the water evaporating from my skin. The way things were arranged out back, a neighbor would really have to be trying if they wanted to see me. And why would they? I had nothing spectacular to show them.

When I was dry I pulled the U-bolt from the greenhouse door latch, went in, and considered my euphorbias. I had forty or so, not counting the less sun-tolerant ones in the shade house, where Casillas had found the abdelkuri stub. Tall ones, round ones, leafy ones, bald ones. The genus is huge, two thousand species or so, with four hundred of them succulent. Everything from *E. obesa*, the "baseball plant," to the virulent but widely grown *E. tirucalli*, known as the "pencil cactus" even though it isn't one. Plus giant tree forms, semisucculents like the crown of thorns, and, as we succulent enthusiasts are so fond of pointing out, the poinsettia.

As I'd told Casillas, it was all in the flowers. The true reproductive organs were always the same—a pistil and a few stamens, maybe some glands. Simple and elegant. What people thought of as the flowers were bracts, colorful leaves that had evolved to serve the same insect-attractant function as petals did on other plants. The gaudy red things on poinsettias were a prime example.

I picked up one species after another. There had to be some clue. I just needed the proper stimulus to pry it out.

I was standing there trying to divine what that stimulus might be when the golden polistes landed on my thigh.

Or maybe it had been there awhile. I don't know. I do know that I felt a tickling sensation, and when I looked down I found an inch-long yellow and black wasp exploring my leg three inches from my bare privates.

7

My ABSURD DREAD OF WASPS BEGAN THE SUMMER I WAS nine, at Camp Los-Tres-Arboles. A kid named Bobby Jewell was crying his head off one day, and the next he was gone. I asked my friend Norman Gonzalez if he knew what happened. "A wasp got him," he said.

"What do you mean, jelly bean?"

"A wasp can sting you ten times in the same place without dying. Each one's worse than the last one. If you're really unlucky you could die."

Since Norman had developed a reputation of knowing all sorts of neat stuff about nature, I took him at his word. And so a week later, when I was walking a log that stretched across Tres Arboles Creek, and when something big and black began buzzing around my head, I screamed my little lungs out, lost my balance, and tumbled into the streambed.

When I regained consciousness they showed me my bandaged temple in a mirror and told me the damage was from a rock. But I knew better. I knew a wasp had stung me. Only once, possibly twice. Enough to let me know that, given the chance, it would inject enough venom to kill me dead.

That was the start of it. From then on—even though I

quickly realized that Norman's grasp of natural history was questionable at best—the mere mention of a wasp drove me into a frenzy. More than once in my ensuing teenage years, I turned off some cute young thing by acting like a total maniac when we encountered one.

I mellowed somewhat with age, and got to the point where a yellow jacket taking a bite of my hamburger merely induced partial hysterical paralysis. I never got stung. But deep down inside I knew someday I was going to be. Ten times in the same place. The wasp wouldn't die. But I might.

❦

I did my dance. To the wasp's credit, it didn't sting me. Nor did it go anywhere.

My yells attracted one of the ding-a-lings next door. "What's going on back there?" said a female voice with a Southern accent. "Sounds like someone's dying."

I muttered, "Not yet," and fled out of the greenhouse into the yard, where the wasp figured out it wasn't wanted and buzzed off. I stood with my hands on my knees, catching my breath. I looked up to see a woman with a colossal shock of red hair grinning at me over the fence. She must have been standing on a milk crate. I managed a weak smile back and escaped into the house.

❦

I braved the rush hour on the northbound 405 and arrived at Lyle's just after six. He lived way up in Sunland by the Foothill Freeway, on a lot that didn't look big from the street but went way back. This gave him room for several greenhouses, lots of outdoor benches, and his mule.

The mule's name was Merlin. He and I didn't get along,

which was odd, since I usually have a good relationship with animals. Take Brenda's canaries, for instance. But the first time Merlin ever saw me he tried to bite my behind, and things had gone downhill ever since.

The minute I emerged from the truck he began braying. This brought Magda out of the house. "Quiet down, you big old bag," she told Merlin. "Joe is your friend." She grabbed his mane and dragged him around toward the back. "Lyle is inside. Please go in."

I went through the screen door into the sunken living room. Native American artwork hung from every wall, occupied every table, overflowed from the mantel. If one were into that kind of stuff, one would be overwhelmed. I wasn't, so I wasn't. I idly fingered a construction of twigs and feathers dangling on the wall between two masks. "Chumash," said Lyle.

I stifled the urge to say, "Bless you," and turned to say hello. He stood up on the riser to the hallway wearing only shorts and sandals. A thick mat of gray and black hair covered his chest and stomach. Lyle was almost ten years older than me, and in far better shape. His stomach muscles still had some definition.

He sometimes wore a full beard, but now he was clean-shaven, although his stubble was obvious from clear across the room. His hair was black, thick, and pulled back into one of those two-inch ponytails that look good on only the rarest of men, of which he wasn't one.

He bounded over and pumped my hand with one of his massive ones. "Picked it up near Ojai a couple of years ago," he said. "Old Indian guy in a cabin. Lived off the land." He fingered the trinket lovingly, patted it twice before stepping away. "Want a beer? How about a joint?" He laughed, a big, hearty, hairy-chested guy's laugh.

"A beer would be good," I said. Lyle offered me dope

every time I came up. One time on a trip to Baja he'd gotten drunk and admitted he'd never smoked the stuff.

We went into the kitchen. Lyle pulled two bottles labeled Kőbányai Korona from the fridge and gave me one. Magda came in and stirred something fragrant in the big pot on the stove. She took a taste with a wooden spoon. "Have some soup, Joe," she said.

I said that sounded good and sat down at the sturdy wooden table. Magda dished us out a couple of bowls. The soup was a flawless amalgam of beef and vegetables and essence of Hungary. It went perfectly with the beer.

When we were done Lyle led me outside and into one of the glasshouses. The sun was on its way down, but it was still hot inside. The greenhouse effect, you know.

Flat after flat of cacti and other succulents lined the benches. Everything from the rarest new finds to common species like the crown of thorns that were fodder for McAfee's and several other local nurseries. As I not-so-casually zeroed in on the euphorbias, Lyle followed behind, briskly straightening out any pot that had gone askew. I pointed at a half dozen abdelkuris, babies three inches high and half an inch in diameter. "Anyone bought any of these lately?"

"Sold a couple at the South Coast show a few weeks ago. These are the first I've grown. Seed's been real hard to get. It sounded from the paper like the one that killed Brenda was much bigger than this. Someone had that sucker a while. I hope they catch the guy."

"Or the woman."

He stopped short in front of a flat of aloes. You could see the wheels turning. "You think it could have been a woman? I never thought of that. I just assumed it was one of her old boyfriends." He looked over at me. "Not you, of course."

"Of course."

"But everyone knows she had a lot of boyfriends."

"Maybe she had girlfriends too."

His nose curled up. "A girl like Brenda? No. I know a dyke when I see one."

I'd have to share that comment with Gina. She could put it in her spreadsheet.

Lyle picked up a plant with little spiny arms growing from a big fat central stem. "Like the caudex on this one?" The fancy term for a big fat central stem.

"Sure. That's a nice one; which is it?"

"Euphorbia restricta." He waggled the plant at me. "Got to watch it with these. You grow them from cuttings, they don't get a caudex. All my caudex euphorbias are grown from seed."

"Nothing field-collected?"

He threw me a look like I'd suggested he engaged in carnal relations with Merlin. "Of course not. I wouldn't sell that shit. Goddamned habitat's being ripped to shreds." He thrust the *Euphorbia restricta* into my hand. "Here, take this."

"Uh."

"For free. As a gift. Like those catalogs my wife's always getting. They'll give you a bra or something to get you to come back as a customer."

"I haven't been gone as a customer."

"Whatever. Come on, take the plant."

"You don't have to do this."

"Fuck a duck, Joe, will you take the goddamned plant?"

It seemed prudent. "Okay," I said. "And thanks."

"You're welcome," he said, instantly calmer.

A minute later I ran across some nice *Euphorbia francoisii,* the colorfully leafed Madagascar dwarf Sam had mentioned, and that prompted me to get back to business. "Several people think Brenda's killing had something to do with plant smugglers."

"I met one of 'em once."

"You did? Where?"

"South Africa. On that trip last year."

"What'd he do, just walk up and say, 'I'm a plant smuggler'?"

This invoked a robust laugh. "I was in a bar in Johannesburg with a couple of the local succulent guys." I could see him there, drinking hearty brews with the hearty South Africans. "This guy in a bush jacket walks in and says hi to the locals. He has an accent, but I can't figure out what kind on account of everyone there talks funny anyway. He joins us at the table. They're all blabbing away, and all of a sudden they start arguing. Turns out the guy's on his way to Namibia to dig stuff up. My two friends are trying to convince him not to, and he tells us about how the market in Europe is dying to have these plants, and so it doesn't matter if they're all dug up. So they go back and forth for a while, and nobody convinces anybody of anything, and as far as I know the guy went off that day and dug up everything he wanted to."

"Did you catch his name?"

He scratched his hairy chest. "It was a German name. One of those *Sh* names."

"Schoeppe?"

He cocked his head at me. "Yeah, that was it. How'd you know?"

"You're sure it was Willy Schoeppe?"

His brow furrowed. "No. Not Willy. It was something else. Hans or . . . Hermann. That was it. Hermann Schoeppe."

"Hmm."

"What?"

"How common a name do you think Schoeppe is?"

"Don't have a clue. Hey. It's getting dark, and we have two more greenhouses to look at."

Forty-five minutes later I drove off with my wallet lighter by the forty dollars I'd spent on the box of plants on the seat beside me. As I pulled away I threw a look back at the house. Merlin was again out by the front fence, regarding me with a baleful eye. I regarded him right back with one of my own.

8

I PULLED INTO A MINI-MART ON FOOTHILL BOULEVARD AND parked next to a Toyota pickup with tires as tall as I was. A young bleached blonde sat in the passenger seat, screaming at several brats who boomeranged around the cab. "I'll break your heads," she said, over and over.

I didn't have any change and went through several minutes of long-distance-carrier bingo before getting Gina's phone to ring. "Hello?"

"Hi, it's me. I'm coming over."

"You can't."

"Whaddaya mean I can't?"

"I have a date with Carlos."

"Is he the volleyball player who likes Hockney or the flower arranger with the great ass?"

"Great ass."

"Cancel."

"I can't. He's taking me to this new coffeehouse. There's a poetry reading."

"You hate poetry."

"I like coffee."

"Fine. Cancel Carlos and I'll come over and make you coffee."

"I thought I might get lucky tonight."

"No way. Carlos is gay."

"What makes you say that?"

"I know a fag when I see one."

A pause. "I can't believe you said that."

"Cancel Carlos and I'll come over and tell you *why* I said it. Here's a hint: It has to do with one of my detecting excursions today."

"You had detecting excursions?"

"Yeah, didn't you?"

"Uh . . ."

"You didn't? You were the one so hot to get us into all this, and you didn't have one single solitary excursion?"

"I had clients."

"I'm coming over. Ditch Carlos."

"Don't be surprised if I'm not here when you get here."

"Fine. You eat yet?"

"No."

"I'll pick up some Mexican."

It took me a while to find my way out of the hinterlands. It was nearing nine when I reached Ten Forty Havenhurst, the West Hollywood condo where Gina lives. She buzzed me in and I went up.

"Where's my tostada?" she said as she opened her front door.

"Right here. Where's Carlos?"

She carried the food into the kitchen. "At the poetry reading, I suppose."

"I hope he didn't take it too hard."

"No."

"I would have understood if you went with him. Especially 'cause you might have gotten lucky."

"Bottom line is, I didn't want to. Carlos is cute, but he has the intelligence of a bowling ball. I'm getting too old for recreational sex."

A couple of minutes later we were shoving food in our faces at Gina's bird's-eye maple dining table. It was typical of the impeccable way she'd done the place up. The living–dining room was all earth tones, with an opulent leather sofa as the centerpiece and several expensive-looking tapestries on the wall. The fixtures in the kitchen were straight out of *House and Garden*; those in the bathroom shone like spun gold. Her bedroom was done up in blues, with hundred-and-fifty-dollar-a-yard drapes that shimmered like a mirage when they caught the light and a down comforter that could have done duty at Buckingham Palace. The carpet throughout was so pristine it made you ashamed to walk on it.

All that expensive stuff—most of which she'd gotten at huge discounts, she was quick to point out—could have made the place seem cold, but Gina'd interspersed enough weird Gina stuff to overcome that. Schlocky tourist gewgaws from Olvera Street. A cello, propped up in the corner of the living room, that she hadn't played since college. The goofy plaster-of-Paris bust of Simón Bolívar her mother had made at the senior center.

I filled her in on my adventures. When I got to Eugene Rand she said, "Sounds like he had a thing for Brenda."

"Definitely."

"Think he'd ever do anything about it?"

"You mean like ask her out? Make a pass at her out among the cacti? Ask her if she'd like him to pollinate her ovules?" I thought it over. "I don't know. What if he did?"

"Is he attractive?"

"He's not a good-looking man."

"Brenda liked her lovers attractive. So she would have

turned him down. And then his disappointment, his resentment would have festered, grown unchecked, until one day he waited in her bathroom and plunged a plant down her throat."

"Half a plant," I said. "Which he later hid the rest of at my place."

"Not likely, huh? Where else did you go?"

She got all excited about the two Schoeppes. "Let's find out if they're related."

"How do you propose to do that?"

"Call the one in Madagascar."

"I don't think they have phones there."

"You're so Eurocentric. Of course they have phones there."

"Out in the bush?"

"They could have cellular. Where's that itinerary you got from Sam?"

"At home."

"I need to put it in the spreadsheet."

"Stop with the spreadsheet."

"I want you to call Madagascar the minute you get home."

"What else do you want me to do?"

"Question some more people."

"Who, for instance?"

"Maybe you could go back to UCLA. Find some colleagues."

I picked up what was left of my burrito and stuck it in my mouth. Sour cream dripped on my shorts, threatened to run down, bounce off the elegant chair, splatter on the spotless carpet. Gina's eyes went wide.

I dabbed at the white stuff with a napkin. "All right, I'll call Madagascar. Christ, maybe I ought to get on the Internet too."

"What's that supposed to mean?"

I told her about Sam's little demonstration the day before. Her eyes lit up. She got up and headed for her bedroom. When she came out she was carrying her computer and a long phone cord. "What?" I said. "We're going to call up the smugglers' computer?"

She was plugging in cables and pushing buttons. "Do you have any idea how the Web works?"

"No, and I don't want to."

"Pull your chair over and watch. And don't roll your eyes at me."

The computer came to life. Gina moused around, boops and beeps sounded, and the computer presented us with a screen full of furniture. *Regina Vela Interiors* marched across the top. "What's this?"

"It's my home page."

"What's it for?"

"People see it and call me up."

"People surf the Internet for an interior designer? How much business has this brought in?"

"None yet, but—"

"Who did this for you?"

"I did it myself."

"You did? Very impressive. Show me some cactus stuff."

She keyed and moused some more. Now the screen displayed something called the Cactus and Succulent Mall. "Watch." She moved down to where it said *Culver City Cactus Club* and clicked the mouse. After an interminable wait some more verbiage appeared. Factoids about the club. Halfway down were the words *Our President*, and suddenly I was staring at a picture of Brenda, with Lyle in the background in his bearded days, and a white spot I thought might be the top of Rowena's head.

"Weird," I said.

We bounced around for three quarters of an hour and ended up back at the Cactus and Succulent Mall. I saw something about Cacti_etc. "Hey, Sam mentioned that."

Gina clicked on it, read what appeared, and got all excited. "We have to subscribe."

"Why?"

"Because it's a mailing list."

"So Sam said."

"We can post a question, and whole bunches of cactus people will see it. We can ask about Brenda."

What could it hurt? "Sign us up."

She read the instructions, pressed, and clicked. "All done."

"Now what?"

"Now we wait."

"How long?"

"It depends on the listserv they're using and—" She stopped when she saw me shaking my head. "What? What's wrong?"

"Gina, Gina, Gina. I knew you when you were a nice girl who didn't use words like *listserv*. Look what's happened to you."

"You have your hobby. I needed one too."

I left around midnight, got a reasonable night's sleep, and rose at eight. I journeyed out to the greenhouse and was relieved to find my metaphysical connection with my plants was nearly back to normal, that Brenda's death hadn't forever soured my early-morning tours. When I was done in there I stayed out back, sipping the last of my litchi tea, enjoying the shifting light as the sun ascended. A mockingbird flew down onto the lawn. She poked around in a yellowed patch and left empty-beaked. Somewhere down the block a car alarm wailed.

Brenda's funeral was at three, and I didn't have a whole lot to do before then. I went in, slid aside one of the sliding mirrored doors to my bedroom closet, and pulled out my one suit. I ironed my white shirt and shined my dress shoes. My rhinoceros tie seemed appropriate. A homage to Brenda, the African connection and all. I threw some normal clothes in a gym bag for after the funeral, in case I didn't come straight home. No point being in a suit longer than absolutely necessary.

Showering and shaving took me up till ten. I sat on the couch with a silent soap opera on the TV, trying to figure out what to do next.

The phone rang. It was Dick McAfee. "We need to talk about something," he said.

"About what?"

"I'd rather not say. Can you come by my house after Brenda's funeral? Say, five o'clock?"

"Sure. Or before, if you like."

"No, I'm heading for the nursery in half an hour and won't be back home until five."

"Aren't you going to the funeral?"

"I don't go to funerals. A little quirk of mine. I prefer to say my good-byes privately."

"I'll see you at five, then."

I hung up and called Gina. "Did we get any e-mail yet?"

"As a matter of fact, we did. Like a dozen already. I'm just looking at them now."

"Anything interesting?"

"Here's a good one. Some guy is defending smuggling plants. He doesn't use that word exactly, but he— Wait, let me page down a little more. Oh, get this. *God put those plants there for our enjoyment, and I don't see anything wrong with digging them up.* He spelled "plants" with an apostrophe, by the way."

"Is he a German?"

"Is Cedar Rapids in Germany?"

"Not last time I looked."

"Then no. And that's the last of it."

"Why don't we send an e-mail of our own?" I said. "We could tell everyone what we're up to and see if anybody has any ideas."

"But what if the killer's lurking out there? He might come after us."

"I hope you're not serious."

"Half."

"I'll leave it up to you, Gi. If you're afraid don't do it. Are you coming to Brenda's funeral?"

"If I finish with my twelve-thirty in time. You're sure it's okay?"

"I don't think they sell tickets. Come if you want. There'll be lots of suspects there."

She said she would try, and we hung up. I still couldn't think of anything to do, so I dug out Sunday's paper and riffled through the Calendar section. The first show of the new Jackie Chan was at eleven. Off I went. But when I got to the theater, I was overcome with guilt. Gina and I always went to Jackie Chans together. I took in the new hit comedy instead. Some Jim Carrey thing. The other six people thought it was pretty funny.

9

I STROLLED DOWNHILL ALONG A CURVED PATH LINED WITH rhododendrons and tree ferns, all maintained with tender loving care. Terrestrial orchids and exotic ground covers carpeted the surface below. The walkway opened up into a picturesque clearing. Topiary animals cavorted off to my left; on the right a terraced garden of azaleas and miniature bamboo worked its way back up the hill. Birds twittered, and dappled sunlight danced on the ground. I'd been at Final Haven two minutes and already I wanted to be buried there too.

A stone building with the near end open stood in the center of the clearing. Abstract paintings and exotic sculptures lay within. Wooden pews faced a simple altar, in front of which a plain wood casket rested.

I sidled off behind an acacia and situated myself where I could see who was coming or going. Coming, more likely; the only one going was Brenda. Rowena Small got there soon after I did and grabbed a seat in the front row. Five minutes later Eugene Rand showed up, wearing a black suit jacket and old chinos and the worst-tied tie I'd ever seen. He looked right at me but didn't or wouldn't recognize me and took a spot halfway back on the right.

Detective Hector Casillas appeared, chatting with Lyle Tillis. Casillas had his suit from Monday back on. Lyle wore no jacket, and the end of his tie hung three inches above his belt. Magda followed three steps behind him, in a simple blue dress.

More people filtered in. Some I vaguely recognized as colleagues of Brenda's. A short cute chubby blond woman. A few more cactus folks, like Austin and his wife, Vicki.

Frank Balter, Brenda's lawyer, arrived, accompanied by a tall woman in a simple black dress garnished with a pearl necklace. She was willowy, with well-defined cheekbones and dark brown, shoulder-length hair, and even if she hadn't been with Balter, I would have guessed she was Brenda's sister, Amanda. Her eyes gave her away. The same odd green as Brenda's, tending toward yellow. The same oval shape. The same long lashes.

Balter had her by the elbow and led her to the front row. Rowena immediately popped up and offered condolences.

Brenda's friend Toussaint Razafindratsira appeared. He was born in Madagascar but had come to the U.S. for graduate school and stayed. His dark face was a unique mix that Brenda'd told me represented both African and Indonesian lineage. He carried a staff with a stylized lemur carved into its head and was wrapped head to toe in a length of colorful cloth—a *lamba*, the traditional Malagasy garment. Brenda'd worn them when she was feeling particularly Madagascan.

He took a position behind the dark wood podium and asked everyone to be seated. As the mourners filtered in I found a spot in the next-to-last row on the left side, on the outside aisle, where I could watch most of the crowd.

When the rustling stopped, Razafindratsira spoke. "Brenda came to Madagascar many times. She grew to understand our people and tried to protect our natural heritage." His accent had been dimmed by his years in the States but still came through as a peculiar lilt, an unusual separation of syllables. "She has requested to be buried in the traditional manner of the Mahafaly, the people of the thorn forest in the south of our island." He paused and his eyes swept the crowd. "We who come from Madagascar believe death is but a milestone in the journey each person travels. So do not grieve for Brenda. She has simply moved on."

He strode over to her coffin and began to speak in what I took for his native language. He stood over it for several minutes, gesturing with his staff at irregular intervals. I got caught up in the whole thing until I remembered I was supposed to be watching the crowd. I casually turned my head to the right. Somebody was watching right back.

His Mediterranean face was tanned and creased and his salt-and-pepper hair precisely cut. He wore sunglasses and a well-cut dark gray suit, a light gray shirt, and burgundy tie. He seemed tall, and a little overweight, until I realized the extra poundage was well-disguised muscle.

He removed his shades. Our eyes locked. His were pale blue. He smiled, a kind of tensing of the upper lip that left the lower one in place. Something glinted gold in his mouth. I turned away.

Razafindratsira seemed to be winding down. His eyes scanned the crowd as he told us some more about death and the Malagasy.

I snuck a peek over to the right. Sunglasses Guy was gone. I turned all the way around. He wasn't anywhere in sight. Instead of him, I saw Gina hustling down the path. She wore the navy suit she saves for well-heeled clients. Her hair dropped in blue-black sheets to her shoulders, save for an errant tress by her left temple. I ran my hand through my hair in the appropriate area. She got the point and smoothed down her own and slid into the spot behind me. "What did I miss?" she whispered.

"Not much. Did you see a big guy with sunglasses on your way in?"

"No."

"Hmm. There was this guy sitting on the other side who didn't look like he belonged. He was watching me. Maybe he's a cop."

Across the aisle, Eugene Rand cast a dirty look and put his finger to his lips. I shut up. Several minutes later Razafindratsira stood beside Brenda's casket, with one hand atop it. "We will now move on to the interment ceremony."

Everyone adjourned to the grave site, further down the hill in a wide meadow studded with a variety of burial structures: a weird pile of rocks, an upside-down stone cross, a wicker tepee. A garland of vegetables rested atop a giant wooden spool. Music flowed from hidden speakers. I picked out accordion, flute, and clarinet.

Brenda's tomb was a white-painted structure about four by eight feet, and three high. On each side a geometrical border in blues and purples ran round an assortment of painted scenes. In one, a light-faced woman and several dark-faced men knelt before a stylized plant. Four wooden poles, about eight feel tall, stood at the corners, each topped by a carving symbolizing an aspect of Brenda's life. One showed her with a plant in her hand. Another had her with a strange tube to her eye. I finally realized it represented a microscope. The third carving included two small figures by a larger one; I guessed it symbolized her teaching. The last had her holding something resembling an overgrown penis. The Malagasy believed in telling it like it is.

When I looked more closely I discovered the tomb was merely a wooden simulation. Its roof leaned against a pile of dirt a few feet away, and inside the walls coffin-lowering apparatus topped a normal grave.

Four beefy attendants carried the coffin down the hill, maneuvered it between the walls, and sent it slowly into the ground. Toussaint Razafindratsira gestured for silence. "We have a saying in Madagascar," he intoned. "A house is only for a lifetime; a tomb is for eternity. Thus it will be for Brenda." Some prayers were said, and that was that.

Everyone milled around aimlessly. Razafindratsira came up to me and we shook hands. "It was a fine service," I said.

"It did go rather well," he said. "It is difficult, though, to compress our ceremonies into the time frame Americans are comfortable with. Major elements must be dispensed with entirely. Keeping the body in state until the flesh is decomposed, for instance. Wanton sexual activity as well." He sighed. "Ah, well. Such is life in America." He moved on.

I went back up the hill to the chapel and walked over to Amanda to pay my respects. She stood where the coffin had been, looking perplexed. I held out a hand and introduced myself. "I'd known Brenda several years," I said as we shook. "I'm feeling quite a sense of loss." Okay, so I'm not good with death. "Of course, not anywhere near as much as you must be feeling."

Off to the side I could see Gina, out of Amanda's line of sight. She clapped her hand to her temple and shook her head.

"Yes," Amanda said. "Brenda mentioned you in her letters. I understand you discovered her body."

I nodded. Why did she have to bring that up?

"Did she look like she was in any pain?"

"No."

"Did she look like she died quickly?"

"Yes. I'm sure she never knew what hit her." Liar, liar, pants on fire.

Amanda nodded. "I'm going to be in town for a few days.

I'd like the opportunity to speak with you. Brenda and I had grown so far apart. I'd like to speak to someone who knew her these last few years."

"That would be good," I said.

"I have a room at the Loews in Santa Monica. Do you know it?"

"Yes. It's quite pleasant." Ever so civilized, that Portugal.

"I need to be alone for a while. You understand. Perhaps you could stop by Saturday night."

"I think I could fit that in."

"Say seven-thirty?"

"That would be fine."

"Room 621." She turned and walked prettily back down to the tomb.

As I watched her recede, a vision blossomed full-blown in my head. Amanda and I would assuage each other's pain by making love all night long. She would cry in my arms, and I in hers. I would kiss away her tears.

Ridiculous. Brenda not in the ground ten minutes, and already I was planning her sister's seduction.

But the vision, insensitive to my guilt, persisted. Amanda would light a cigarette. "For Brenda," she would say, and we would share it. In the morning I would leave, never to see her again.

"You're having one of your sex fantasies," Gina said.

I whipped my head around. She stood a few feet behind me, grinning like a maniac. "How could you tell?"

"Your nostrils were flaring and you licked your lips."

"I did not."

"Did. You gonna go?"

"Of course. She could be valuable to our investigation."

"Valuable to your sex life, you mean. But, hey, why not? She *is* kind of cute, in a Midwestern corn-fed sort of way. Nice eyes. Come on, let's get out of here."

We left the mourners behind, made our way up past the natural wonders on the hill, found our vehicles. "Now what?" Gina asked.

"I'm supposed to go see Dick McAfee. Want to come?"

She followed me to Dick's place. He and Hope lived on Warren Avenue in the nice part of Mar Vista, near Santa Monica Airport. Huge evergreens overhung the street; their invasive roots buckled the asphalt. It was a nice block, a family block. Kids rode bikes. Couples walked dogs. A gardener trimmed the eugenias at the house next door.

I'd taken off my jacket and tie when we left the funeral, but the suit pants and dress shirt were still too confining. I reached into the truck bed and grabbed the gym bag with my everyday clothes. I could change in Dick's bathroom.

We walked up the driveway and onto the front porch. Dick had festooned it with pots of big barrel cacti. A foot-wide ferocactus was in bloom, though its purple flowers were closing up for their evening's rest. A gigantic *Boweia volubilis*—a climbing onion—sent its shoots twirling around a pillar all the way to the roof.

I rang the bell. The strains of "La Cucaracha" resonated inside. After a decent interval I rang again. This time it was the first few notes of "Lara's Theme."

"Ring it a few more times," Gina said. "See if you can get the macarena."

"Maybe he's in the back." I pressed my face up against a window, shaded my brow with my hand. A dining room. Nothing out of the ordinary. "Yeah, let's go try the back."

We clomped off the porch, followed the driveway along the house, went through a big wooden gate. A giant syca-more dominated the backyard, its branches spreading from one property line to the other. The spiny brown fruits—we called then "itchy balls" when I was a kid—littered the ground.

Dick didn't have a greenhouse, though shade cloth protected several tables full of plants. An eight-foot wood fence ringed the yard. In the back, sugar-snap peas clung to green mesh. Passionflower vines covered one side; on the other he'd planted a pereskia, a primitive leafed cactus resembling a climbing rose more than a denizen of the desert. He must have kept it trimmed; it formed a nice neat hedge. Unchecked, I knew from painful experience, pereskia would cover the side of a house in no time.

"Dick?"

"He's not here," Gina said. "You've been stood up. Come on, let's go get some ice cream."

"He's got to be here. Dick is the most responsible man I know. Maybe he's in the garage."

"Fine. Go look in the garage. When you don't find him we'll go to Baskin-Robbins."

The side door to the garage was ajar. I poked my head in and flicked on the light. He had an old Buick in there—early fifties was my guess—that he was restoring. Scraps of fabric and pots of glue were scattered about. I walked in and took a quick look at the dash. I've always had a fascination with dashboards. "Neat," I said.

I turned around. Gina stood in the doorway, wearing an expression I'd seen only once before. "You're not going to believe this," she said.

We stared at each other for a good ten seconds before I said, "Where?"

"Behind the big tree."

She stepped aside as I walked out of the garage and followed me as I went across the lawn and around the sycamore. When she caught up with me, she slipped her hand in mine and held on as if she'd never let go. The two of us stood gaping at the spectacle draped on the back side of the tree.

A wooden cross had been nailed to the trunk. Dick

McAfee was tied to the cross-member by lengths of cord around his upper arms. His head dropped to one side and his eyes were closed. His naked feet dangled six inches above the ground.

His arms were spread wide, and somebody had driven spines through his hands. Three inches long, wickedly sharp, from *Euphorbia grandicornis* was my guess. And, adding insult to injury, whoever had pulled off this heinous stunt had taken a branch of *Euphorbia milii*, and twisted it into a ring, and tied the ends together with a thin green plant tie. They'd placed the ring on Dick's head, pushing it down so it would stay in place. The spines had opened dozens of tiny cuts that were the least of Dick's troubles.

Euphorbia mili. Common name: crown of thorns. Supposedly the plant Jesus wore on his head when he, like my cactus cohort Dick McAfee, had been crucified.

10

Two hours later Gina and I were standing with detective Alberta Burns on the McAfee front sidewalk. She and Casillas had come and done their cop stuff, while Gina and I hung out with a gaggle of uniformed officers. Someone had found Hope at the homeless shelter she volunteered at on Thursdays and brought her back home. A knot of onlookers had gathered; most still hung on. All those kids with bikes and couples with dogs.

Speaking of dogs, the local news hounds had already sniffed the situation out. Two of their vans were parked a few houses away. Across the street the blonde from Channel 6 rehearsed a stand-up.

"He was already dead when they strung him up," Burns was saying. "There was a blow to the head."

"Blunt-force trauma," I said.

My impressive command of police lingo surprised her, I think. "The thorns through the hands were a nice touch," she said. "Don't you think?"

"Spines."

"Excuse me?"

"Botanically, they're spines, not thorns."

"I see. By the way, where were you when he was killed?"

"When would that have been?"

"Late morning, according to the coroner investigator."

"We spoke on the phone around ten. He said he was going to the nursery in half an hour. Whoever it was must have come right after I talked to him. Christ."

"What's the matter, Mr. Portugal?"

"If I'd rushed over after we talked, I might have saved him."

"How would you know there would be something to save him from?"

"Oh, yeah."

"Were you somewhere we could verify between, say, ten and noon?"

"I went to the movies at eleven. Somebody there should remember me. I was the one who wasn't laughing."

"We'll check it out. What about you, Ms. Vela?"

"I was with a client from eleven until two-thirty."

She nodded. "We'll need a name and number."

We answered some more questions. When she told us we could go, I hustled Gina off toward our vehicles. I'd gotten her into hers and had the Datsun's door open when Casillas materialized. "What's in the bag?"

I'd been clinging to the gym bag like a life preserver since I first walked around the sycamore. It dangled from my fingers, all sporty and blue with a white Dodgers logo. "Clothes," I said.

"That all?"

"A hanger. To hang my suit up."

"One always wants to hang one's suit up, doesn't one?"

I tossed the bag on the ground. "Just open it, okay? Just be done with your harassment so I can go home."

He spread his hands. "If you insist." He knelt by the bag, fumbled with a zipper that hadn't worked right since I left it out under the sprinkler the previous summer. When at last it opened he reached in and pulled out a T-shirt. Joe Walsh, olive green, early eighties. "Very nice," he said, tossing it on the ground. Next came my denim cutoffs. A pair of white socks. Cheap canvas sneakers from Payless Shoe Source. And finally, with much dramatic widening of eyes, a roll of green plastic plant ties.

It was a different interrogation room than the one on Tuesday, but most of the details were the same. Only the gouges in the table were distinctive. Someone had raked their fingernails across it after Casillas whipped their face with a rubber hose.

He and Burns had the good-cop–bad-cop thing down to a science. First he'd browbeat me for a while. Then Burns would replace him at the table and soothe me with her dulcet tones.

It was Casillas's turn. "Jeez," he said. "Things keep turning up on you, don't they?"

"Listen just once more, because I'm not telling you again. I left the bag in the back of the truck at the funeral. Anybody there could have planted the ties in it. Any of the cactus people. Even Brenda's sister. Even *you*."

"Accusing L.A.'s finest of planting evidence?"

"Look," I said. "Given that you think I'm stupid enough to shove a plant down a woman's throat and leave the stub lying around my yard, do you really think I'm so *monumentally* stupid as to do the same kind of thing again? Talk to anybody. Ask them if they ever saw me use a thin plastic tie. Everyone knows I like the soft, wide kind."

While that statement didn't convince anybody of anything, it was dumb enough to shut them up. I jumped into the breach. "Do you have someone watching me?"

"Watching you?" Burns said. "As in, following you around?"

"Yeah."

The two of them exchanged looks. "You tell him," Burns said.

"What?" I said. "Tell me what?"

Casillas pulled off his glasses and rubbed his eyes. "This isn't the only case we have to work on, you know."

What was he doing, going for the sympathy vote? "Go on."

"We've got a gang-killing in Venice, another over by Mar Vista Gardens, and a body dump in Ballona Creek. We're not just working your goddamned serial succulent killer."

"And this means what to me?"

"Everybody else around here has the same kind of case-load. You think we've got the manpower to spend following you around?" He and Burns swapped glances again. She frowned and shrugged her shoulders. "Why don't you go home," Casillas said. "And do me a favor. Don't go finding any more dead bodies."

"I'll try my best." I got up and hurried toward the door, certain he was going to call me back any second. It was a cruel joke. He would throw me in the hole. Cockroaches would be my friends.

It didn't happen. I emerged into the hall. Burns waited long enough to let me feel stupid and came out and escorted me up front. Gina sat waiting for me in the lobby, all worried-looking. She jumped up when she saw me, hugged me fiercely, led me out to her car, and took me home.

Sometimes things get so depressing or so weird that you need something to remind you of a better time and place. Or a simpler one. When people you knew didn't end up with spines through their hands and the only plant you put in your mouth was marijuana. Certain record albums can be counted on as such a reminder. Neil Young's *After the Gold Rush*. Jefferson Airplane and *Surrealistic Pillow*.

At nine thirty-five on this particular Thursday evening, it was *Beggar's Banquet*, which, as far as I'm concerned, was the last really good Rolling Stones album. "Parachute Woman" blasted through the speakers in my living room, and Gina's ears perked up. "Did he say what I thought he said?"

"You mean about 'blow me out'?"

"Uh-huh."

"That's what I've always thought he was saying. But I've been known to get lyrics wrong. For decades in some cases." I took a sip of Snapple. "Who do you know that would want to set me up as a murderer?"

"Could be anybody. What are you going to do about it?"

"I'm getting on the phone to Madagascar. You work on your spreadsheet or get back on the Internet or something."

She went out to the car for her computer, and I rooted around for Brenda's itinerary. By the time I found it, Gina was on the couch with the computer in her lap and was mousing away.

Brenda's travel plans had put her in Antananarivo for only one day. Her companions would already be in the bush, unless Sam's cable had reached them and persuaded them to stick around town mourning or something. I dialed a ton of digits and was rewarded with the news that all circuits were busy. I put down the phone and dropped down next to Gina.

"There's, like, fifteen more messages since this morning," she said.

"Did you send one like we talked about?"

"Uh-huh. Wait a minute, I'll show you. Here."

I squinted to make out the screen. She'd paid three thousand dollars for her computer, and you couldn't read the damned thing. *Anybody knowing anything about the death of Brenda Belinski or any of her affairs before her death please e-mail privately to designwoman@aol.com. Weirdos and murderers need not apply.*

"Not bad," I said. "Short and to the point. Did you get any replies?"

"I'm not sure. Let me wade through the rest of this stuff. It all gets mixed up with my regular e-mail, which is mostly junk anyway."

The doorbell rang. "Who's got their kids selling chocolate bars at this time of night?" I said. The bell rang again. "I'm coming. Hold your damned horses."

My father always taught me to ask who it was when I answered the door. My father probably had more reason than most to do so. But what good would it do? If the killer were out there, he could just shoot me through the door.

So I pulled it open. It wasn't a kid with a Rubbermaid full of sweets. It was a grown-up. His face was reddish, his blond hair combed straight back, his mouth crooked. He appeared to be in his mid-fifties, with crinkly facial skin from which sprouted a couple of days' growth of blond stubble. His clothing was brown and rumpled. "Mr. Portugal?" When I uh-huhed he held out a hand.

"Very nice to meet you. I'm Willy Schoeppe."

11

I TOOK THE OFFERED HANDSHAKE IN A BIT OF A TRANCE.
"Hi," I said. "I just tried to call you in Madagascar."

"I don't suppose I was there."

Gina jumped up from the couch, introduced herself, and
maneuvered him and his battered leather suitcase through
the door. As he passed into the living room, she raised an eyebrow at me. I shrugged. "Make yourself at home," I said.
Once he had, I asked, "To what do we owe the honor of this
visit?"

"Sam Oliver told me I should speak to you." His accent
wasn't quite as thick as I would have expected. He spoke
quickly, with everything sounding like it came through
pursed lips. "I spoke to him from the airplane."

"Sam's in Tucson."

"Yes, I know. I spoke to him in Tucson. Isn't it wonderful
now, you can pick up a telephone from the back of the seat in
front of you and call anywhere in the world."

"You're telling the wrong guy how wonderful it is,"
Gina said.

"Call anywhere except Madagascar, that is," he went on.

"I tried to reach Doug Hammer numerous times since I left there but was unable to get through. Ach." He shifted his weight, trying to find a comfortable spot on the couch. "I have spent the last three days in airports and on airplanes. Air travel to and from Madagascar is not difficult if you are prepared well in advance, but last-minute arrangements are troublesome. I had to transfer in Ouagadougou. I spent the night there as well. Have you ever spent the night in Burkina Faso?"

"Can't say as I have," I said.

He asked for a glass of water, and Gina brought him one. He held it up to the light, saw we were watching him, smiled. He was always smiling, like everything in life was a big happy merry-go-round. "One gets in the habit of inspecting one's water when one spends time in Madagascar. Not that one can see all the nasty things inside. However." He downed half the glass, placed it carefully on the coffee table. "So. I came as soon as I heard. It is a terrible thing, no?"

"It is a terrible thing, yes," I said. "Assuming you're talking about Brenda's murder and not the water in Antananarivo."

Yet another smile. None of them real big, but a constant stream. "Yes, of course. I truly wished to be at the funeral, but the airline situation prohibited it. I am sorry to have missed it." He rubbed his chin and appeared surprised at the stubble he found there. "I understand you are investigating Brenda's demise."

Gina nodded. "And Dick's."

For the first time Schoeppe's expression wasn't so happy-go-lucky. The ever-present smile gave way to a puzzled frown. "Dick's? Who is this Dick?"

Of course. No one knew but Gina and me and anyone Hope had managed to call. This was my big chance. I could telephone everyone I knew and gauge their reaction to Dick's death. Eugene Rand and Henry Farber. The entire Department of Botany at UCLA. Anyone who'd ever been to South Africa.

Only one problem with that: the news vans at Dick's. The local TV news fiends were already all over the story like flies on a carrion flower. The story had doubtless been on Channel 6 already. *"New developments tonight in the shocking death of UCLA professor Brenda Belinski . . ."*

We filled Schoeppe in on Dick. "This Mr. McAfee," he said. "Was he involved in conservation?"

"Some," I said. "He had a letter in the *Journal* a few months back. Called the plant smugglers some pretty nasty names."

"They sound so dangerous," Gina said. "Evidently they macheted a ranger."

"Sam told you that," Schoeppe said. A statement, not a question.

"Yes," I said.

"I do not believe that incident happened. These people . . . they are not violent. That is why I find it difficult to believe they were involved in Brenda's death."

I cleared my throat. "May I ask you something?"

"Yes?"

"Do you know a Hermann Schoeppe?"

That momentary retreat of the smile again. "Yes, I do. Why do you ask?"

"Are you related to him?"

"He is my brother. Has Hermann's name come up in this business?"

I told him about my conversation with Lyle. When I was done he sighed deeply. "Hermann is what you would call the black sheep of the Schoeppes. Even when we were boys, he was always looking for—what do you Americans say—an angle. I have not seen him in several years. But I have heard much about my brother's adventures." He held his glass out to Gina. "May I have some more water?" I got the feeling he wasn't thirsty, that he was stalling. When she returned he put the glass on the table without touching its contents and rubbed his eyes with his fingertips. "What you have heard is true. It is most uncomfortable for a man like me, a man deeply concerned about our natural heritage, to rub shoulders with my colleagues knowing my own brother is one of our adversaries."

I said, "Do you think—"

"That he had something to do with Brenda's death? No. I do not." His smile was resigned now. "Whatever else you may say about Hermann, he is not a violent man. He may be clever and devious, but he would never hurt anyone."

Except for the thrum of the refrigerator, we sat in silence. Gina broke it. "I've been hearing all this about the plant smugglers. About this CITES thing. But how exactly was Brenda involved? What did she hope to accomplish?"

He sipped his water, licked his lips. "She was on the verge of a breakthrough with the Malagasy government. While they have in general been cooperative, until now harsh economic realities have kept them from giving us support. That was about to change. We were going to collect some final data before returning to Antananarivo to sign an agreement that would enact the harshest of penalties against anyone caught smuggling plant material out of the country. Up to and including death."

It seemed draconian, but who was I to say? "So these plant smugglers—the evil ones, as opposed to your brother, who is merely a crook—maybe they sent someone to prevent her coming."

He shrugged. His eyes drooped, and his words came slowly. "All of this is mere hypothesizing. As I have said, I do not have any reason to believe plant smugglers had anything to do with Brenda's death." He stood suddenly, regarded Gina and me in turn. "But I have intruded quite enough. Perhaps we can speak tomorrow, when I am rested. I only wanted to make your acquaintance this evening, Mr. Portugal. Ms. Vela, it was quite enjoyable making yours as well."

"Where are you staying?" I asked.

"At the Loews in Santa Monica. I always stay there when in Los Angeles. It has a lovely view of the ocean."

"So I've heard. Brenda's sister is staying there too."

"I shall have to make her acquaintance."

I called him a cab, and we watched as he drove off into the night. It was just past eleven but still warm out. Next door a bug zapper zapped. A guy with one arm and one leg hobbled in; the big-haired Southern woman sashayed out. She saw me, said, "Hi, good buddy. I see you got dressed," and waggled out to her El Camino, chuckling at her cleverness.

"What?" Gina asked.

"A wasp story."

"Oh."

Next door a bug fried particularly loudly. "Come on," I said. "Don't we have some e-mail to look at?"

"It's from Succuman at L.A. dot cheapnet dot com," Gina said. "An unfortunate choice of ID, I'd say."

"Any idea who it is?"

She shook her head. "No signature either." She'd shown me earlier how some of the more ardent e-mailers attached signatures to their messages. Little blurbs that told who they were, maybe their affiliation, and whatever else they wanted to clog the phone lines with.

She passed the computer over to me. "Here, look."

It took me awhile to tilt the screen to the right angle, and when I did it hardly seemed worth the effort. The subject was *This may help*. The message was *Look for the milii with stripes*.

I glanced over at Gina. "What the hell does that mean?"

"How do I know? They're your friends."

"There is no milii with stripes."

"That's the crown of thorns thing, right?"

I nodded. "Like on Dick's head."

"Maybe it's some crank."

"Maybe some crank killed Brenda. We have to follow up on it."

"Why?"

"Because I don't have anything else to follow up on, that's why."

"Don't get snippy with me, Portugal."

"Sorry. Let's put another message of our own out. Ask if anybody knows anything about it."

Gina prepared our inquiry. *Anyone knowing about a* Euphorbia milii *with stripes please e-mail privately.*

"Well done," I said. "Okay, send it. And send one direct to Succuman too. Ask who he is."

Tap, tap, click, tap, tap, click. "Done and done. Now what?"

"In the morning I'll call around and see if anyone knows anything about a striped milii."

"And if that doesn't pan out?"

"Maybe check up at the Kawamura. And after that . . ."

"What?"

"I have no idea. Look, I'm exhausted. I need to go to bed. You going to stay?"

"No, I've got to get to the Design Center early. I've got a full day, and then I have a date with Carlos."

"You do?"

"Couldn't put him off again. We're going to Luna Park for performance art."

I walked her out. She asked if I wanted a ride back to Dick's to pick up my truck. It was only a couple of miles, but it seemed like a million. I told her I'd figure something out in the morning, and she slipped into her Volvo. She fired it up, sat there a couple of seconds, switched off the ignition, came back out. "I have to tell you something," she said.

"What?"

"Remember when you said it was hard to believe somebody you slept with was dead and I said I knew what you meant and you said how could I?"

"Uh-huh."

"Well . . ."

"What?"

"Come on, Joe, don't make me spell it out."

I'd have gotten it more quickly if I wasn't so pooped. When I did I fixed her with a steely glare. "After all the times you gave me hell for supposedly hitting on your girlfriends, you slept with Brenda?"

"It was later, like two years after you and her. I ran into her at a yoga class, and one thing led to the proverbial other. It didn't last long."

"Thank heaven for small favors. A one-night stand?"

"Two."

"Oh."

"And Sunday."

"Sunday? Not all day?"

She nodded.

"You did all day Sunday with Brenda? *I* never got to do all day Sunday with Brenda."

"Well."

"I didn't know she was into girls."

"Neither did she, until then."

"You turned her into a lesbian."

"No."

"Into a bisexual, then."

"No. She decided she didn't like it."

"It took her two nights and all day Sunday to decide she didn't like it?"

"It only took her the first night. She didn't like it emotionally. But she liked it well enough physically—"

"To keep it up all weekend. That's our Brenda. Wait a minute. Is this why you were so hot to get me to dig into her murder? You weren't carrying a torch, were you?"

"Of course not."

"You sure?"

"Sure I'm sure."

I looked into her eyes. She wasn't as sure as she said she was. "How come you didn't tell Casillas about this?"

"He didn't ask."

"Withholding evidence? Hey, you didn't kill her, did you?"

"Sure, and then I did Dick so it would look like a serial succulent killer. Joe? Are you okay with this?"

"Why shouldn't I be okay?"

"I don't know."

"I'm fine. Why didn't you tell me before?"

She shrugged, a kind of shrug I've come to recognize as I don't really know and I don't want to figure it out and I don't want to talk about it anymore. I told her again everything was fine and I hugged her and when she drove away I stood in the street watching her taillights recede. Gina and Brenda. Who would've thought?

12

Friday morning the June gloom was back. I woke at eight but thought it was earlier because it was so dark outside. I flipped on the TV while I made my tea. The weather lady on Channel 6 was jabbering about the marine layer and the Catalina eddy. They were always talking about the Catalina eddy. Someday I'd have to find out what it was.

After my greenhouse communion I pulled out the NordicTrack, intending to do half an hour, ten minutes more than usual. I'd been missing quite a few mornings, and I was feeling guilty. I slid Volume One of Rauh's *Succulent and Xerophytic Plants of Madagascar* off its shelf and carefully balanced the huge book on the rack I have hooked up to the machine. Nothing like a little light reading with your exercise.

Within thirty seconds Rauh was on the floor with a big ding in his corner. I climbed off and picked up the book. I glanced over at the NordicTrack. I looked back at the book.

The book won. The exercise gods would forgive me if I slacked off until the Brenda business was done.

I gathered some Grape-Nuts and half a cantaloupe and took them out to the Jungle, along with both volumes of

Rauh. I'd bought them when they came out, at over a hundred bucks a pop, looked through them once, and promptly put them back on the shelf to gather dust. They intimidated me. More than two thousand photos of the island's plant life and an endless stream of descriptions.

Now I scanned the pages for anything about *Euphorbia milii*. The books' arrangement frustrated me; they were laid out by region of the island, so that to look at euphorbias you had to go to one area, find them there, move on to the next, find them, et cetera, et cetera. It took me an hour of page-turning to satisfy myself that there was no picture of a *Euphorbia milii* with stripes.

But there were other books. The same publisher had produced a ten-volume set called the *Euphorbia Journal*, and CCCC's library had most if not all of the volumes. Sometime today I'd have to get hold of our librarian, Austin, and convince him to turn them all over to me. Normally a member couldn't get so many books at once, but I figured my position of authority in the club entitled me to some perks. After all, with Dick gone now, I was the highest-ranking officer, and—

"Holy shit," I said.

I ran inside and called Gina. "Boy, am I glad I caught you."

"I'm just on my way out the door. What's going on?"

"Brenda was president of the cactus club."

"So?"

"Dick was vice president."

"Mm-hmm. What's your point?"

"I'm the secretary. I'm next."

"Next in line for the leadership? Congratulations. I'm glad you called to share this with me, but—"

"No. Next in line to be killed."

Silence on the other end.

"Gi? You there?"

"Sure. Now, look. What do you think are the chances that whoever's behind this is systematically knocking off the leadership structure of your cactus club?"

"Stranger things have happened."

"Not to anyone I know."

"Maybe it's a disgruntled member."

"And what? They're going to kill off the whole board of directors? Oh, and then they work their way through the appointees. Let's see, you've got the person who's in charge of the refreshments, the—"

"Okay, stop already. I guess it is pretty far-fetched."

"There's got to be a connection between Brenda and Dick besides being club officers. Hey, look. I know it sounds weird, but maybe they—"

"Stop right there. If you knew Dick and Hope, you'd know how ridiculous the idea is."

"Meaning?"

"I have never seen two people so in love. Even after all those years of marriage, they were always holding hands, whispering sweet nothings, all that kind of stuff. Trust me on this. There's another connection. Maybe I was right. Someone really is going after all the officers."

"If they plan to knock you off, why would they be setting you up for the other murders?"

"Because it'll look like, filled with remorse, I did myself in. It's a perfect scheme."

"You think that's how it works?"

"I don't know. I don't know how criminals' minds work."

"Maybe it's time you found out."

I knew what she meant. I knew it like I knew where she got the gun from. I knew it like I always know when she's talking about my father. "He wasn't into this kind of thing."

"Are we in heavy denial today?" She let me think it over. "He's a good resource. You should use him."

"Maybe I'll run by over the weekend."

"'Maybe you should run by this afternoon."

"Don't you want to go?"

"I think you should see him alone. *Mano a mano.* You can talk about babes, and football, and killing."

I glanced down and discovered I'd twisted the phone cord into a brainlike mass. Impenetrable, like the murders. "I'll go over there this afternoon. I promise."

"Do that. Look, I have to get off. You know how those boys in the showrooms get their panties in a knot when people are late."

"Gina, if we're going to keep hanging out together, you're going to have to stop with the homophobic remarks."

"I'll watch myself. Keep me posted."

"Okay, see you—wait. Did you get any more interesting e-mail?"

"No. But I did find out they've got all the old messages archived, going back several years. You think it's worthwhile downloading them?"

"Sure. Download away."

"Okay, I'll do it tonight while I make myself pretty for my big date with Carlos."

"Carrying coals to Newcastle again?"

"You're sweet."

"Gi?"

"Yeah?"

"Are you feeling okay?"

"Sure, why?"

"I just wanted to make sure there were no aftereffects from the Cygon."

"Not that I can tell. If I grow another head I'll let you know. And now I really have to get going. Bye."

"Bye."

I wanted to ask somebody about the striped milii. Sam

would have been my best bet, but he was out of town. I'd gotten Brenda's itinerary from him but stupidly forgotten to get his. Lyle seemed like a good alternative. I could tell him about my kill-the-officers theory too. He was the treasurer; he ought to know. I gave him a buzz at work, but he was in a meeting. I left him a message.

I thought about heading up to the Kawamura and remembered I had nothing to head up there in. Why hadn't I let Gina drive me to my truck last night? Sheer idiocy was the only answer that came to mind.

After a brief flirtation with calling a cab, I decided to walk. I took Venice Boulevard, passing a string of South American and Caribbean restaurants and dozens of the ubiquitous two-story apartment buildings with fan palms or giant birds of paradise or yuccas with elephantine bases out front. I hoped the repeated impact of my feet on the pavement would jar a clever idea from some crevice in my brain. It didn't happen.

The overcast began to burn off. At Inglewood Boulevard a car backfired, and I jumped a foot up in the air. When I came down a couple of Latino teenagers across the intersection were in hysterics. They had shaved heads and long T-shirts and baggy shorts. I threw them a weak smile. "Too much *café*, man," one yelled.

By the time I reached Centinela Feed and Pet, I could see my shadow. By the time I turned north on Beethoven, I wished I'd worn shorts, and by the time I crossed Rose, my shirt was stuck to the small of my back and I was panting like a puppy.

I got to Dick's at a quarter to eleven. A length of yellow police tape littered the lawn. I wondered if such trimmings were still apparent at Brenda's. Or if it were opened up now, so her sister, Amanda, could go in and gather effects, so someone could collect the canary supplies and take them to whatever new home the birds managed to find.

All the aloes fronting the Kawamura Conservatory had been torn out of the ground. A couple of broken-off leaves were the only hint they'd ever been there.

The front door wouldn't budge, so I walked around the building in search of another entrance. A chain-link fence, about six feet high, followed the building's perimeter, I guessed to keep vandals from breaking the glass and wandering around inside. Around back, additional fencing lined with vertical redwood slats outlined a sort of patio under a slanting Plexiglas roof. The gate into it was open, and I went in. Plastic pots sized from two inches up to five gallons formed neat stacks along one side. Sacks of soil and amendments were piled along the other. A bag of pumice had fallen on its side, and the eighth-inch particles formed a little white mountain where they'd spilled out.

At the far end of the supply area, an open door led into the conservatory. I stuck my head in. "Hello?"

No answer. I carefully made my way in through a corridor between two fifteen-foot plant benches topped with vertical lathwork. Vining cacti had overgrown the lath, forming a tangled nest of snakelike stems. Selenicereus, the "queen of the night," along with the rest of the royal court. Some had reached the top of the lath and been trained over to the other side, forming a living arbor. New buds thrust, and spent blossoms drooped.

I moved down to the end and stuck my head around the corner. "Hello? Anybody here?"

I knew what I would find. I'd make my way over to the

euphorbias and discover Eugene Rand lying there, his eyelids knitted together with tiny spines. An old hollow euphorbia stem would pierce his jugular. His blood would stain the gravel.

Resisting the urge to flee, I continued between the benches, throwing a hello out here and there, always making sure I had an escape route.

The place looked like the world's biggest botanical garage sale. Dozens of pots hung from a peaked roof. Succulent plants of all shapes and species, in various stages of neglect, cloaked the benches. I spotted a multiheaded mammillaria—a nipple cactus—that had rotted from within. All that remained was an exoskeleton of hooked spines. Over near the wall a whole tray of sansevierias had turned to tufts of brown. It was supposed to be impossible to kill a sansevieria, but there you were.

Within the green hodgepodge, though, you could find some gems. Amidst a cluster of gallon pots holding what looked suspiciously like poinsettias, I spotted the biggest *Pachypodium decaryi* I'd ever seen, with several four-foot stems poking out from a football-shape and -size caudex. Big oval leaves and oleanderlike white flowers burst from the tips.

Although the vents just below the roof were wide open, the air was hot and humid. The first was good, the second hot. Fungi love succulents. I located the exhaust fans; they sat motionless.

I worked my way over to a concentration of euphorbias, craning my head, looking for bodies. Just as I realized I'd reached a dead end, I heard a tiny noise behind me. I whipped around and jumped back. "Go away," I shouted.

Eugene Rand's reaction was a mirror image of my own. "Ack!" he cried as he leapt backward.

He wore thick leather gloves and in them clasped a three-foot chunk of *Euphorbia ammak*, one of the tree species from

Africa. Thick half-inch spines studded its four-sided stem. He held it like you would a baseball bat, if you'd never played baseball before. When he sprang back, the tip clobbered a hanging pot of rosary vine. It removed itself from the water-line it hung from and smashed to the ground at his feet. Strings of heart-shape leaves detached and scattered. "Ack!" he repeated. Again the ammak smacked a pot overhead, but this one, a foot across and filled with the spindly leafless stems of *Euphorbia antisyphilitica*, merely swayed alarmingly.

"It's me," I told him.

"Me, who?"

"Me, Joe Portugal. Remember? I was here the other day."

He squinted mightily. Just before the tip of his nose reached his forehead, he recognized me. "You."

"Right. You want to put your bat down before you destroy any more foliage?"

He stared at his club like he'd never seen it before. Then down at the rosary-vine wreckage. Then back up at me. "Right," he said. He leaned the euphorbia up against a bench. It promptly slid to the floor. White latex oozed from multiple wounds. "You can't be too careful."

"No," I said. "You can't."

"First Dr. Belinski, and now this McAfee fellow—I've just chosen to prepare myself."

"And you've done it well. That's quite a bat you've got there."

"I have several distributed throughout the conservatory. The parent plant is rather unattractive now, but it's a small price to pay."

"Speaking of euphorbias, did you ever have an abdelkuri in here?"

"We did, and we still do."

"How about a milii with stripes? Ever seen one of those?"

"A milii?"

"Yes."

"With stripes?"

"Yes indeed."

He squinted again. I could almost hear facial muscles contorting. "No."

"Word is that Dr. Belinski was working on a striped milii."

"I don't know anything about it."

I thought he did. "Word is that she had several specimens right here in the conservatory." It was nice to know my new talent for making it up as I went along hadn't atrophied overnight.

"Word is this, word is that. Everyone says they know the word about Dr. Belinski. Even the people on the television. They don't know anything about her. You don't know anything about her."

Contrary to popular belief, I am capable of being a prick. Not often, but when I choose to do so, I do a real good job of it. "Oh, I'd say that isn't true. I know a fair amount about her. I used to sleep with her, you know."

Every muscle in his face distorted. His jaw slid down. His nostrils flared, once, twice. His ears wiggled. "You bastard," he said. "You perfect bastard." He snatched up the euphorbia bat.

This was why I'm not a prick very often. It always gets me into trouble. "It was a long time ago," I said, mounting a conciliatory smile. "And only a couple of times."

"You weren't good enough for her."

"Yes, you're probably right. I wasn't good enough for her. She thought so too. Which is why the whole thing never happened. I made it all up."

He swung the euphorbia. He had a swing like a rusty-hinged barn door, but when your bat's a spiny, virulent-sapped plant, that's not necessarily a liability. He missed me by three feet and moved in for another try.

I needed defense. I spotted a length of pipe under a bench, bent, grabbed it just as he swung again. This time he was closer. A foot and a half.

Trying to remember everything I'd ever learned from Jackie Chan, I held the pipe at arm's length in front of me, parallel with the ground. Rand untwisted himself and prepared for another pass. I fixed my eye on his weapon. Once more he wielded it. The tip flew by, mere inches from my face. It continued down, smacked into the pipe, and fractured.

The tip went flying one way. Rand let go the rest and it glided off in another. Sap flew. I instinctively closed my eyes. It sounded like Eugene Rand had not. He was screaming.

I opened my eyes. He had his hands over his. He whirled around and around, certain to crash into something. I dropped the pipe and rushed over to him. "Your eyes?" Joe Portugal, master of the obvious.

"Yes," he wailed. "Help me. Please help me."

I threw my arm around his shoulders. "Is there a hose? A sink?"

He stuck an arm out. "A sink. Over there." Unfortunately, he was pointing at a blank wall.

"Right." I got him going and moved up an aisle. Down another. Eventually I found the sink, almost hidden by some epiphytic cacti. I maneuvered him over there, turned the water on, and stuck his face underneath. "Keep the water on your eyes," I said. "I'm going to get help."

"Aeonium," he said.

"Whatever you say. Hold on tight." I straightened up, ran halfway out, realized what he had said. I scurried back. His wailing continued. "Where is it?" I asked.

"Outside. With the first-aid kit."

I ran out and found it in the pot-storage area. A mangy little cluster of leaves in a three-inch plastic pot sat atop the first-aid kit. It was missing its label, but the pale green rosette said aeonium to me. And, unless I missed my bet, it was *Aeonium lindleyi*. Supposedly a treatment for euphorbia sap. I grabbed it, ran back to him, snapped off a couple of leaves, and poked him in the eye.

I wouldn't have believed it if I hadn't seen it. Within seconds his agonized writhing ceased. His eyes were red and raw, but he had no trouble keeping them open. I broke off another leaf and prodded some more.

"I guess I shouldn't react so strongly when someone admits to being one of Brenda's lovers," Eugene Rand said. He'd given up the pretense of calling her "Doctor."

We were sitting on a couple of cheap plastic lawn chairs in the shade of the Kawamura's toolshed. Rand held a piece of aeonium leaf between his fingertips, and every little while he'd jab himself in the eye with it.

"Not that I've ever taken after anyone with a piece of euphorbia before. It's just all the pressure, the killings and all." He poked his eye again. "It's not like she was promiscuous, you understand. But she was never without a man. When she was done with one, she would move on to the next. Before I would ever have a chance to make my intentions known."

"You never told her how you felt?"

He shook his head. "She knew, of course. I knew she knew, and she knew I knew she knew, and so on in this great big complicated charade."

I wondered why he was being so reasonable all of a sudden. Perhaps I was too close on his trail and he realized his outburst would make me more suspicious. "It must have been tough working with her," I said.

"It was indeed. But I really love my job." He saw the look on my face. "Oh, I know the place looks awful. But it's only half as awful as it was when I started. Slowly but surely I'm making progress. As I told you the other day, we're short of funds."

"I know this is difficult. But I have to ask. Do you know who Brenda was involved with before she died?"

"Of course I do. Masochist that I am, I made it my business to know who all her lovers were." He got up, went into the shed, and came out a minute later with some pencil scribblings on a Post-it. "He's actually not a bad fellow," he said. "Somehow, that made it a bit less difficult. Those of her lovers that I met, at staff functions or wherever, were all nice fellows. You're a nice fellow too. I'm sorry I attacked you."

I glanced down at the note. Rand's handwriting was miserable, but the letters and digits swam into focus. The phone number had an 821 prefix, which made sense since the address was a boat slip in Marina del Rey.

The name I knew. Henry Farber. The guy Brenda'd broken up with four years earlier when she started seeing me. The guy who had promised revenge.

13

I'D BEEN SITTING IN THE TRUCK FOR A QUARTER HOUR, chewing on my latest discovery, when it hit me. Brenda was recycling old lovers. If she were going through them in order, and if she'd just stayed alive a few more months, she would have gotten to me.

It had been a year and a half since I'd gone out with anybody more than once or twice. Or made love to anybody. If Brenda were still alive and dumped Henry again, I'd have found myself back under the blue canopy, engaging in the ancient Malagasy sexual arts, with the oils and the chants and—

But Brenda wasn't still alive. She wasn't going to be making love to anybody anymore.

Henry Farber was a professor, and since I was at UCLA it seemed like a handy place to start looking for him. I found a pay phone and called the English department. They'd never heard of him. I tried History next. They'd heard of him, but he had the day off. I called the number I'd gotten from Rand

and reached a machine. Leaving a message seemed a bad idea. *"Hi, this is Joe Portugal, the guy who took Brenda away a few years ago. Sorry I didn't get the chance this time around. By the way, did you whack her?"*

As long as I was on campus, I thought I might as well check out the Botany department. I talked my way into the lot at the Mathias Garden, parked in the shadow of the Botany building, and made my way in. I monkeyed around for fifteen minutes trying to find, in order, a bathroom, a directory, and Brenda's office. The corridor I found the last of these in was plastered with announcements for esoteric plant workshops and cartoons reflecting lame graduate-student humor. Weird botanical items rested on the floor and on randomly placed tables. Cypress knees, dried pods, that sort of thing. A plastic pot with a dead-looking spider plant. But you can't tell with spider plants. Unlike people, they can look dead and still come back.

Brenda's office door was locked. What else did I expect? I stood with my hand on the knob considering which clever gambit to try next.

"May I help you?" It was a zaftig woman in a light blue blouse and jeans. She stood by one of the doorways halfway down the hall, carrying a white plastic bucket.

"I'm looking for Dr. Belinski."

"Haven't you heard? She's dead." She said it in the same cheerful tone of voice in which she would have said, "She went to Wisconsin to visit her sister."

"Yes, I know." *Don't tell me she's dead, lady, I found the damned body.* "I meant I was looking for her office."

"You've found it."

I walked down the hall to where the woman stood, now clutching her bucket close to her ample bosom. She was short, five-two or so, and younger than I'd thought at first, no more than twenty-five. I usually go for slim women, but I liked the way the little bit of extra poundage worked on her. Her face was round and pink, almost cherubic, with no makeup. Her eyes were hazel and her hair a shiny blond that couldn't have come from a bottle. I remembered seeing her at Brenda's funeral.

"What's in the bucket?" I asked.

"Kelp. The police don't have any leads. Isn't that fascinating?"

"How do you know that?"

"It was on the noontime news. I always watch the noontime news when I'm in the lab. It keeps me in touch. They had a detective on. Carillos or something."

"Casillas."

"Yes. Did you see the news too?"

"No, but it's funny you should mention Detective Casillas. I'm helping him out with the succulent part of the investigation." I held out a hand. "Joe Portugal. I was a friend of Dr. Belinski's."

"Iris Bunche," she said as we shook. "Like the flower and the U.N. guy. Oh, just look at your face. Everyone looks like that when I tell them my name. My parents weren't even thinking. Irises were my mother's favorite flowers, they still are, and so when I was born—well, you get the picture."

"Did you know Dr. Belinski well, Iris?"

"Sure I did. She was my faculty adviser."

"I didn't know she was into kelp."

Confusion preceded a glance into the bucket. "Oh, this. This is for my garden. It's used kelp. The algae people down in the basement are done with it." She seemed to realize how closely she held the bucket and dropped it into a one-handed grip. "I have to go down to the herbarium now. Do you want to come with me? We can talk about Brenda."

She deposited the algae inside a lab, and we went down to the ground floor and into a claustrophobic room lined with row upon row of bound botanical journals. At the back of this repository, a steep metal staircase, barely more than a ladder, led upward. I followed Iris up it, trying to ignore the sway of her full but firm behind, and not succeeding.

The room at the top was filled with dozens of dark green metal cabinets. Each bore the name of one or more families of the plant kingdom. I'd never been in a herbarium before, but my boundless botanical knowledge told me the cabinets were filled with pressed plant remains.

Iris delved into the Didieriaceae, a family of spiny succulents endemic to Madagascar. She grabbed a sheaf of manila folders, positioned them carefully on a wooden table, and sat. I took a seat across from her and asked if the didierias and their friends were her research subject.

"They sure are. Everyone says the Portulacaceae are the closest other family to the cacti, but I'm out to prove that it's the Didieriaceae. It's all in the DNA. That's what Brenda always used to say, isn't it?"

I'd never heard Brenda use those exact words, but no matter. "Yes. She often did say that. Have you done any work with euphorbias?"

She shook her head most delightfully. "No, they're too nasty for me. That latex is horrible. Oh."

"What?"

"I knew I knew your name. You found Brenda, didn't you?"

"Yes. Can you tell me what she was working on?"

"Was it hard?"

"Was what hard?"

"Looking at her. I've never seen a dead person."

I put on a sad face. It didn't feel like one of my better ones. Eight years of acting only in commercials had dulled my instrument. "I'd rather not discuss that, if you don't mind. Let's talk about Dr. Belinski's work."

Maybe my instrument was sharper than I thought. Iris

reached a pink hand across the table and placed it gently atop one of mine. She wore a college ring with a big red stone. "You poor, poor man. I'm so sorry to bring up bad memories." She patted my hand a couple of times, like you would a small dog, and withdrew her own.

I felt a stirring. Those pats were the most intimate feminine contact I'd had in months. My mind took off in unexpected directions. Ridiculous directions. Iris was barely half my age. "You were talking about Brenda's research."

"Oh, yes. She did some work with gene splicing, you know. And she was working on her new classification scheme for the Madagascar euphorbias. It was based on DNA sequencing."

"It's all in the DNA."

That elicited a winsome smile. "She hoped to publish her findings in about a year and a half. And now she never will. Poor, poor Brenda."

Now it was Iris's turn to look sad. I reached out and returned her pats from earlier. I left my hand on top of hers. After a bit she pulled hers out and mine clonked to the table. I could hear Gina. *"Serves you right, you dirty old man,"* she was saying.

"Maybe you could pick up her research," I said.

Iris gave me a look that said I clearly didn't understand how this research stuff worked. "That would be impossible." She glanced down at the folders. "Look at me. I haven't even opened one of these yet. You're a bad influence on me, Joe."

"Maybe I ought to get going, let you do your work. Just a couple more things. Did you ever hear about a *Euphorbia milii* with stripes?"

"No. That would be odd, wouldn't it?"

"It would. One last thing. You know about Brenda's fight against the plant smugglers, right?"

"I know about it, but I don't pay much attention to that kind of thing."

"As far as you know, did anyone ever threaten Brenda because of that?"

"I never heard about any threats, no, but—it was funny. In some ways Brenda was my friend, and in others . . . it was like she had compartments in her life. She never talked to me about the conservation stuff."

I pulled out a pen, found a scrap of paper, wrote down my phone number. "If you think of anything else . . ."

"Then I'll call." She took the paper, tore it in half, slid the part I'd written on into a pocket. "It was very nice meeting you, Joe." She wrote on the other half and handed it back. "And if you need to ask me any more questions, here's *my* number."

"Thanks. Nice meeting you too."

I left the table, climbed down the infernal staircase, paused at the bottom. Some preposterous part of me wanted to go back up and ask Iris out on a date. Maybe I was old enough to be her father; so what? She *had* given me her number.

When I'd climbed back up to the herbarium, I found her with one of the didieria folders open, intently studying a desiccated scrap of vegetation. She looked up when she heard me and smiled. "Did you forget something?"

"Sort of. Forgive me if this is out of line, but I was wondering—"

"Yes?"

I couldn't do it. She was too young, too blond, too . . . alive.

"I was wondering if Brenda ever mentioned a man named Schoeppe."

"She did. One of the men she was going to meet over

there in Madagascar. I met him once." She giggled. "Very cute. Nice beard. Did you ever wear a beard, Joe?"

"A long time ago, in a galaxy far, far away."

"You'd look good with a beard."

"So I've been told. Sorry to take up more of your time."

"You can take up more of my time anytime."

That seemed like an invitation. But could I be sure? I was terribly out of practice. Mumbling incoherently, I beat a hasty retreat. Too much was going on. I didn't need to get involved with anybody while under suspicion of murder. Later, if—no, when—things turned out all right, I could march back here and ask her out and get my dollop of romance. Sex too, if the gods were willing.

🌵

I needed to go home to check the phone machine, which, a week or so earlier had mysteriously stopped delivering messages remotely. It wasn't good for an actor, no matter how loosely you use the term, to be cut off from his telephone, and I'd intended to get a new machine this week. But with all that had happened since Monday night, I just hadn't gotten around to it.

I was on the southbound 405 when I spotted an early-seventies Chevy Malibu in the lane to my right, one car back. It was in beautiful condition, not a dent, not a scratch, with the sheen of new polish overlaying its bright red paint. I slowed down to let it pull even, admired it some more, shifted my eyes to check out the driver.

It was the big guy I'd seen at the funeral, sunglasses and all. Burns and Casillas were full of shit. They were tailing me.

I stomped on the brakes, letting him zoom past and provoking much horn-blowing and finger display from the Jeep behind me. I cut in behind the Malibu, zipped across three lanes of traffic, and sped onto the ramp to the eastbound 10. Sunglasses Guy was boxed in and couldn't follow. "Eat rubber!" I shouted out the window.

There were two calls on the machine. The first was from Elaine.

Back in the late sixties and early seventies, after Dad went away and Mom died, Elaine was my roommate at my parents' place. She's five years older than me, which was just enough to make her an authority figure, and she kept me from going off the deep end while I spent my teenage years getting in and out of a dozen bands and twice as many serious fixes. She moved out when she married Wayne, leaving me to fend for myself, at least until Dad got out of stir.

Years later, when she became an agent, she kept trying to make a client out of me. But by then I was too much of a theater snob to try out for commercials. Finally, in '88, when I'd just given up on the Altair, I broke down. I let her send me out for a Toyota spot, and I got it. That was the beginning of my commercial career. It was also the end of my theatrical one.

Elaine's message said the client was very pleased with my work on Wednesday and was considering a long-term campaign. Also, I had an audition at ten-fifteen Monday for Burger World. Unlike McDonald's commercials, which tended to play a couple of weeks and disappear, Burger World spots ran and ran and ran. If I got it I'd be set for six months and would get to gorge on free burgers all day.

The second call was from Detective Alberta Burns. Just checking in, she said. Had I had any thoughts that might help out their investigation?

I reached Burns at the station. I told her I had nothing new. I didn't bother complaining about their damned tail, but in retribution I kept the striped milii stuff to myself. I asked if they'd gotten anywhere tracking down Brenda's men friends. She said they were following up on all appropriate leads. I asked if they'd checked Henry Farber—they had—but didn't reveal what I knew about his recent reappearance on the scene. Follow me around, would they?

After I hung up I realized I hadn't asked Burns anything about Dick. My subconscious was trying to soft-pedal the possibility the two killings were related, because to admit they were gave credence to the theory that I was next in line.

Thinking of Dick reminded me I hadn't called Hope with my condolences. I looked up their number but got a busy signal.

I called Elaine back. I confirmed my appointment for Monday, and we chatted about the Olsen's shoot and her daughter Lauren's boy problems. That killed a quarter of an hour.

Now what? I could call the Huntington and check on striped miliis. But you could never reach anyone up there. I could drive up instead, seek out the curator of the Desert Garden. But the prospect of schlepping all the way to San Marino and finding out nothing was too discouraging. Although it might be fun trying to lose my tail at one of the Pasadena Freeway's five-mile-an-hour exits.

I tried Hope again and got another busy. I gave Austin Richman a call. If he was home I'd drive over there and pick up the ten volumes of the *Euphorbia Journal.* I could spend the rest of the afternoon paging through them, looking for God knew what.

But Austin wasn't home or, more likely, was out in the yard and ignoring the phone. I left a message.

I ransacked the refrigerator and came up with an overripe mango. I ate it with my fingers, letting the juice run down my chin, enjoying a rare primitive moment. Upon my return to civility I flossed the strings from between my teeth. I considered the mango pit and decided to plant it. By the time I'd picked out the right soil and the right pot, I'd killed half an hour. It was two o'clock.

I checked out the backyard. I checked out the greenhouse. I went inside and looked in the refrigerator again. I ate a sour pickle.

I examined the driveway light. It had simply unscrewed from its socket. I screwed it back in.

I got out my checkbook in preparation for a trip to Best Buy for a new phone machine. I got halfway to the front door and stopped. Because I knew what I was doing. I was stalling. I was stalling because the next significant thing I had to do was visit my father and have a conversation I'd been putting off for years.

I could quit stalling if I gave up the idea altogether. But I couldn't give it up. Because I'd promised Gina I would, and I never broke a promise to Gina.

Dad got out of prison in '79, during the period I was managing the Altair. He moved back home, and the two of us constituted a household for four years. Then, at age sixty-two, he suddenly got religion. He started talking about moving up to the Fairfax district, "where all the Jews are." One day he said, "The house. It's yours." He'd made some wise investments with his ill-gotten gains before he went up the river, and money was not an issue. Next thing I knew he was living on Hayworth Avenue with Leonard, who's Jewish, and Catherine, who's not.

When I got up there around three-thirty, Leonard answered the door. He's barely over five feet, has one clouded eye and one glass one, and always wears a blue yarmulke perched atop his bald spot. I've never been able to figure out what trick of physics he uses to keep it on, and he's never volunteered the information.

Leonard said my father was in the backyard, "tending to his posies." Dad discovered gardening in his golden years, which gave us at least one point of reference. As Leonard led me back through the place, Catherine popped out from the kitchen. She's thin, almost severe, and has jet black hair by Clairol. Though Dad would never admit it, she looks a lot like my mother.

Leonard and Dad like to refer to Catherine as "our little shiksa," even though she's taller than either of them. When they say this they exchange glances and get this creepy carnal look in their eyes. Or at least Dad does; Leonard doesn't get much of any kind of look in his eyes anymore. They insist everything is platonic, and at their age I tend to believe them. But who knows? Sometimes I think Dad gets more nookie than I do.

I would have sworn he couldn't see me when I came through the back door, but the second I did he said, "That you, Joseph?"

"Sure is, Dad."

"Come here. Help me with my posies." Anything short of a rosebush is a posy to him.

He was kneeling on the foam-rubber knee protector I'd bought him, planting a patch of impatiens, a plant he loves and deposits in every available cranny. I went over, got down on my knees, and troweled out a hole. He dropped in a pink-flowered specimen and carefully tamped the soil around it. "Good job, son." He stood slowly, pulled out a checkered handkerchief, and wiped his face. "Nice day."

Dad has all the requisite wrinkles, but they don't make him look old, merely a little less young. He's got most of his hair, though it's all gone gray. His blue eyes are as piercing as ever. He's gotten skinny though, almost too much so, and sometimes I worry about that.

The handkerchief barely made a dent in the perspiration coating his head and sticking his Farmer's Market T-shirt to his spindly chest. "You should take it easy, Dad," I said.

"Eh." He flapped a hand to dismiss the thought. "So I keel over here in the posies. So you and Leonard can bury me, and the rabbi can do a *barucha*."

We sat at the teak table and chair set Gina had gotten them for nearly nothing in some freight-claim fiasco. Catherine brought out a tray with iced tea and some Hydrox cookies. "If I'd known you were coming, I'd have baked," she said.

"These are fine," I said, and thanked her, and she went inside.

Dad pulled off his garden gloves. He took one of the cookies, twisted the halves apart, and scraped the good stuff with his teeth, which he still had all of. "So," he said. "What brings my son Joseph to see me on a Friday afternoon?"

"I was wondering if you remembered what our original name was."

He knew I was full of crap, but he answered anyway. "Patchkivatchki. Something like that."

Each time I asked he came up with a different name, with only the initial *P* in common. Once it was Poltergeist.

"How did they get Portugal out of Patchkivatchki?"

"How do I know? Was I there? You didn't schlep all the way up here to ask about Ellis Island."

"Uh . . ."

"Come on, boy, spit it out."

"I need your special expertise, Dad."

"What kind of special expertise does an old man like me have? I tend my posies, I read my science fiction, I go to shul on Saturday."

"You know what I mean, Dad."

"So say it. Don't beat around the posies."

I sighed. "Okay, then," I said. "I need to talk to you about murder."

14

Until i was ten i thought my father worked at an office. Because I was at school all day, I never realized how irregular his schedule was. And during summer vacations, when they sent me off to Camp Los-Tres-Arboles, I was having too much fun to care. Later I found out that was exactly why they sent me to sleep-away camp—so I wouldn't start asking questions about Dad's weird schedule.

As my eleventh summer began, I fell victim to a hepatitis outbreak that they traced to a sewage backup in the school cafeteria. Five days after school ended and four before camp was to begin, I got terribly sick. Dr. Greene figured out what was wrong right away and put me in the hospital. Dad came each day and spent the whole afternoon with me. When I went home he stayed with me a couple more days until I got my appetite back. Only then would he trust Mom with me.

Over the next couple of weeks, I started to notice how weird his hours were. Some mornings he would be up and out before the crack of dawn; others he wouldn't leave until noon. He'd work evenings on occasion, even stay out all night. I'd already known this last part, but other kids' dads worked nights sometimes, and it didn't really seem strange until I put it together with his daytime schedule.

Then there were his business associates. They dropped by once in a while, and they'd always bring me presents. But they scared me. They had sharp faces and sharp outfits. Whenever one would come by, he and my father would go off into the den and close the door, and a night or two later Dad would stay out all night.

After five or six weeks at home, I was feeling fine, just waiting for my bilirubin to come down to par so I could go outside. I was crazed, and I was crazing my mother too. I'd done about a hundred jigsaw puzzles and knew all the characters on *The Guiding Light*.

Finally, I asked her. "Mom, who does Dad work for?"

"He's a businessman, honey."

"But who does he *work* for?"

She looked at me with those warm brown eyes. "He's an *independent* businessman, Joey."

"What's that mean?"

"It means he works for different people. He's kind of a consultant. Do you know what a consultant is?"

She was a smart lady, my mother. She got me off the subject. But the next week they had a *Highway Patrol* festival on Channel 6. Two episodes a night instead of one. Somewhere among all the 10-4's I figured it out.

"Dad's a crook, isn't he, Mom?" I said one morning over Sugar Smacks.

By the horrified look in her eyes, I knew I'd struck gold. "He is, isn't he, Mom? Does he have a gun?"

"No."

"No, he isn't a crook, or no, he doesn't have a gun?"

Tears brimmed from her eyes. "Finish your cereal."

"Okay, Mom."

I went back to my room and plopped onto my bed with my hands behind my head and a big grin on. My own father, an outlaw. I wondered what kind. He couldn't be a killer, because killers were bad. He had to be a robber. He'd steal from the rich and give the money to the poor. Wow. Wait until the kids heard about this.

That night I was in my room mangling a plastic model of the *U.S.S. Forrestal* when my father came in. He closed the door behind him and sat on the edge of my bed. His eyes toured the room like he'd never seen it before. Eventually, they came to rest on me. "Your mother told me you had some questions," he said.

This was it. He was going to fill me in on all the details of his criminal empire.

But it was not to be. Dad deftly circumvented every crime-oriented query I directed at him. He neatly filled the conversation with lots of a-man's-gotta-do-what-a-man's-gotta-dos and your-father-loves-you-very-muches. When he was done I was more convinced than ever he was a crook, and just as unclear as ever about the specifics.

🌵

"I don't like to talk about those days," my father said.

"I know, Dad. But I'm in a bit of a fix."

"Yes." He nibbled a bit of Hydrox, cast the rest aside, picked up another, and toothed out the filling. "I read about it in the paper," he said proudly, as if it were a big deal that at his age he still read the newspaper.

"You know, I've never really heard the real story about what got you . . . got you . . ."

"Put away? You've heard that story a thousand times. It's old news. Better we should talk about—"

"Not the real story. Just what Elaine told me. Dad, I'm forty-four years old. I'm old enough to be a grandfather. Isn't it time you leveled with me?"

He wiped his head again, sipped his iced tea, picked at his teeth with a finger. "They used to call me Harold the Horse, you know."

"I know. Quit stalling."

He looked me over, slowly got up, went inside, came back out with a fat cigar. He removed the ring. For a second I thought he was going to give it to me, like when I was a kid. I wanted him to do that. But he placed it carefully on the table. "There are only two reasons why people kill other people," he said. "Love and money."

Good. That covered both the routes I was following with the Brenda thing. Old—or wannabe—boyfriends, and plant smugglers. "What about power?"

He made a dismissive gesture with the cigar. "Power is nothing. What can you do with power? You can get money, that's what."

"Which was it with you?"

He made a big show of lighting the cigar with a worn Zippo he pulled from his pocket. He drew in some smoke, blew it out, watched it dissipate in the quiet afternoon air.

"Dad? Which was it? Love or money."

He rubbed the side of his nose. He had a discolored spot on his cheek. I thought of Sam and his skin cancer.

"I don't want to talk about it. I'm not involved with any of that anymore."

"You're involved enough to have found a gun for Gina when she needed one."

He gave me a look like he'd just discovered his only child wasn't an idiot, following it with the slightest of nods. "Who asked those guys to horn in on our hijacking?" He downed his tea, set the glass down, and leaned forward. "It was the worst feeling I ever had in my life."

"Killing that guy."

He nodded. "We'd stop the trucks and the drivers would get scared and everything would be real simple. Who knew on that night some other guys would pick the same shipment?" He puffed out his lower lip like he did when he was thinking, or angry. "They were just a couple of two-bit schmucks like us, trying to make a buck the easy way. But when they showed up it got crazy. They were new to the game, thought they'd do better pretending to be cops making a traffic stop. It was a big mess. When it was over a guy was dead. Your father shot him."

"Do you remember what it felt like?"

He took a big pull on the cigar and dumped some ash on the lawn. "Like someone took out my stomach and put in a balloon. He was a young kid, maybe twenty-five." He looked up at the sky and shaded his eyes. "I don't remember pulling the trigger. That part is a big blank. But when it was over I had the gun in my hand, and there were real policemen."

"Are you sure you did it?"

"What? What kind of a stupid question is that? Of course I did it."

"I mean, maybe one of your partners did it and put the gun in your hand."

"It was my gun. I used to keep it up on the top shelf of the hall closet."

"Where you kept my Christmas presents?"

He raised an eyebrow. "Those were Chanukah presents."

"Back then you called them Christmas presents. You're sure you don't remember pulling the trigger?"

"Why do you care?"

"Because you're my father, and I'm getting a little

concerned you may have been framed. Since someone seems to be trying to frame me, this is a good thing for me to know about."

"Framed, shmamed."

"Come on, Dad, take this seriously. I'm trying to find out a little about the emotions that go with taking someone's life. So I can look for them in my suspects."

"Suspects, you have. Why don't you tell me about these suspects?"

I sat there in the hot sun and did as he asked. After a while he put the cigar out, saving the rest for later. We were still there as the sun went behind a pepper tree, affording us some welcome shadow. When it came out again, its harshness gone for the day, it found us still engaged in conversation, the longest one I'd had with my father since he'd gotten out of the slammer.

We'd reached the amazing-appearing plant ties when Catherine came out the back door. "You going to stay for dinner, Joe?"

"Catherine will be lighting the Shabbat candles," my father said.

"Catherine will be doing no such thing," she said, holding back a smile. "You want someone to light candles Friday night, Harold Portugal, you get yourself a Jewish lady. You want me to light candles, you come to Mass with me Sunday."

They both looked at me expectantly. It wasn't as if I had anything better to do. "Sure," I said. "I'd love to stay for dinner."

Three and a half hours later, Dad walked me out to the truck. I stepped out into the street and checked both sides for red Malibus. Dad asked what I was doing.

"Somebody's following me."

"Somebody's following you?"

"Didn't I just say that?"

"Who would be following you?"

"I think it's a cop."

"What makes you think it's a cop?"

"He looks like one."

"Describe this cop."

"He's big and Italian-looking. Nice suit for a cop. Oh, and he wears sunglasses all the time."

He pushed out his lower lip. "I wear sunglasses, Joseph. They shade my old eyes. Even Leonard, who can barely see his penis, wears sunglasses, and he is not a cop."

I got into the truck and rolled the window down. "Dad, I'm a little scared that someone might really be killing off the officers of my club. Do you think I should carry a gun? For protection?"

"You? A gun? What would you do with a gun?"

"You gave Gina a gun."

"Her? She would know what to do with a gun."

"Thanks for the vote of confidence."

"You're welcome."

"You ought to get that spot on your cheek looked at."

"It's an age spot. You'll have them, too, when you get to be my age. You want to go to shul with me tomorrow morning?"

"I can't. I have things to do."

"Soon, then."

"Soon, Dad. I promise."

🌵

I caught the tail end of the news on Channel 6. There was a little item about Brenda and Dick. They ran a graphic behind the anchorman. CACTUS KILLINGS, it said, with a silhouetted saguaro and a smoking gun. Thank God they didn't spell *cactus* with a *K*.

According to the report, the police said they had no suspects. "But," the toupeed anchorman said, "Channel 6 has exclusively learned that detectives have interviewed this man." They ran four or five seconds of film from a Rice Krispies commercial. The guy in it was me. "Now, let us emphasize," the anchor went on, "this man, actor Joe Portugal, the discoverer of both bodies, it not a suspect. However, he has been interviewed."

The phone rang. "You're on the news," said my father.

"I know, Dad."

"You looked thin."

"That commercial was three years ago. You just saw me an hour ago. Did I look thin then?"

I got him off and the phone rang again. This time it was Elaine. After she hung up a few more people called. The last was Rowena Small. "I *knew* you were a suspect," she said.

After the ringing stopped, *Nightline* came on, and I fell asleep on the couch. These two events can be counted on to go together.

Another ring of the phone woke me. I snatched it up. "Yes, I know I was on the news, and no, I'm not a suspect."

"You were on the news?" said Gina.

"Oh, hi. Yeah, I was. What time is it?"

"Midnight."

"Why are you calling me at midnight?"

"It's this archive stuff I downloaded," she said. "I've been looking it over. I think I found something."

15

GINA OPENED HER FRONT DOOR FOR ME AT A QUARTER TO one Saturday morning, wearing her glasses and a Frankie Goes To Hollywood T-shirt that reached her knees. She held a quart of Dreyer's strawberry in one hand, a spoon in the other. She led me into the dining room, where her computer and printer were set up. A small stack of letter-size paper sat between the two. More sheets littered the area.

"I guess your date with Carlos didn't go very well," I said.

"Medium." She led me to the table, made me sit, and handed me the top sheet off the pile. "Look at this." It was an e-mail from someone whose ID was madagasprof@ucla.edu.

"Brenda?"

"Uh-huh. Look at the signature."

It said she was with the UCLA Department of Botany and that *if we don't save the wild species they won't save us.* The message itself was a response to someone who had asked some arcane question about the differences between two varieties of *Euphorbia viguieri*. Ironic, given how this whole thing had started, but certainly of no help to Gina and me.

"So?" I said.

"Just setting the stage." She handed me another e-mail,

dated the previous December. In it Brenda was taking the plant smugglers to task, referring to them as *rapists of the landscape* and *mechanics of destruction* and various other inflammatory epithets. She ended by saying that anybody who violated CITES should be *strung up naked and have all the hairs in their body picked out one by one, until every inch of their skin is defoliated, and see how they like it.*

I looked up. "Very Brenda."

Gina held out a third sheet. "Now check this out."

This one was from someone whose moniker was Adolfwax. I smiled. "A German."

"Yes. Read."

The first couple of paragraphs agreed with some of Brenda's points, politely disagreed with others. Moderately interesting, but nothing to get excited about. Until the end. *One should be careful if one makes threats one cannot carry out. To suggest the plucking of another's hair, no matter how mercenary he who is plucked, is an idea that can only backfire on the source.*

"I like that," I said. "*He who is plucked.* But this is probably some wienie with too much time on his hands. I don't think what you see here represents a threat to Brenda, if that's what you're getting at."

"It's not. But keep going." She pushed the rest of the stack over.

The next one was from Brenda. Very simple. *Are you trying to scare me?*

Adolfwax: *Not at all. I'm only pointing out that this list is monitored by persons not as civilized as you or I.*

Brenda: *I will not, repeat, not be scared off. The fact of the matter is, I have received private e-mail far more threatening than anything I've seen here. These people will stop at nothing to gain their nefarious ends.*

Adolfwax: *Who have you gotten threats from?*

Brenda: *It would be unwise to say.*

The last sheet was from someone whose signature identified him as the mailing list's moderator. *Will you all please take this off-line? It's getting too close to flaming, and the group doesn't want to hear about it.*

I looked up. "Flaming?"

"When people get into nasty personal discussions in a public forum. They start yelling and—"

"How can you yell on a piece of paper?"

"You type in all caps. It's very obnoxious."

"The whole thing is very obnoxious. Too much technology." I wagged the sheets in the air. "But now we know someone threatened Brenda. All we have to do is download that threatening e-mail she got and—"

Gina was giving me that pitying look she gets when one of my eight-tracks self-destructs.

"What?"

"I can't just download Brenda's private e-mail. That's why it's called private."

"Oh. Makes sense, I guess. Would she still have it on her computer?"

"If she didn't delete it. And I know if *I* got threatening e-mail I wouldn't delete it." She saw the look on my face. "No."

"Why not? I've still got the keys."

"What if the police are watching the place? The-killer-always-returns-to-the-scene-of-the-crime kind of thing."

"We have every right to be there," I said. "We're coming to feed the birds."

"The birds probably aren't even there. Weren't they going to take them off to the SPCA or something?"

"For all we know, they're starving to death. Killing off the weakest and eating them." I got up. "Put on some clothes."

"Right now? You want to go sneaking through Brenda's house at one in the morning?"

"You got a better time?"

✽

We took Gina's car, stopped back at my place to pick up the keys, and reached Brenda's a little before two. We parked half a block beyond the house and walked stiffly back, jumping at the tiniest noise. There wasn't any crime-scene tape to avoid as we slunk up to the front door. I unlocked it, we slipped in, I closed it behind us.

"It's pitch dark in here," Gina said.

"Let me turn on a light." I reached for the switch.

"No." She punched me in the side.

"Ow."

"Sorry. I was trying to grab your arm. People would wonder why a dead woman had the lights on."

"Which people? Everyone's asleep."

"Not Mrs. Kwiatkowski. She has insomnia. She told me when I used her shower. She also has arthritis, severe heartburn, and loose—"

"Spare me. Why don't you go out to the car for a flashlight?"

"Why don't *you* go out to the car? Anyway, I don't have one."

"Everyone has a flashlight in their car."

"Not me."

We felt our way into the bedroom, and Gina turned on the computer. It gave off enough light to check the bird cage, which was deserted.

Soon she was mousing away. A screen showing a photo of the Madagascar thorn forest quickly gave way to a more computerish one. "Her e-mail," Gina said.

She poked around for a few minutes, viewing all the saved

messages. I was too antsy to look and figured she'd let me know if she came across anything. I paced. I stuck my head in the corridor to greet the cops, who were sure to burst in on us. I went to the bathroom, pointedly avoiding looking at the tub, even though it was too dark to see anything that might be in there. When I came out, hoping my aim had been true, Gina was muttering. The thorn forest reappeared. "It's not there."

"How about something on the striped milii?"

"No, although . . ."

"What?"

"Ssh. Let me think." She did, then said, "Maybe she archived it. She could have moved the threats out of the e-mail program. She doesn't seem to have kept anything older than a month or two."

"Can you find them?"

"Given time, but they could be anywhere on her hard disk."

"We've got time. We've got till morning at least." To emphasize my point I made myself comfortable on the bed.

"Yeah, but I don't really know what I'm looking for."

"That's what makes it fun."

Somebody was shaking me. "Joe, wake up." I burrowed into the bed. "Get up now."

"Go away."

"There's a hive full of wasps in the room."

I was on my feet instantly, flailing like I'd never flailed before. Several fun seconds later I realized Brenda's bedroom was stinger-free.

"That was really nasty," I said. "Being cooped up with a bunch of wasps is my worst nightmare."

"It was the only thing that would get you up. I found them."

"You found what?"

"Will you wake *up*? I found the old e-mail messages."

"You did? What do they say?"

"I didn't look yet. I wanted you to be there for the discovery." She sat back down at the keyboard, and I knelt beside her. She clicked the mouse, and a file glimmered into life. We paged down through what appeared to be every e-mail from the previous year that Brenda's seen fit to hide away. Things she'd said in confidence about other members of her department. A very steamy missive from somebody named Conner. Nothing the least bit threatening showed up until, in the middle of October, *You'd better stop or else* popped into view on the last line of the screen. The subject line of a message. Gina reached out a finger to bring the accompanying text into view. The doorbell rang.

Gina's finger froze in midair. We stared at each other like Hansel and Gretel when the witch showed up. "Ignore it," I said. "They'll go away."

They didn't. Instead, they rang the bell again.

"They don't know anybody's here," I said.

"Why else would anyone ring the doorbell at three in the morning? I doubt it's a kid selling candy."

"I'll go look." I stumbled to the living room, parted the drapes, peered outside.

Someone was out there, but it was too dark to see who. They pressed the doorbell again. I jumped, crashed into a bookshelf, and made a terrible racket.

"Who is that in there?" inquired the inharmonious voice of Mrs. Kwiatkowski.

I felt my way to the door and swept it open. "It's me, Mrs. K.—Joey the Cactus Boy."

"Joey? What are you doing here at this time of the morning?"

"I couldn't sleep, Mrs. K. And then I thought maybe the police had forgotten about Brenda's canaries, so I decided to come over and check on them. How did you know I was here?"

"I saw the TV in the bedroom, that's how. Why do you have the TV on?"

"It's not the TV, it's the computer. The lights don't work in the bedroom, so I turned it on so I could see."

"The lights don't work?" Before I could stop her she'd swept her hand across the wall switch. Three lamps sprang to life. "The lights work in here." Mrs. Kwiatkowski's plump face was crowned with an assemblage of curlers that could have brought in Alpha Centauri. She wore a chartreuse robe that said QVC all over it.

"I'm sure it's just the bulb," I said. "Anyway, it turns out the birds aren't here, so we can just go—"

"Where's your truck?"

"My truck?"

"Your truck. Your white truck."

"I walked, Mrs. K."

"Who walks at three in the morning?"

"I do. Whenever I can't sleep I go for a walk. And now if you'll just—"

"Hello?"

Mrs. Kwiatkowski and I turned in unison to see who stood in the doorway. It was Officer Benton. When he stepped aside, Officer Jones stood revealed.

"Not to be disrespectful," Officer Benton said, with his hand lurking not terribly far from his gun. "But what are you two doing here?"

"I was about to ask you the same thing," I said.

"It's our job," he said. "Finding lights on at dead people's houses at strange hours."

"Well, I came over to feed the birds, and Mrs. Kwiatkowski here came over to see what the ruckus was about."

"You made a ruckus feeding birds? Wait minute. There aren't any birds. We took 'em to the SPCA. We told you we'd take good care of them."

"Yes, well, I forgot."

"How'd you get in here?"

"I have the key."

"Maybe we should take you down to the station."

"Look, Officer Benton, I'd really rather not. I've been down to the station twice on suspicion of murder, and I hated every minute of it, so why would I do anything that would get me brought down there again?"

"I don't know . . ."

Officer Jones spoke up for the first time. "Come on, Marlon, he's harmless."

Benton nodded slowly. "All right then. But you'll have to leave."

"Fine," I said. "I'm leaving. I'm leaving right this minute."

"And since you know the birds are in good hands, I won't expect to see you here again."

The four of us walked out, and I locked up. Benton and Jones drove off in their patrol car, Mrs. Kwiatkowski toddled off to her place, and I crept away down the street. I circumnavigated the block until I spotted Gina skulking back to her car. I caught up without giving her more than a small fright. "That was a waste of time," I said.

"Not really." She held up a computer disk.

"I don't get it."

"I dumped all Brenda's old e-mails onto it while you were partying with Mrs. K."

"You're a genius."

"Any moderately accomplished computer user could have done the same. Come on, let's get out of here."

We drove back to Gina's condo. We started her computer up and stuck the disk in and found out what we had. Which was nothing.

16

THE LITTLE BOX ON THE COMPUTER SCREEN SAID SOMEthing about a *fatal disk error*. And interesting choice of terms, I thought.

"I cannot goddamned believe it," Gina said.

"But it worked in Brenda's computer."

"Sometimes this happens. You put a file on a diskette and go back to read it and you can't. But usually I have another copy on my hard disk, so it's no big deal."

"So we go back and get another disk."

"You go back. Hiding in the haunted bathroom when the cops came was quite enough excitement for one evening."

"But this could be our big break."

She made a show of taking the disk over to her kitchen sink and dropping it into the garbage can underneath. "I'm exhausted," she said. "You're exhausted. If we go back we'll get caught again."

"Maybe we can just sneak in, take the computer, and have at it at our leisure."

"I believe they call that burglary."

"Oh, yeah." I was fresh out of clever ideas, and trying to

think of them hurt my head. "I'm going home to get some rest."

"You could stay here."

"I hate sleeping on your couch. It's too sturdy."

"I could sleep on the couch."

"Gina, I'm not kicking you out of your bed."

"We could both sleep in the bed."

"I don't think we should both sleep in the same bed."

"Why? What could happen?"

"Nothing. That's one reason I don't want to."

"What's that supposed to mean?"

"I have no idea. Look, like you said, I'm exhausted. I don't know what I'm talking about. I'm going to go home and get some sleep."

Outside, the world was beginning to light up. It took *The Who Live at Leeds*, loud, to keep me awake long enough to get home.

I was dreaming of Amanda Belinski. She lay in Brenda's bathtub, wrapped in a *lamba*, trying out various positions, asking me over and over, "Is this how you found her?"

The telephone rang. I groped for it, thinking it was Amanda, calling to ask why I hadn't shown up last night. Just as I found the phone I realized that couldn't be the case, because our appointment was on Saturday night and Saturday had just begun.

It was Lyle Tillis. "Hope I didn't wake you."

"No, I've been up for hours."

"Good, good. Sorry I didn't get back to you sooner. It's just been kind of crazy up here, with Dick's getting killed."

"No need to apologize. I probably shouldn't even have

bothered you." I got my hand around the alarm clock, twisted it so I could see it. Nine-fifteen. I'd had three hours' sleep.

"Yeah, well, life goes on. Damn, I miss him already."

"Me too." I didn't, though eventually I might. "Look, I thought of something yesterday that I wanted to bring to your attention. Brenda was the president of CCCC and Dick was vice president."

"Right."

"So somebody might be making their way down the list of officers."

"Wow." I heard braying in the background. Was Merlin inside the house? "So that would put me next."

"No, it would put *me* next."

"No, no, treasurer's next."

"I don't think so."

"Treasurer's more important. No offense."

"No, you're right, but I think on the list in the newsletter I'm next. Isn't that how they usually do it? Secretary's always listed before treasurer. Let me go find a newsletter." I jumped out of bed, dragging the phone with me.

"I have one right here. Hey, you're right. You're next."

"But you bring up a good point. Would they be going in the listed order or in order of importance? Assuming there is a *they* and, if there is, that they're going in any order at all." It was too overwhelming to think about on three hours' sleep. "When did you hear about Dick?" I asked.

"Hope called last night."

"How's she holding up?"

"Fair. Magda and I are helping her out as much as we can with the funeral and all. Well, not really a funeral; he's going to be cremated after the cops are done with him, and there'll be a private service. Although we're talking about having a memorial on Monday. Anyway, we're headed down there in a little while to see Hope, so I'd better get going."

"You be careful, okay? Just in case somebody really is after one of us."

"Will do. See you."

"Okay. Hey, wait a minute. What I called about yesterday—"

"Right, striped milii. No, I never heard of anything like that. Would be pretty weird though. Probably could sell a lot of them."

After we said good-bye I continued standing in the bedroom, holding the phone, because I couldn't get it together enough to do anything else. I had that gnawing feeling in my stomach from lack of sleep, and I thought I had to pee but wasn't sure. Also, someone had stuffed cotton batting in my mouth.

The phone rang, startling me, and I dropped it noisily to the floor. When I picked it up I heard a tinny Austin Richman saying, "You there, man?"

I fumbled the handpiece to my face. "Yeah. How are you?"

"Fine, man. You still want those books? You could come and get them now if you want."

I wanted. I could run up there and check on Sam's stuff on my way back. I did my greenhouse tour and showered and gobbled some shredded wheat. When I opened the door to leave, I found Detective Hector Casillas on my doorstep.

He's been talking to the uniforms, I thought. He knows I was poking around at Brenda's last night, and he's come to arrest me for trespassing in the first degree. "Hector," I said, none too cleverly, "to what do I owe this visit?"

"Why didn't you tell me your father was a hood?"

"I don't think *hood* is quite the appropriate word."

"He went to prison for murder. What would you call it?"

"My father is a fine man who was in the wrong place at

the wrong time." Even I realized how lame that sounded. "And anyway, even if he was the Hillside Strangler, what's that got to do with me?"

"Life father, like son, I always say."

"Do you, now? What did *your* father do for a living?"

"He was a cop."

So much for that clever ploy. "Yeah, well, just because you followed in your father's footsteps doesn't mean I did. Listen, get this straight. I didn't kill Brenda. Or Dick. I'm trying to help you guys figure out who did, because they were friends of mine."

"Yeah, well, just stay out of our way, why don't you."

"Yeah, well, go work on your body-dump case, why don't you. Or do you suspect me of that too?"

"Smartass. We've got an eye on you. As soon as you make a mistake . . ." He raised the back of his suit jacket and showed me his handcuffs.

"Very impressive," I said. "And now, if you'll excuse me, I have business to attend to." I stepped out, locked the door, and brushed past. Halfway to the curb I stopped and turned. "By the way, tell the guy you've got tailing me I like his car." I left Casillas standing there with his mouth hanging open.

I took Pacific Coast Highway and turned up Topanga Canyon Boulevard. It's an odd road to call a boulevard, a winding two-lane highway that zigzags up through a rocky cleft in the mountains. After a few miles it passes through the loose assemblage of buildings that's the village of Topanga, eventually reaching the dreaded San Fernando Valley thirteen miles or so from where it started.

Topangans like to view their community as a place the

nineties haven't yet reached, perhaps not the eighties, and on a good day not even the seventies. A countercultural refuge where the hippies never went straight and where, if you squint, you can imagine you're living off the country. They're fooling themselves, I think; it's only a matter of time before Starbucks shows up.

Austin's and his wife Vicki Neidhardt's place lay two miles and three turns off the Boulevard, and if you didn't know where it was you weren't going to find it. I did know and still I barely made it. I walked around their gigantic A-frame and found Austin in the vast backyard knee-deep in squash vines. He was smoking something hand-rolled that was too fat to be a joint, one of his homemade cancer sticks.

His long blond hair was parted down the middle like an Allman Brother, and he had a Fu Manchu mustache to match. He wore overalls with nothing underneath, and Earth Shoes. He was the only person I knew who could say things like "far out," "right on," and "out of sight" and not seem like an idiot. He didn't have a job and hadn't in thirty years, though I'd always suspected he pulled in a certain income from a marijuana patch somewhere in the hills behind the house.

It didn't matter that he didn't work, because Vicki was a corporate stooge. I use this phrase only because she used it herself. She *liked* being a corporate stooge. She loved the commuting and the power clothes and the jetting around the country. She was a vice president of a major investment-banking firm downtown, and she probably made more money than anyone else I knew. She and Austin had two teenagers, a boy and a girl, and, regardless of the apparent disparity in their lifestyles, were the second-closest couple I knew, surpassed only by Dick and Hope. Which I guessed meant they were now number one.

"Hey, man," Austin said. "Come on over and check this out."

"This" was crawling around his palm. A hairy caterpillar with little green spots on it.

"I found it munching on my squash leaves," Austin said. "Can't have that, you know. Let's take it to higher ground."

We trekked up a hillside that Austin had spent countless hours landscaping with cacti, euphorbias, agaves, and other desert plants. Little dust clouds rose up and made me sneeze. Austin found a suitable place for the caterpillar on a palo verde branch, stepped away, and sat down on a rock. "I heard about Dick on the radio," he said. He began field-stripping his cigarette. "It's a damned shame, man. What's wrong with the world, Joe, do you think?"

"Don't know, Austin."

He nodded, solemnly, like I had said something significant. "It's the truth. Shit, I try to think why anyone would knock off a cool chick like Brenda, and I just don't get it."

"I've been not getting it myself." I found a rock of my own to sit on. "Fact is, Austin, I've been digging into the whole thing a bit."

"Far out." His face got all weird. I was afraid he was having an acid flashback. "That's right. You and she were balling some time back. No offense meant."

"None taken. It *was* a long time ago. But I just kind of felt I owed her something."

"Cool. Find out anything?"

I filled Austin in on my adventures over the past few days. When I told him about Eugene Rand's unrequited love of Brenda, he nodded thoughtfully, saying, "Now, *there's* an uptight dude." When I got to the part about Gina and the e-mail, he put on this big serious expression and pointed a weather-beaten finger at me. "You ask me," he said, "you and Gina need to get together."

"I didn't ask you," I said with a smile on my face.

"Everyone needs a good woman." He shrugged. "But suit yourself. So what happened with the e-mail?"

"Nothing much yet. Somebody told us to watch for a striped milii."

"Hmm."

"Hmm, what?"

"I've got one."

"Got one?"

"A striped milii."

"You do? Where'd you get it?"

"Brenda gave it to me."

"What? When?"

"Let's see. Would've been three years ago."

"Can I see it?"

"Sure."

"Where is it?"

He pointed. "Right there over your shoulder."

I flung my head and shoulders around but didn't see anything.

"Higher up. Behind the golden barrel."

I scrambled fifteen feet or so up the slope. "Holy cow."

It was three feet high, branched both at the base and higher up. The gray stems were three quarters of an inch thick and studded with spines. Four-inch stalks displayed clusters of tiny flowers with blood-red bracts. The leaves were elliptical, three or four inches long. Nothing out of the ordinary there.

What *was* extraordinary was that the leaves were, as advertised, striped. Actually, *chevroned* is a better word. Each leaf was adorned with alternating V-shape areas of red and green. Each *V* pointed down toward where the leaf sprang from the stem, with the mid-rib at the base of the *V*. The stripes varied from a quarter to a half inch wide.

Austin came up behind me. He had another home-rolled job in his mouth. I said, "She just gave this to you?"

"Sure did. She said she wanted to see how it would grow in the ground. And 'cause I'm the best in-ground grower we got, she gave it to me."

"How big was it then?"

"Oh, it was a little guy." He held his palms about a foot apart. "Maybe like this."

"Were there more?"

"I don't know, Joe. This was years ago." He grinned. "And remember, people say I've destroyed a lot of my brain cells."

I fingered the leaves. "Could I get a piece of this?"

"Sure could. As a matter of fact, I've got one already cut. Part of it was growing the wrong way, would have run into that big mound of mammillaria over there. Just haven't got around to sticking it back in the ground, but I didn't really know where I was going to put it anyway."

We descended the hill and walked around to his potting area. He reached down to a low shelf and pulled out a chunk of milii, about two feet long, with a couple of branches of a foot apiece.

I pumped Austin for more info on the plant, but he didn't have any. "You're not Succuman, are you?" I asked, and he asked me what the fuck I was talking about. I never-minded him, thanked him profusely, turned down his invitation to smoke a joint, and headed back to the city.

I was almost to the Coast Highway when I remembered the books. Screw them, I thought. I've got something much better. If I needed the books I'd come back over the weekend, and maybe that time I'd take Austin up on the joint.

I pulled over at Gladstone's 4 Fish and ordered a sandwich. While they were building it I found the pay phone and called Gina.

"Are you rested?" I asked.

"No."

"Me neither. I found the striped milii." I related what had happened at Austin's.

"Now that we have it, so what?" she said.

"I guess we try to figure out where Brenda got it. What have you been up to?"

"Looked in the archives a little. Nothing there. I went to Barnes and Noble and bought a computer book."

"You didn't."

"I'd barely cracked the cover when my mother called. She wants me to come over and pick out which of her jewelry I want. The Virgin told her she's about to die."

"Again?"

"Yeah, but it's been a whole, what, two months? So I've got to go over sometime this afternoon and convince her she's not about to kick off. Where are you off to next?"

"I have to run up to Sam's and check on his plants."

"Why don't I go too? I want to see this vaunted plant. And I can put off Mom a little longer."

We agreed to meet in the Gelson's lot in the Palisades. I went outside and made my way east on Sunset. Several minutes later I remembered my sandwich. First the books, now my lunch. Alzheimer's was setting in early.

I came around a curve and zoomed past Final Haven. I had some time to kill before Gina would reach Gelson's, so I hung a U-turn and a couple of minutes later drifted down the garden path. A half dozen people were visiting one or another of the weird grave sites, but Brenda was alone. I sat on the grass in front of her tomb and we chatted. It was a nice conversation, though I did most of the talking.

I pulled into the Gelson's lot in time to see Gina exiting the market, peeling the wrapper off a Häagen-Dazs bar. She had on gray shorts and a light blue tank top with no bra, and why was I noticing a little detail like that all of a sudden?

I showed her the plant from Austin's and drove us up to Sam's. "You know," I said when we'd exited the truck, "last time I came to someone's house when they were out of town—"

"Shut up."

I did, but I'd managed to scare myself, and Gina too. We approached the cabin. I peered into the window, alert for feet sticking out from behind furniture. There weren't any.

We glanced at the greenhouse and back at each other. "I'm not letting you out of my sight," I said.

"Why not?"

"Every time I do you find another dead body."

We advanced on the greenhouse. I opened the door and poked my head in. "Sam?" No reply. "Sam?" Again, louder. He didn't answer. And one wouldn't expect him to, considering he was in Tucson.

Unless he was lying dead with a euphorbia violating some part of his anatomy. I remembered what he'd said Tuesday. *"I'm probably next."*

We slipped in and walked up and down the aisles. I came around a corner and looked down under a bench. "You'd better see this," I said.

She came up behind me. "Is it?"

"Yes," I said. "It's another striped *Euphorbia milii*."

This one resided in a gallon plastic pot. It was smaller than the first, with thinner stems and fewer leaves.

"Did everyone but me have one of these?" I asked no one

in particular. I pulled it out and inspected it, then ran back to the truck, got my piece, compared the two, put Sam's back.

I checked what I was supposed to check, and we left. When we got back to Gelson's, Gina sighed and said she'd better get over to her mother's. "And you?" she asked.

"Me?" I said. "I thought I'd go dig up Henry Farber."

🌵

Back in the seventies Marina del Rey was the singles capital of the Westside, if not the entire Los Angeles metropolitan area. Every weekend hundreds of hormone-crazed pilgrims would flock to places like T.G.I. Friday's to engage in inane conversation and elicit casual sex. As the years went by, the singles grew old or got married or contracted an STD, and their meeting places shuttered or became copy centers and record stores. But the real marina, home to sun-browned men and women in deck shoes occupying boats with funny names, went on as always.

I drove down streets named after south-sea islands. Mindanao and Bali and Palawan Ways. Eventually I gave up trying to figure out where Farber's slip was and looked for someone to ask. When I found her she was sixty years old, had skin like a steer, and towed a mastiff with a head the size of Ohio. I tried not to stare at her facial fissures as she directed me to the third row of boats. I parked and walked over.

The ever-present gulls wheeled over Henry Farber's boat, the *Zinger II*. It was a nice boat, I guessed, with brass trimmings and antennae and things. As I approached, a dark-haired woman, around thirty-five, popped out of the cabin. Tall, with the irresistible combination of black hair and blue eyes. She had on a Dodgers cap, a well-filled electric blue bikini top, and short white shorts. Picture the classic blond

California girl, give her dark hair, and you've got the picture.

"Hi," she said. "You must be Dutch. You're early." Her voice was deep for a woman. Bacall-ish.

I resisted the urge for a geographic comeback. "No, I'm Joe."

"I thought you must be Dutch, because I know all Henry's friends except Dutch."

"I'm not one of Henry's friends. Giving a party?"

"Eight or ten people. Basketball playoffs."

"I'm afraid I'm more of a hockey fan. Is he here?"

"No. But I expect him any minute. He went to the market. We ran out of toilet paper."

"I didn't know you used toilet paper on a boat. I thought there was a big hole in the bottom."

She smiled. I smiled. We stood there smiling until I said, "Are you Henry's girlfriend?"

"Uh-huh. Maria. And who are you?"

"I'm Joe."

"You said that. But who *are* you?"

"Does the name Brenda Belinski mean anything to you?"

She hopped onto the dock. She was barefoot, but even so she was as tall as I was. "That's that girl Henry used to see who was killed."

Used to see. How interesting. "Right. I'm a friend of hers. I'm just trying to track down old acquaintances, see if I can get any idea who might have wanted her dead." I tried a winning smile. "How long have you known Henry?"

"A year and a half. Do you want to come aboard? I can give you a daiquiri. Or some iced tea, if you like."

"Tea would be good." I followed her aboard and sat down in a white plastic chair up against a railing in the back of the boat.

"Lemon? Sugar? Equal?"

"Straight." She bent over to drop a napkin in my lap,

bringing me closer to a glimpse of a female nipple than I'd been in well over a year. She handed me a pink plastic glass. I took a sip. Instant, but not bad. "You live here too?"

A nice smile. "No. I like the creature comforts too much to be a live-aboard. I generally come up from Long Beach on Friday night or Saturday morning and leave Sunday night."

"Is it serious?"

"Is what—oh, you mean Henry and me. I don't—you certainly ask a lot of questions."

"I'm a curious kind of guy."

"I see." Maybe she saw, but she sure wasn't going to tell me if it was serious. "Henry should be here any minute."

"We've established that." We smiled awkwardly at each other. I considered asking her if she knew he was seeing Brenda again. But I'd already been a prick once that week, and it nearly got me bopped with a euphorbia. No. I'd wait until Henry showed up, get him alone, ask him stuff. Why screw up her life? "If I remember correctly, when I met Henry he had the boat docked in Long Beach."

"That was *Zinger I*," she said. "He sold it and bought this when he got the position at UCLA and moved up here."

"This one bigger?"

"Actually, a little smaller."

"Sometimes smaller is better."

"So I've heard. Here comes Henry now."

The years had not been overly kind to Henry Farber. I remembered him as thin, with nice features, not a bad-looking guy to have tirading around your living room accusing you of stealing his girlfriend. He was still slim but had developed a belly that jutted out almost comically above the waistband of his shorts. He'd lost enough of his hair to be noticeable. Tufts of graying chest fur sprouted around his orange tank top.

I stood and stepped away from my chair, trying to appear

calm, casually sipping my tea. He climbed onto the boat, casting a quizzical expression through the wire-framed glasses that had replaced his former horn-rims. He carried two sets of grocery bags, paper inside plastic, with a six-pack of Charmin under his arm. He dumped the provisions, keeping his eye on me, appearing to know me but not from where. "And who would this be?" he asked anyone who would answer.

"This is Joe—what *is* your last name, Joe?"

"It's Portugal. Hi, Henry."

His mouth froze. His eyes widened momentarily, then narrowed. His fists balled. "You."

"Right, and I'm hoping we can let bygones be bygones. I'm hoping—"

But Henry Farber never found out what else I was hoping. Because with three great leaps he ran over to me, and he pushed me, hard, and before I could do a damned thing about it, my iced tea and I plunged over the railing and into the not-particularly-clean waters of Marina del Rey.

17

I HAD WATER UP MY NOSE.

I also had water in my mouth and in my ears and I was freezing my balls off, but it was the nose that really got me. I'd hit the surface ass-first, sunk down a fathom or two, and thrashed my way back to the surface. I continued thrashing, which is as close to swimming as I get, until I more or less stabilized, treading water in *Zinger II*'s shadow. I trod long enough to get my breath back, and when I did I felt the burning behind my palate that meant water had gotten up my nose, and I cursed Henry Farber out at the top of my lungs.

My pink plastic glass floated by, followed by a catsup packet from Burger World with an unidentifiable yellow-green glob on top. I splashed it away and vocally reaffirmed my opinion of Farber. I swam to the dock, climbed up on it, and stormed up to the boat. It was a half-assed storming because one of my sandals now rested at the bottom of the marina. It's tough to storm when you're walking lopsided.

Farber obviously hadn't thought his action through. He must have figured when I went over the side I'd disappear forever, that there were man-eating mackerel down there or something. Now that I was back aboard his pride and joy, he put his hands up in front of him and stepped back, mumbling, "Now, now." He inched over toward the cabin until I said, "Hold it right there."

He held it. I got in his face and flicked water from my hair at him. "You are *such* an asshole," I said.

"It was instinctive," he said. "I saw you there with Maria and I remembered what you did before."

"No," I said. "Protective can be instinctive. Angry can be instinctive. Pushing me off the goddamned boat isn't instinctive." I wheeled toward Maria. "Has old Hank here told you he was seeing someone else?"

A tiny shrug. "I kind of figured."

"He was seeing Brenda again, you know." I threw a glance back at Henry. There was always the possibility Eugene Rand had given me a bum steer. God knew what that love-starved wienie was capable of. But no. By the caught-red-handed look on Henry's face, I knew I'd hit the bull's-eye.

Back to Maria. "Has he ever threatened you? Slugged you, done anything violent?"

She didn't say anything. But she wanted to.

"Come on, Maria. Let it out."

"I went out to dinner with an old friend. A man. He got angry."

"How angry?"

"He grabbed my arms and shook me."

"And?"

"That was it. I had little bruises. Not too bad. Henry isn't very strong." A slight turn of the head. "Are you, Henry?"

"So I got a little mad once. That doesn't mean I did anything to Brenda."

I raised my eyebrows. "No one said you did."

"The police came and asked me questions. They didn't suspect anything."

"Didn't they?"

"It doesn't matter if you believe me. I didn't do it." He roused himself and went over to Maria. "Honey, she didn't mean anything to me. It was just a fling. Only once or twice."

"Christ, Hank," I said. "You went to faculty parties with her and everything. While poor Maria here stayed home down in Long Beach watching reruns of *Cheers.*"

I watched them, hoping she'd get mad, hoping the whole thing would get emotional, with yelling and screaming, so Henry would lose control and let something slip. But instead, Maria got a little teary-eyed, and Henry told her he was sorry. He tried to put his arms around her. She shrugged him off. But not very forcefully, and I was afraid if he tried again she would let him. I didn't want to be around to see that. I didn't want to see yet another asshole getting the girl while nice guys like me slept alone. So I got off the boat.

Someone new was walking up, a big red-haired lug carrying a six-pack of Blackened Voodoo. "You must be Dutch," I said, and went somewhere else to dry off.

I found a towel among the debris in the truck. But my shirt was still wet, binding, and uncomfortable, so I pulled it off and drove home bare-chested. A guy without a shirt in a pickup. All I needed was the backward baseball cap to complete the redneck image.

When I got home I threw my orphaned sandal in the Goodwill bag atop Mrs. Kwiatkowski's jogging suit and checked the phone machine. My father had called. So had Magda Tillis. Both said the machine was making weird noises and they were hoping I'd get the message.

Dad wanted to know how I was doing. Were the cops still following me? I called him back and told him everything was fine and that I hadn't seen my shadow again. He told me to be careful. I said I would.

Magda told me Dick's memorial service was Monday at ten-thirty at a small cemetery in the hills above Santa Monica, where his ashes would already have been interred in front of a select few on Sunday. She hoped I could make it.

This presented a small dilemma. My ten-fifteen Burger World audition should be over by ten-thirty, but it was way over in Hollywood. The earliest I could get to the service would be eleven. I briefly considered calling Elaine to cancel the audition. But I couldn't afford to blow off a shot at a Burger World.

After I put the chunk of milii in the greenhouse, I phoned Gina. We exchanged stories, mine about Farber and hers about her mother. Mine was more exciting; hers scored points for human interest.

She was prepping for her encore with Carlos. We joked about how it was the first time in a year either of us had seen the same person two nights in a row. And about how she might get lucky. "I thought you were getting too old for recreational sex," I said.

She waited a long time before answering. "I guess two dates in a row takes it out of the recreational category. Maybe not quite meaningful, but close enough. I've been celibate too long. You too, Joe. It's making me nervous."

I showered and shaved. This made three days out of four shaving, way above my average. I emptied my wallet and dried the contents as best I could with my hair dryer. I spent fifteen minutes inspecting my wardrobe before settling on my blue Dockers and a chambray shirt Gina'd gotten me for my last birthday, and I left for my assignation with Amanda Belinski.

I stopped at American Flowers, picked out half a bouquet, asked myself what the hell I was doing, and carefully returned them to their containers. But I broke the stem off one iris, so I paid for it and threw it on the floor of the truck.

The flowers went back because it wasn't a date. It was fact-gathering with someone who could be invaluable to my investigation. The fact that she was attractive and I was suddenly horny had nothing to do with it. Besides, what kind of putz would come on to a woman whose sister had just been murdered?

I was halfway up Main Street in Ocean Park when the eight-track ate the Dave Clark Five. I jerked the cartridge out, reeled in four or five feet of tape, and threw the whole mess on the floor. It landed atop the iris. This reminded me of Iris Bunche and of her substantial yet attractive tush. They say men think of sex every six seconds. I'd been way behind, and all of a sudden my hormones were playing catch-up.

It was a quarter after seven by the time I pulled into the circular drive in front of the Loews. Twenty-five after by the time I'd discussed the rates with the parking attendant and opted for a place several blocks up the street. Twenty-five to eight when I knocked on the door to Room 621.

Amanda came to the door wearing a diaphanous white blouse over something lacy. Her dark gray slacks faithfully followed the curve of her hips. She wore a little more makeup than when I'd seen her before—a bit of color on her cheeks, some highlighting around the eyes—and ear studs with pale blue stones. Her dark brown hair hung straight down the sides of her face, framing it perfectly. She had a nice perfume on, subtle but sexy.

"Shall we go to the restaurant downstairs?" she said.

"That'll be fine."

She grabbed a sweater, and we took the elevator down and walked through the lobby. I'm not usually a fan of fancy expensive hotels, but the Loews works for me. A huge atrium arched all the way to the roof, with plants all over the place. All relatively tasteful. And right at the beach.

We'd just about reached the restaurant when I heard someone call my name. I turned to see Willy Schoeppe approaching. He was clad in khaki pants, a matching shirt with epaulets, and his ever-present smile. He came up and pumped my hand Teutonically. I introduced him to Amanda and told her how he knew Brenda, while wondering why he hadn't looked Amanda up before.

"Have you eaten, Mr. Schoeppe?" she asked.

"I have not," he said. "But I would not want to intrude."

"Nonsense. Mr. Portugal and I are here to talk about Brenda. I would be happy to have you join us."

He looked at me, and I nodded. A few moments later we were seated at a window table that afforded us a splendid view of the sunset. Little rows of delicate high clouds transformed from pink to purple in a minute's time. A lone pelican winged by over the bay.

The waitress came by and recited the specials. None of us took her up on them. When she went away I broke the ice. "You said at the funeral that you and Brenda'd grown apart."

Amanda nodded. "Especially since our parents died. Seven years ago. Within a month."

"Sometimes it's like that," I said. "When people are really close, when one goes, the other doesn't want to——"

She shook her head. "They weren't close at all. They divorced when I was two. They just happened to pass away the same month. And as for Brenda and me, a lot of the time I lived with my father and she stayed with Mother. And even when we were living in the same house, we didn't play together much. She was nine years older than me." Which put Amanda around forty. Old enough. Unlike Iris, who——

Jesus, Portugal, I told myself, get your mind out of your gonads.

The sun squashed itself down atop the horizon, turned redder and redder, and winked out. I kept an eye on Amanda, waiting for some sign this was affecting her emotionally, waiting for the big breakdown. *"I wish I'd known her better,"* she would gasp out between sobs. *"I wish I'd gotten to tell her that even though we hardly ever saw each other, I loved her."*

It didn't happen, and by the time our entrees arrived, I knew it wasn't going to. Pasta with chicken for me, a steak for Schoeppe, lamb curry for Amanda. In L.A. a lot of people had given up lamb and veal. The whole baby-animal thing. Things were different in Wisconsin.

I didn't taste much of my meal. I was too involved in the conversation. And in watching Amanda Belinski eat.

She did so with amazing intensity. She loaded everything into her mouth with strong, discrete actions. Like a robot would eat, if robots had to. First a shrimp cocktail she'd cached while Schoeppe and I ate our salads, then her lamb curry. Fork in food, fork up, fork over, fork in mouth. I was especially taken by the way she shook the salt. With vigor. Strong, discrete shakes.

We got to talking about Brenda's burial place. Schoeppe had been out there twice. "A fine example of the Merina tradition," he said.

"I knew Brenda was into all things Madagascan," I said, "but I had no idea she would have herself buried like one."

"It was probably my doing. She was always fond of the plants, but I insisted on introducing her to the culture, and in short order she was more of a devotee than I."

But that was the last time Brenda entered the conversation for quite a while. Mostly, Amanda and I swapped life stories, while Schoeppe acted avuncular. She taught geology at a medium-size private college in Bow Springs, Wisconsin, where she'd lived for the last twelve years. She'd never been married, had no immediate prospects, and lived with a dog and a cat and a pair of lovebirds named Lucy and Desi.

When the check came, everyone grabbed for wallets and purses. The waitress had Schoeppe's hundred-dollar bill before my hand even reached my pocket. "Please, allow me," he said. "It has been a great pleasure."

Amanda and I filed halfhearted protests. Schoeppe pooh-poohed us, got his change, threw a big tip on the table. Smiling more broadly than ever, he said, "I think you two young people would like to be alone now."

I hadn't been called a young people in quite a while, and the term made me grin. Amanda made a lukewarm attempt to get him to stay, but he said he had to get up early and arose from the table. I got up to shake his hand. He held my grip, got a faraway look in his eye, and temporarily lost his smile. "As I spend time here in Los Angeles," he said, "I grow convinced plant smugglers had nothing to do with Brenda's death."

"Why is that?"

"This is not their milieu. I cannot imagine these people in this city. They are people of the desert."

"I've read that climatically, L.A. qualifies as a desert."

His eyes returned to the room, and his smile did too. "I have read that the same is true culturally. Although personally I do not agree." He gave my hand a final squeeze and strode off through the lobby.

Amanda carefully placed her water glass in the exact center of her napkin, stood, put on her sweater. "Let's walk outside."

We went down to the concrete boardwalk along the beach. The sky was clear, with a fair number of stars. A faint marine odor ran through the air. To the north, Santa Monica

Pier jutted into the bay, filled with lights and tourists and skeeball games.

"Let's walk up to the Promenade," I said.

"You mean that big shopping center?"

"Just north of it. A pedestrian mall. Great urban-renewal story, yada yada yada. Restaurants, people-watching. Bookstores. You like bookstores?"

"It sounds fun. Let's go."

We'd gone halfway up the boardwalk when a grizzled old homeless guy, smelling of burlap, popped out of a doorway to ask for a handout. Amanda shrank back and took my arm. I dug in my pocket for some change. The man said, "God bless you," which was big among the homeless that year, and returned to his lair.

A block later Amanda abruptly stopped and twisted me around to face her. Her hair fluttered in the breeze. Her eyes searched my face. "Why are you trying to find Brenda's killer?" she said.

I studied her features. Her eyes, so like Brenda's. Her lips, cool and refreshing. "How do you know I am?"

"Call it woman's intuition."

"I see." It was a good question. I still wasn't sure of the answer. "She was a friend."

"The police will find him."

"Eventually, maybe. I think they're off on the wrong track. They suspect me, for instance."

"Did you do it?"

"Of course not. Did you?"

"No."

"I thought not."

She let go of my arms and got me walking again. We continued in silence, listening to the surf and the occasional insomniac sea gull.

18

THE THIRD STREET PROMENADE IS A MONUMENT TO UR-
ban regeneration. They took a three-block stretch you
wouldn't want to venture into after dark and turned it into a
major entertainment center. It's full of fun things to do, if
you're the type who's into fun things.

Maybe the evening hadn't started out as a date, but to the
casual observer it would have looked like one. Amanda
would touch my forearm to get my attention, then point at
some street clown or balloon twister or fancy bubble blower.
I would grab her hand to keep from losing her when we
pushed through the crowd. We browsed in a used bookstore
but didn't buy anything.

Around nine-thirty we wandered into Yankee Doodles.
The place was packed. People leaned intently over pool tables. A dozen TVs showed highlights of the basketball game
earlier, as well as hockey and baseball, tennis and golf.

We found a place in the corner. The monitor nearby was
tuned to what had to be Trash Sports Network. Bungee
jumping and skyscraper climbing and reruns of *Battle of the
Network Stars*. A waitress came and we ordered drinks, a

greyhound for me, a Manhattan for her. In old books, people were always drinking Manhattans. My mother liked them. I hadn't seen anybody order one in years.

We watched the pool players and exchanged confidences on how bad we both were at the game. This seemed to demand signing up for a table. Twenty minutes and another drink later, one came available. After two games had confirmed our ineptitude, we turned in our cues and paid our bill.

We walked back south along the Promenade. I started picking up a two-ships-passing-in-the-night vibe. Like something meaningful, or at least not totally frivolous, was supposed to pass between Amanda and me that evening. What form it was going to take was unclear, and if we weren't alert enough to spot it when it came along, it probably wouldn't happen at all. The emotional buzz had been missing for a long time, and when Amanda reached out and took my hand, I felt a physical one as well. We walked silently for a block or two, thinking our own thoughts. As we turned west on Colorado, she said, "Brenda liked you a lot."

"How do you know that?"

"She wrote me. We traded letters once or twice a year. She said she'd met this guy and he was something special."

"Is that all?"

"I don't remember the details. It *was* four years ago. I wrote back telling her how happy I was for her, and the next time she wrote she said that it was over."

"Yes."

"You don't want to tell me what happened."

"There's nothing to tell. She got tired of me."

She looked me over. "Self-pity doesn't look good on you."

My lips were dry. I licked them. "Sorry."

"She just dropped you?"

"More or less. She went off to Madagascar and said she felt I should see other people while she was gone. And when she came back we just never got back together."

"Did you try?"

I said nothing.

"You didn't, did you?"

I shook my head. "No. I just sort of let the whole thing slip away."

"Maybe she was waiting for you to come after her."

"Maybe."

She nodded, as if this explained everything. "But you remained friends."

"Yeah. A year or so later we worked together on a succulent exhibit for the county fair, spent a couple of days out in Pomona together, and we found we still enjoyed each other's company. So we began to hang out. She was one of my closest friends."

"Your closest being this Gina woman who keeps creeping into your conversation."

"Does she?"

"Like clockwork."

I looked away, pondering the significance of what she'd said. The guy who'd been following me was across the boardwalk. He stood on a staircase leading down to the beach, several steps from the top, with only his head and torso visible. He'd ditched the suit and wore one of those fancy polo shirts gangsters in the movies have on when they're taking calls at poolside. He still had his shades though.

I told Amanda, "Stay here," and dashed out to intercept him. When I reached the staircase he was gone. I stomped halfway down to the beach, far enough to see that he wasn't down there.

When I got back to the top, Amanda was waiting for me. "What was that all about?"

"The damned cops have somebody following me around. Come on. I'm going to find him."

I pushed through the crowd, headed back toward land, more or less dragging Amanda by the hand. I nearly knocked down a woman tending an incense stand. Somewhere not too far away a calliope chugged. "The carousel," I said.

Everyone's seen Santa Monica's resident merry-go-round in *The Sting*. It reopened a few years ago after a long period of inactivity and delights kids of all ages once more. We ducked in and plunged through the throngs inside. The calliope clanged out "A Bicycle Built for Two." Little kids screamed for just one more ride. Horses took riders up and down, while less adventurous folk rode benches.

We followed the wheel's perimeter and stopped directly across from the entrance. I scanned the crowd, but I knew I wasn't going to find Sunglasses Guy. "Damn it," I said.

"Are you giving up?"

"Yes," I said. "I'm not going to find him. He must have taken Melting Into the Crowd 101 at the academy."

She laughed. "Too bad," she said. Another laugh. "That was a lot of fun."

I turned to her. "Fun?"

She was a little out of breath, and a tiny bit of perspiration stood out on her forehead. Her eyes were slightly glazed. "Yes, fun. Like being Julia Roberts in a thriller movie. This kind of thing never happens in Bow Springs."

Julia Roberts, was she? If she could be Julia Roberts, I could be Mel Gibson. I put my arm around her and pulled her tight and I kissed her. I expected her to resist. I was wrong.

It was a lovely kiss, nearly a perfect kiss. Earlier, her lips had looked cool and refreshing. They were refreshing all right, but warm, very nicely warm. They were soft, too, and pressed up against mine sweetly, at first tentative and then with more insistence. The quickest brush of tongues, and suddenly it was over.

Somewhere in there she'd gotten her hand entangled in my hair. She gently pulled my head back and looked quizzically at me. "Oh, my," she said.

"Oh, yours indeed."

We stared at each other for a moment, then turned simultaneously and began to walk toward the exit. I slipped my arm around her shoulders. There's a delicious feeling of anticipation that goes with putting your arm around a woman for the first time. Will she, in turn, place hers around your waist? Or will she decline to do so, leaving your limb lying there like a dead fish, until you can find some excuse to remove it without feeling like too much of an idiot?

The question was answered quickly. After only two or three seconds of suspense, she slid her hand across the small of my back and snapped it into place against the waistband of my Dockers. I leaned over and kissed her hair and escorted her off the pier. I threw a perfunctory look over my shoulder, in case the cop should be following, but when I didn't see him I let him disappear from my mind.

As we turned south on Ocean I felt a chill. Probably that darned Catalina eddy. I drew my arm a bit tighter around Amanda. Ten minutes later we came to the Datsun. "That's my truck," I said.

"Really? You don't seem the pickup type." She giggled and disengaged herself from me. She went to the truck and peeked in the window.

"It's kind of dirty," I said.

"So I see." She inspected the truck bed, ran a finger along the side, stood by the cabin. "I want to sit in it," she said.

"You do?"

"Yes."

I unlocked the door and held it for her and she got in. She

inspected the interior wonderingly, as if she were in some mansion instead of the cab of a '72 Datsun, touching the gearshift and the steering wheel and the sun visor, looking very much like a woman who'd never been in a pickup truck before.

She rolled down the window and smiled out at me. "I've never been in a pickup truck before," she said, then patted the seat on the driver's side and added, "You come sit too."

I went around and got in next to her. She smiled again and took both my hands in hers and gazed into my eyes. "Take me back to your place," she said.

"Are you sure?"

"Of course I'm sure. Why wouldn't I be sure?"

"I wouldn't want us to do anything we shouldn't."

"We won't, Joe."

That was good enough for me. I started the engine and pulled out into the waning Saturday night traffic.

19

H ER LOVEMAKING WAS ACCOMPLISHED WITH QUICK, PRE-
cise movements, as if what she was taking in would soon be
gone. Our rhythms didn't mesh, but it didn't matter because
we were both so in need that the whole thing was over in a
minute or two. Afterward we lay there watching each other's
eyes in the flickering light from the candles I'd lit before-
hand. She began to cry, not the huge, racking sobs I'd pictured at the funeral, but a tiny flow of tears, slipping off her
face onto the pillowcase. I reached out a hand to comfort her
and she smiled. "I'm so silly," she said, and I felt wetness in
my own eyes. When the first drop trickled out she kissed it
away. Her lips drifted down to mine and lingered.

I wrapped my arms around her, and she rolled over on top
of me. This time around we had the luxury of getting in sync
with each other. We tried this and sampled that until there
was nothing left to try, no treat unsampled.

When we were done we lay there, head to toe, sweating
and out of breath. I offered to go out to the garage for the
fan. She said that was sweet but she'd be fine.

I snuggled my head on her thigh, traced the curve of her

stomach with a fingertip. She smiled and took my hand. "Do you want to hear something odd?" she said.

"What?"

"At the hotel, right after the funeral, right after I met you. I imagined this might happen. Isn't that strange? Here my sister had just been buried and I was thinking about sex."

"I had the same thought. Only I had it *at* the funeral. Remember that Woody Allen movie, *Love and Death*?"

"No."

"The point is, love and death, they sort of go together."

"Joe?"

"Yes?"

"We're not dealing with love here, are we?"

"No." I sat up, lay back down with my head next to hers. "When I had my fantasy I pictured you pulling out a cigarette afterward. We would smoke a toast to Brenda."

"I've never smoked a cigarette in my life."

"Me neither. Not tobacco, anyway."

"You mean you've smoked . . . other things?"

"I used to light up a joint now and then."

"I've never tried marijuana." Several seconds later: "Do you have any?"

I should have just said no. "There's some in the freezer. I haven't touched it in two or three years. I don't even know if it's still good."

"I'd like to try it."

I got up on an elbow, looked down at what I could make out in the candlelight. "No, you don't."

"I do. I've already witnessed a heathen burial ceremony and engaged in casual sex. Why don't I just get this other new experience out of the way?"

"Not to mention riding in a pickup. Wait. You've never engaged in casual sex before?"

"No. I suppose you do this kind of thing every day."

"If you consider a couple of times a decade every day. Anyway, this isn't exactly casual."

"Oh? What would you call it?"

I thought it over. All things considered, on the casual scale of one to ten, it was about an eight. "Okay, you win on that one. You really want to smoke some grass?"

"I do."

"I'll go get it."

Twenty years before, on a particularly dope-addled evening, I'd painstakingly taken a jar of Spice Islands marjoram and cut and pasted letters from other jars until it said MARIJUANA. Now I hopped out of bed and retrieved my handiwork from the freezer. I unscrewed the top and slipped a joint out. I lit it, took a hit, and passed it over to Amanda. "Don't take too much the first time. Just draw a little into your lungs, hold it as long as you can, let it out."

I heard her suck it in, saw the end glow, let the sweet scent bring random memories. After ten seconds or so she said through clenched lips, "Is it all right to let it out yet?"

I told her it was and she did. "Are you sure you haven't done this before?" I asked. "You're supposed to be gasping and wheezing."

"I swear." She passed the joint back over. I took another hit and sent it back. She inhaled again, held it, let it out. "When do I start to see planets?"

"That's LSD."

"You don't have any of that, do you?"

"Not for about the last quarter century. How do you feel?"

"Fine."

"You don't feel anything strange?"

"No."

"Take some more." She did, and I did, and she did and I

did. I lay there obsessing on her failure to cough. Maybe she'd done this before and wasn't admitting it. A fib. Perhaps one in a long line of fibs. Everything she'd said was a lie. She was lying to cover up the fact that she'd killed Brenda. Some sibling rivalry going back three decades. Brenda had dissected her Barbie or something. This did nothing to explain Dick getting knocked off, but that could have been a smoke-screen. Amanda had killed Dick to make it appear there was some succulent connection. How ruthless. How insidious.

How ludicrous. Amanda making Spartacus out of Dick McAfee? "I'm Spartacus," I said.

"Excuse me?"

"Oh. It's from a play I did. Called *Bleacher Bums*. All these Cubs fans are out in the bleachers, and one of them does something bad, throws a hot dog at the center fielder or something, and when the guard comes to throw him out, everyone claims they did it, to protect him, and they all stand up and say, 'I'm Spartacus,' like in the movie."

"What movie?"

"*Spartacus.*"

"Oh. I never saw it."

"It was a double bill with *Love and Death*. Oh, God, I'm babbling. I guess the dope is still good."

"I think it must be."

"Why?"

"Just a second ago I thought of Brenda's funeral, and that strange tomb, and it made me think of my parents' vault back in Eau Claire, and how odd it was that they were buried together even though they were divorced, and then I was thinking of my father and how he always put a little note in my lunchbox when I went to school and how he always signed it, *SWAK, Dad.* Sealed with a kiss. And when I was done I realized this whole thought process had taken only a second or two." She giggled, a nice girlish titter.

"Time compression," I said. "You're high, all right. Next thing you'll be wanting a bag of Cheetos. Hey. Maybe in your altered state you can think of something that might help with the investigation. Some little tidbit about Brenda from your childhood that bubbles up and makes the whole thing clear. So lie there and think."

"I'm lying. I'm thinking. Give me some more marijuana, please."

The joint had gone out. I dug a roach clip out of my jar and lit it. "Here."

"Thank you kindly." She drew it in, held it, flushed it out. "Here's something. Brenda really liked *Mr. Ed.*"

"The horse or the program?"

"Both. She used to watch religiously. She kept a list of episodes in her diary and—"

"She kept a diary?"

"Yes."

"Maybe she still keeps one. Kept one. Maybe I can find it and—" She clapped a hand over my mouth. "Ow."

"Sorry. No, she stopped doing that after college. She didn't want any incriminating evidence."

"Too bad. Some incriminating evidence is what we need right now. Anyway, I don't think we're going to get anywhere with the Mr. Ed connection. What else?"

"Did you seduce me so you could interrogate me?"

"No. It's an added benefit."

"Hmm. It's so hard because our relationship was so distant. I used to send her birthday presents, for instance, but she seemed uncomfortable even with that, so I stopped."

"Uncomfortable?"

"She didn't like to receive gifts."

I nodded. "Yeah, she was a little odd about presents. I bought her a couple of things, nothing very significant, and she got all weird. Almost angry that I'd given her something without warning her so she'd be able to have something to give back. It was such a hassle I never did it again."

"Probably my mother's influence. She was rather a strange woman. Oh, dear, I probably wouldn't have said that if it weren't for the marijuana. I'm hungry, by the way."

"A well-known effect of dope smoking."

"Are there others?"

"It's supposed to enhance sex."

"Is it now?" Suddenly she was on top of me again, her face looming above my own, her hair hanging down and tickling my cheeks. "Show me," she said.

So I did—show her, that is—and she showed me a thing or two she'd left out the first couple of times. When we were done making up for lost time, I slipped off into a dreamless sleep.

I awoke to the sound of a toothbrush. I jumped out of bed, grabbed the condom wrappers, and tossed them in the wastebasket, wondering a bit after the fact if the golden oldies I'd dug up in my nightstand had been up to their job. I pushed the bathroom door aside, and found Amanda brushing away, with strong, precise strokes, like she did everything else. Her breasts gently echoed the up-and-down motion of her hand. I watched them. She watched me watch them.

When she'd done enough brushing she searched around the sink. "I use my hand," I said.

The expression on her face was so pained I ran into the kitchen for a glass. When she was done I put my arms around her, hugged her tight, enjoying the soft press of her flesh against mine. "I had the worst taste in my mouth," she said.

"Munga mouth. The downside to marijuana."

"I found the toothbrush under the sink. I hope you don't mind that I opened it."

"Of course not." I let her go. "Do you want to leave while I use the toilet?"

"Oh. Yes, I think that would be best."

When I returned to the bedroom she was already half dressed. I went to hug her again, trying to give her a big romantic kiss. She hardly responded. I drew my head back. "I was going to take a shower," I said. "I thought you might want to join me, but you seem to have your clothes on already. Something wrong?"

She pulled away and gave me a wan smile. "Only that I'm getting on an airplane today and I'll never see you again. So I need to separate myself."

"How do you know you'll never see me again?"

She picked up her blouse, pulled it on, did a button. "Let's not kid ourselves. What happened last night had nothing to do with you and me. It had to do with Brenda."

It didn't seem worthwhile to pursue it. It never does. "Okay. I'm still going to get a shower."

"I'll shower at the hotel." She finished with her blouse. "I'd better go back as soon as you're finished. My plane's at three, and I haven't packed."

"It's only"—I glanced at the clock—"a quarter to nine. Plenty of time."

"Please, Joe, don't make this any harder."

I watched her for a few seconds and nodded. "Okay."

I showered quickly and dressed and was ready to leave in fifteen minutes. When I opened the front door, Casillas was standing there.

"Now what?" I said.

"How interesting," he said. "The old boyfriend and the sister."

"That's none of your business. What do you want from me now?"

"Henry Farber called and said you were giving him a hard time."

"I was giving *him* a hard time? He pushed me off his goddamned boat."

"He says it was self-defense."

"Self-defense, my ass. If you're looking for murder suspects, Hector, that's where you ought to be looking. Have you checked out his alibi?"

"Yeah, that Maria girl, she'll vouch for him and— Hey, who's asking the questions around here?"

"He's got that Maria girl wrapped around his slimy little finger. I'd look a bit more closely if I were you."

"Which you're not, thank God. You're not a cop, Portugal, and I wish to hell you'd stop trying to act like one."

"How's this? You stop accusing me of killing Brenda, and I'll stop trying to figure out who really did."

"No can do."

"Then neither can I."

"I didn't think you would."

"How about this? At least stop having that guy follow me."

His eyes flitted skyward for assistance with the idiot in front of him. "I told you before, we don't have anyone following you."

I stared at him and thought, he really is good at this. If I didn't know better I'd swear he was telling the truth. "If you'll excuse us," I said, "Ms. Belinski here has a plane to catch."

He glared. He fumed. He thought bad thoughts about me and turned and went back out to his el cheapo Chevy.

I ushered Amanda into the truck and we got going. We

briefly discussed Casillas. Uncomfortable silence followed until, as we turned right onto Pacific, she said, "Your friend Gina. Was that like Brenda?"

"What do you mean?"

"Is she an old lover too?"

It took me a minute to answer. With Gina, sometimes I think I imagined it. "Yes. But that was a long, long time ago. She's a friend now, nothing more. Like Brenda was."

Ten minutes later we stood in the Loews lobby. "Do you want me to walk you up?"

"No. I'm fine." She held out a hand. "It was nice meeting you, Mr. Portugal."

I stuck out my own and took hers. "And you, Ms. Belinski." We stared at each other for a couple of long seconds. She pulled herself closer, gave me a fierce squeeze, a quick, soft kiss, and drew away. She walked a half dozen paces and turned. "Find the bastard," she said, and disappeared from my life.

20

I MADE IT A FEW STEPS OUT THE DOOR, REVERSED FIELD, and found a pay phone. I dialed Gina's assortment of numbers, but she didn't answer at any of them. I wondered if she'd gotten lucky too and she and Carlos were waiting for the phone to stop ringing to continue their lovemaking. Or maybe she'd just gone out to buy a paper.

Austin was next. I called and told him I was on my way up to get the books. On the way I could stop at Gladstone's and see if they were still holding my sandwich.

I sat in the phone booth wondering why I'd let Amanda go so easily. Yeah, it probably wouldn't have worked out. Long-distance relationships seldom do. Not to mention that we didn't have a thing in common. But I could have at least made the effort. I could have volunteered to visit her in Bow Springs, see if we could stand each other for more than an evening.

I forced her out of my mind. If I suddenly woke up in a week with an irresistible urge to see her again, I knew where to find her.

I got to Austin and Vicki's around ten-fifteen. They were out back, soaking up sun, reading the paper, listening to the Grateful Dead with their two impossibly hip teenagers. Vicki was my age, with long wavy red hair, blue eyes, pale skin, fine features. I'd always found her incredibly attractive and always felt guilty about it.

Austin had the books waiting for me. He'd brought out Rauh's Madagascar volumes too. I said I already had them. He said, "Far out, man."

Vicki offered me breakfast, and I took her up on it. When the kids left a little later, Austin asked if I wanted a joint. I turned him down. I didn't smoke dope anymore. What had happened the night before was an aberration. I hoped.

It was pleasant being there with them, talking about things other than Brenda and Dick, idly paging through the books. One of the Rauh volumes, before getting into the plant stuff, had a section on Malagasy culture and showed a picture of a Mahafaly tomb similar to Brenda's. Something gnawed at my brain when I saw that, but I couldn't zero in on it.

Eventually I checked my watch. "It's nearly two," I announced. "And I haven't gotten anything done today."

"What is it you want to do, man?" Austin asked.

"Track down clues."

"Bring us up to date."

They were fascinated about Sunglasses Guy, and Vicki wove intricate webs with which I could entrap him, all highly imaginative and utterly impractical. Then she said, "Maybe he isn't a cop."

"Huh?"

"Maybe Casillas is telling the truth. Somebody else is following you."

"Who else would be following me?"

Austin picked up the thread. "Could be the same guy who killed Brenda and Dick."

"No way."

He shrugged. "Seems as likely as the cops."

Once they got me started on that, it seemed perfectly logical. I'd been an idiot. The killer had been stalking me, and I didn't even know it. In fact, I'd chased after the guy like I was the hero in a Hitchcock movie.

No, that was ridiculous. It had to be a policeman who was following me around. "This Brenda business," I said. "It's just too complicated. I can't get a handle on it."

"See," Austin said, "there's your problem. You keep calling this the Brenda business. You're ignoring Dick."

"But can we be absolutely sure the murders are related?"

"Of course they're related, Pollyanna," Vicki said. "And I don't believe for a minute that someone is working their way down the list of officers. There's some link between Brenda and Dick, and as soon as you find it the whole thing will fall into place."

"But—"

"There's no buts. Shut up and think about it a minute."

She was right. I'd been so bent on avenging Brenda that I'd been ignoring a whole other path of investigation. So I picked up the books and went back to the city to look up Hope McAfee.

🌵

Traffic on P.C.H. can be brutal during beach weather. I got stuck around Chautauqua and didn't get home until nearly four. I checked the machine. There wasn't anything there, from Gina or anyone else. I called her but didn't get an answer. I didn't leave a message.

I tried Hope, and she answered on the first ring. "Yes?"

"Hi, Hope. It's Joe. Joe Portugal. I'm sorry about your loss."

"Thank you, Joe."

"I was also calling to see if you needed anything."

"No, no, I'm fine. As fine as anyone could be, given the circumstances. Now that we've put Dick's ashes to rest I've been able to start— Oh, who am I kidding? I'm miserable. Everyone's gone and left me by myself."

"Let me get you out of the house."

"What do you mean?"

"I'll come over and take you for a drive."

"That's not necessary."

"I think it is." I hung up before she could protest further.

🌵

Hope waited out front, dressed in a gray sweatshirt and jeans. Most of the color was gone from her face; for the first time since I'd known her, I could believe she was a sixty-year-old woman. She wore sunglasses, which hid most of the redness around her eyes.

As she approached the truck I gathered the euphorbia books into a semineat pile on the floor. "Anywhere special you want to go?" I asked when she got in.

"I'd really like to go to the beach. That's where you're supposed to go to think about things after the loss of a loved one, isn't it? But I don't think I could stand all the volleyball players and the children with pails and shovels."

"I have just the place."

Dockweiler Beach consists of several miles of sand south of Playa del Rey, and sometimes, before the really hot weather sets in, some sections are nearly deserted, especially late in the day. I took Hope down there, found a place to park, led her down to the water. We found a spot where there wasn't anybody around for thirty yards. "How's this?"

"It's perfect." She sat on the sand just a bit above the high-tide line, drew her knees up close to her, locked her arms around them. She gazed out to sea. Out on the horizon I could just make out a tanker. Above us a gang of gulls squawked and soared.

"Dick never liked to go to the beach," she said.

I dropped down beside her. "Why was that?"

"He said the salt air gave him headaches. And that he didn't want people to see his scrawny chest. What I wouldn't give to see that scrawny chest again. What I wouldn't give to hear his mumbling again." She looked at me, indulged in a little smile. "After the first ten years I got to the point where I could make out just about everything he said. It gave me a kind of perverse pleasure watching other people try to understand him."

"It wasn't that bad."

"Yes it was, Joe, and you know it. Do you have any idea who killed Brenda yet? Oh, don't give me that look. I know you're nosing around. Lyle told me. And that nice boy who came by, Eugene Rand."

"Eugene Rand came to see you?"

"Yes," she said. "That seems to surprise you. Why is that?"

"I didn't know he knew Dick."

"He knew him from the club. That's what he said."

"Oh, right."

"No, something's wrong here. Tell me what it is."

"I don't want to upset you."

She put a hand on my forearm. "Do you really think anything you say could make me more upset?"

"All right. You've been to club meetings. Have you ever seen him at one?"

"No, but I only go to one or two a year. I went last Tuesday to give Dick moral support in dealing with Brenda's death. Succulents really aren't my thing."

"Rand isn't in the club."

"Of course he is. Why else would he say he is?"

"I'm the secretary. I know who's on the list. He's not."

"Perhaps he didn't actually mention the club."

I grabbed onto that. "Yeah, that must be it. He must have known Dick from other succulent stuff. I just never saw them together."

"There's something you're not telling me, Joe."

I sighed. "Do you think Dick's death and Brenda's are related?"

"They would almost have to be, wouldn't they? Although it's hard enough for me to understand why anyone might want to kill my Dick, let alone both of them."

I thought about turning the conversation another way. Why make anyone else suspect Rand if I had only nebulous reasons to suspect him myself? But if I was going to get to the bottom of this, it wasn't going to be by dropping things whenever the going got a little sticky. I'd seen how that worked in my love life. "Rand had a huge crush on Brenda."

"How would that connect to Dick?"

I shrugged. "I have no idea. I really don't have anything else on him. It's simply that I don't know why he would come to see you unless he was involved in some way. Eugene Rand's a bit socially backward. I can't see him making a condolence call for someone he knew barely, if at all."

"He seemed nice enough. Although he was awfully quiet. Sat in the corner. There were a lot of people there at the time."

Two runners passed by, a man and a woman, both prime specimens. The man nodded a greeting and I waved one back. "You didn't happen to get a visit from a man named Henry Farber," I said.

"No, I don't remember that name."

"Good."

"Who is he?"

I shook my head. "Doesn't matter. Hope, I got into this thing because Brenda was a very good friend of mine. Dick and I were never what you would call close. I need to get an okay from you to dive into that end."

"Please, Joe, whatever you can do. The police certainly don't have any good ideas."

"What do they have to say?"

"They asked me a lot of questions Thursday night, after you and your girlfriend discovered Dick's—"

"Did you tell them anything they seemed excited about?"

"No. As far as I know, Dick didn't have an enemy in the world. His competitors all respected him. His employees loved him. The nursery is a union shop, something Dick was very proud of, and the employees are well-paid and have a health plan and all. We've closed down for a few days, but we're reopening Tuesday. You can come speak with people if you want." She ran her hand under the surface of the sand, let it drift down between her fingers. "No, I had nothing to give the police. They call each day to see if I've had any thoughts, and I haven't. They tell me there are some leads they're following up on, but I assume they always say that."

"What leads?"

"They didn't say. I got the feeling it wasn't anything very significant, that the person who did this was very careful about fingerprints and such."

"Do you know of any connection, any at all, between Dick and Brenda?"

"Only club things, and you would know about those far better than I. They worked on the annual show together, of course, and they had their board meetings. But we certainly didn't socialize with her. I don't remember ever seeing her at the house, except when we had a board meeting there. Wait. She did come over once. Two or three years ago. Right around Christmas, I remember, because she brought us a poinsettia. But they started talking about plant things and I left them alone."

"You don't know what kind of plant things?"

"No."

"Did Dick ever have e-mail?"

"Several years ago he subscribed to America Online for a while, but he found electronic mail too impersonal and gave it up."

"Did he ever say anything to you about a *Euphorbia milii* with striped leaves?"

"Oh, dear. That's the plant they found on his head, isn't it?"

I nodded.

"If he did, I don't remember. But I must admit, sometimes when he went off about his plant collection, I tuned out. I think all married couples do that after a while. You get to know when it's important to hear every word your spouse is saying and when it isn't."

A tear ran out from under the edge of her sunglasses. Her face crumpled. A couple more drops made their way down her cheeks. For the tiniest second the reaction seemed forced. These could be crocodile tears sliding down her face. Hope had done it, wiped Dick out for God knew what reason, after treacherously killing Brenda to deflect suspicion.

God, I was getting paranoid. Hope killing Dick? About as likely as me offing Gina.

I scooted over and awkwardly slipped an arm around her. She cried for just a minute, reached into her purse, and pulled out a tissue. "What were you asking me about again?"

"It's not important."

"Of course it's important, or you wouldn't have asked it.

Oh, of course, about that plant. He might have mentioned such a thing, but, as I said, much of what he said about his plants went in one ear and out the other."

"Do you mind if I take a look in the yard when we get back?"

"It will be dark."

"Not if we leave now."

"I'm not ready to go back yet. There won't be anyone there. Lyle is dropping Magda off at eight. She's going to spend the night."

"Sorry," I said. "I have a flashlight in the truck. I can use that."

Neither of us said anything for a long time. The sun got bigger and redder and tinted the sparse clouds pink. Off to our right two sea gulls had an altercation about some scrap. They resolved it without my intervention. The salt air got cooler, the ocean smell more noticeable.

The two runners went by in the opposite direction, the only people I'd seen in a while. I looked around. Fifty yards away a young couple was shaking out their blanket. Twice that far, parents waited while their kid got in his last splashing of the day. And back on the path, near where our car was parked, someone sizable was watching us through a pair of binoculars.

"Stay right here," I told Hope. She tried to get up, but I pushed down on her shoulder and she dropped back to the sand.

"Joe, what in heaven's going—"

"Just stay there, okay?" I ran toward the figure. The sand sucked at my sneakers, making me bounce back and forth like one of the aliens from that fifties sci-fi movie *Invaders from Mars*.

I reached yelling distance. "Stay right there! I want to talk to you!" This clever action motivated the watcher to drop the binoculars from his eyes, indulge in an exaggerated take, and head for his red Malibu.

By the time I reached the path, he was in the car. I kept coming, dodging an Accord to get across the road, and I actually got a hand on the rear fender before he spun the wheels and pulled out from under me. I chased him up Vista del Mar, because in the movies the hero can outrun a car. This wasn't the movies. He disappeared around a bend.

I angled over onto the sidewalk, put my head down, and wheezed. Next I rubbed the stitch in my side. By the time I'd finished that activity, Hope had caught up with me.

"I told you to stay put," I said, a bit unkindly.

"Was that man involved in Dick's murder?"

"I don't know. He was at Brenda's funeral, and I've caught him following me several times since."

"Not a very good surveillance man, is he?"

"What?"

"Aren't they supposed to stay hidden?"

"Jeez, Hope, I don't know the rules for this kind of thing. I know he's supposed to see me. Whether or not I'm supposed to see him isn't on my instruction sheet."

"Did you get the plate?"

"The plate? What plate is— Shit. What kind of moron am I? There I was with his license plate three feet from my face and I didn't get it."

When I got over being pissed at myself, I herded Hope back to the truck. As we drove back I found myself wondering if Austin and Vicki had been right. What proof did I have that the guy following me was a cop? He did sort of look like a character from a Martin Scorsese movie. Maybe the Mob was involved. They'd horned in on plant smuggling, and I was getting in their way. Soon I would sleep with the fishes.

21

WHEN WE ARRIVED AT HOPE'S, LIGHTS BURNED IN THE LIV-
ing room and someone moved about in the kitchen. "Looks
like Magda let herself in."

"Yes. We exchanged keys years ago, for vacation emergen-
cies and such."

I escorted her inside, swapped greetings with Magda, and
took my flashlight out back. It took ten minutes to spot
some red and green stripes at the periphery of the flashlight's
beam. Two leaves only, one half brown, the other relatively
healthy. The plant itself was two feet tall, unbranched, in a
rusted-out coffee can.

I went into the garage. The Buick awaited a restoration
that would probably never come. I found a cardboard box,
slipped the plant in, carried it into the house. "You mind if I
take this with me?"

Magda gave me a funny look. Hope said, "That stick? Be
my guest."

"Thanks. Anything else I can do?"

She came over and gave me a little hug. "No, Joe. You've
done enough. If I can just make it through the memorial service, I'll be all right. You'll be there?"

"Yes, though I'll probably be late. I have an audition."

"That's fine, dear. Do what you have to do."

"I could cancel if you want. I could—"

"Joe."

"Yes?"

"You have to make a living. Go to your audition. Dick would want it that way."

When I got home I put the euphorbia in the greenhouse and went into the kitchen to scramble a couple of eggs. I'd just cracked them into the bowl when the phone rang. I rushed to pick it up. "Hi!"

"Joe Portugal?"

"Yes?"

"This is Willy Schoeppe."

"Oh."

"You seem disappointed."

"Sorry. I was expecting someone else. What can I do for you this evening?"

"I am calling to tell you that you can eliminate the plant smugglers as the possible murderers of our mutual friend."

"How did you come up with that conclusion?"

"I have been in contact with them."

"You have? All of them? You've been in contact with all the plant smugglers in the entire world?"

"You seem upset, young man."

"I'm sorry. I get like this when I haven't had my dinner. Please, tell me everything." I dropped down onto the floor with my back against the back of the couch.

"I have been on the telephone all day. I finally tracked down my brother, Hermann, in Nairobi. He, in turn, contacted his colleagues. They are very upset."

"What do they have to be upset about?"

"That suspicion has been pointed at them. They assured my brother they had nothing to do with Brenda's murder."

"And you believe them."

"Yes."

"You are a more trusting soul than I, Mr. Schoeppe."

"Consider the circumstances. These people do not wish to have attention brought to themselves. A murder would certainly do so."

"What about that guy who got macheted? I suppose they had nothing to do with that too."

"I have told you that incident did not occur."

"I see. Thanks for the information. It'll help me concentrate my efforts somewhere more fruitful."

"You are certainly welcome."

"Maybe we can get together again before you leave."

"It is doubtful. I am scheduled to fly back to Germany tomorrow evening. And I have a very busy schedule until then."

"I see. Have a safe trip, then."

"Thank you. Good-bye."

I sat there propped up against the couch, with the telephone in my lap, wondering what was wrong with what Willy Schoeppe had just told me. The phone went off again. I answered halfway through the first ring.

"What were you, sitting on the phone?" Gina said. "Waiting for a call from your new girlfriend?"

"Huh? You mean Amanda?"

"Of course I mean Amanda."

" 'Girlfriend' is a bit of an exaggeration. Though I did get lucky last night."

"Congratulations."

"But in the morning she didn't want to have anything to do with me."

"I take back the congratulations."

"So how'd it go for you last night?"

"I got lucky too."

"You did? But you said you were getting too old for recreational sex."

"I also said two dates in a row took it out of the recreational category."

"Oh."

"Joe?"

"Yeah?"

"Something wrong?"

"No."

"There is. Tell Gina."

"I guess it's that you have somebody now. While my somebody flew off back to Wisconsin this afternoon."

"Sorry. If it'll make you feel better, I'll call him and tell him that was the end of it."

"You would do that for me?"

A pause. "It sounded good when I said it."

"Okay, fine, let's drop it, okay? What did you do all day?"

"I brought the spreadsheet up to date. I'm beginning to think I should have used a database instead; I could've indexed everything much—"

I cleared my throat.

"What? Oh, sorry. And I went back through some more of the archives. Brenda hardly popped up at all, and when she did it was some technical discussion about spine sizes or something. And I went to the gym. I haven't gone all week and I felt like a slug. And I did some grocery shopping and went to the Gap and sat in the park and read."

I filled her in on my exploits. She said, "I'm not sure I trust this Schoeppe guy. His story sounds a little too pat."

"I'm not sure I do either. Maybe I should sic Casillas on him."

"What do you have on the agenda for tomorrow?"

"I have an audition, then Dick's memorial. You coming?"

"I haven't been invited."

"Everyone thinks you're my girlfriend. No one will be upset if you come. And I know you can't stay away. Your woman's natural curiosity is whetted."

"That's about the most sexist remark I've ever heard you make."

"And it wasn't very, was it? Aren't I a peach?"

"Yeah, a real peach. Joe? Are we okay?"

"Why shouldn't we be okay?"

"You sounded really out of sorts when we started talking."

"Maybe I was. I'm going through some stuff. Suddenly in touch with my mortality. Needing to perpetuate my genes. That sort of thing."

"You want to talk about it?"

"No, I'm okay. Let me give you directions to Dick's service."

"In case my woman's natural curiosity gets the best of me?"

"You got it."

After we hung up I went in the kitchen and stared at my eggs. The two yolks stared back. I covered them with Saran Wrap and stuck them in the fridge. I could eat them in the morning. Somewhere in the back of my mind, my mother was holding forth on the proper storage of eggs. I was setting myself up for botulism, she said. Well, Mom, I thought, if I keel over at Dick's service we'll know for sure.

The high point of my Monday morning greenhouse rounds was the discovery of seed pods on one of my pachypodiums. There was a certain life-reaffirmingness to the event, which started the day off nicely.

The casting director for Burger World had requested the "casual dad" look, so I dressed myself in Dockers and a nice button-down. I thought about bringing my suit for Dick's memorial service. Somehow it didn't seem necessary. Besides, if I took the time to change after my audition, I'd show up at the service even later.

It was a glorious day, unseasonably cool, with only a few frilly clouds infringing on the broad June sky. Traffic was light, and I got to the audition ten minutes early.

Something was up. A score of casual dads—way too many—milled about the magazine-strewn waiting room. All late-thirties to mid-forties, nearly all in button-down shirts and Dockers or Dockers surrogates. An equal number of teenage-daughter types worked on their makeup or read the trades.

I signed in and found out what was going on. There'd been a burglary and someone had made off with the cameras. Shortly after I arrived they dug up another and went to work on the backlog. I didn't get out of there until eleven-fifteen. I took Sunset west, avoided traffic, and made it to the cemetery in half an hour.

Dick's resting place was on a hill with a view down to the ocean. It was peaceful, quiet, well-landscaped—all the things a proper burial ground should be. Very traditional, in contrast to where we had said good-bye to Brenda. By the time I got there, the service had ended and everyone was milling around the wall full of urns where Dick's remains would spend the next several centuries, unless the Big One came along and dumped him into the Pacific along with the rest of us. I paid my respects to Hope and said hello to Lyle and Magda, the only cactus people present. I milled as long as seemed necessary and headed back to the parking lot, where Detective Alberta Burns was leaning against one of the department's Chevrolets. I walked over. "Find out anything?"

She watched me for several seconds. "Nothing I can disclose at this time."

" 'Disclose at this time'? Do you always have to talk like a cop?"

"I *am* a cop. Unlike some people I know. Which reminds me, you got anything you want to tell me?"

"Nothing I can disclose at this time," I said with a grin.

She smiled too. "Okay, I get the point. Fact of the matter is, it doesn't bother me your sticking your head in, like it does Casillas and some of the other older guys. I came out of South Bureau. South-Central, to you. There you need all the help you can get. A lot of the stuff we turn up comes from the citizenry. You want to poke your head in, that's okay with me, long as you keep out of our way."

"Hope McAfee said you hadn't really turned anything up."

Burns shook her head. "Everybody thinks we have a million hours to spend on every case. Because of that damned O.J. thing. But no one has the luxury of working full time on one case. Casillas and I have a half dozen more open homicides besides Cactus Girl and—"

"Very nice, Detective. Very sensitive. You got a name for Dick too?"

She nodded. "Jesus Boy."

"I had no idea the LAPD was such a bunch of comedians."

"Anything to make the job a little easier." Again the head shake. "People just don't understand. They see *Lethal Weapon* and think we have all day to run around chasing one set of crooks."

She eyed a couple of people leaving the service. "Casillas is going to talk to Henry Farber again today because of what you said yesterday morning. Why the look? Casillas isn't going to ignore information from you just because he thinks you did it."

"Do you think I did it?"

Her dark eyes searched my face, as if she were just then formulating her opinion. "I'm not convinced you didn't," she said, and got in her car and drove off.

I turned and surveyed the hillside below and the water beyond. Dick's eternal view. On clear days like this he'd be able to see Catalina.

Everyone drove back to Hope's to stand around and offer vague emotional support. Lyle answered the door and told me Hope was in the kitchen. I found her there leaning against a counter, absently chewing on a celery stick, looking like she needed to sleep for a week. Her shoes lay beneath the pink Formica ice cream table. The charcoal jacket from her mourning outfit was draped over one of the matching chairs.

Magda sat in the other chair with her elbows on the table and chin in her hands. She barely acknowledged me. She had big raccoon eyes and seemed in worse shape than Hope did. All the stolidity she'd been showing over the past several days, all the being there for Hope, had collapsed.

I gave Hope a quick hug. "How are you doing?" Clever repartee from Mr. Portugal.

"How am I doing? Lousy, Joe, that's how I'm doing. It's as if till today he could have come walking through the front door, saying it had all been a mistake, that was someone else stuck to the tree, he was in the garage working on his Buick all along. But when I went back to the cemetery and realized he'd been there all night—"

"Ssh," I said. "I didn't mean to upset you." I retreated to the living room, where Lyle and a bunch of strangers were reminiscing about Dick. I had no patience for the anecdotes and escaped back to the kitchen. "I'm going," I told Hope. "Anything I can do?"

"I don't suppose I could get you to take me to the beach again." When I hesitated she said, "No. You have a life to lead." She placed a tiny kiss on my cheek. "Find the bastard," she said. She sat down at the ice cream table, and I went out.

I was out of dead ends. It was time to find a live one. I sat in the truck and concocted a plan. I would go back to UCLA to try to find Henry Farber again. Then I'd proceed to the Loews, where I would hope to track down Willy Schoeppe before he took off for Germany.

I thought I'd check in with Gina first. I found a pay phone and called her cell number.

"Where the hell have you been?" she asked.

"Dick's memorial. You weren't there."

"I never said I was going. Doesn't matter. Wait'll you see what I found out."

"What?"

"It's about our friend Willy Schoeppe."

"What about him?"

"He's not."

"He's not what?"

"He's not Willy Schoeppe. He's an impostor."

22

THE PACIFIC DESIGN CENTER IS A BLOCK-LONG GLASS BE-
hemoth at the west end of West Hollywood. The part facing
Melrose Avenue is surfaced in blue glass, and everyone calls it
the Blue Whale. There's a newer, green section in the back,
which some dreamer once suggested be called the Emerald
City, but it didn't catch on and the whole structure goes by
the original nickname.

The PDC's filled with interior-design showrooms, selling
everything from modular office furniture to oriental rugs.
On any given weekday there's a fair chance you can find
Gina there, and that's where she told me to meet her. She was
preparing to visit some showrooms with a new client. "Some
sub-sub-adjunct to a city councilwoman," she called her.
With visions of decorating the houses of the entire Los Angeles municipal hierarchy dancing before her eyes, she insisted
she couldn't put the client off and that the only way she'd
show me what she had to show me was if I met her in the
lobby before the client arrived.

I reached the PDC just as a brunette in a Jaguar backed
out of one of the diagonal spaces out front. I parked on her
nickel and trotted into the building. Gina was sitting at the

west end, by the escalators. I walked up and she handed me a sheet of paper. "I was checking some more of the archives, and they mentioned this web page."

I scanned it. I examined it more closely. I squinted at it. "I'm not sure this tells us anything," I said.

Her eyes opened wide. "What do you mean? That's not the man who came to your house."

The picture showed several participants at a meeting of the International Organization for Succulent Plant Study several years back. According to the caption, Brenda and Willy Schoeppe were among those depicted. But the lighting was poor and the printing grainy. I could convince myself the woman really was Brenda, but the angle on the man was bad, and I couldn't tell if it was the guy calling himself Schoeppe or not. He had a beard, but beards come and go, and Iris had told me Schoeppe had one at some point.

"I don't think it's conclusive," I said.

"I'm telling you, that's not him."

"The printing's awfully blurry, and—"

Her eyes flashed. "Don't go dissing my printer. Portugal, you can be so obstinate. Look, I saw the actual web page, and it's a lot clearer, and I tell you it's a different guy."

I gestured at her computer. "Why don't you call up the web page now so I can see?"

"Do you see a phone jack around here? You can be such an idiot."

Before Gina could get her hands around my throat, a short Asian woman in a blue pantsuit came up. "Shit," Gina muttered. She introduced me, told her client she'd be with her in a minute, and led me off behind the escalator. "Trust me, Joe. It's not him."

"Okay, if you say so. Put it in your spreadsheet."

"Don't patronize me, okay?"

"I'm sorry. It's just that—"

"I've got to go with my client." She stormed off. By the time she reached the woman, she'd plastered her sincere interior-designer smile back on. They glided off, discussing fabric samples and edge details.

I glanced down at the picture in my hand. It could have been a different guy. It could have been the same one. I folded it and slid it into my pocket and walked out to the truck.

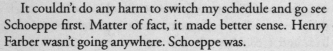

It couldn't do any harm to switch my schedule and go see Schoeppe first. Matter of fact, it made better sense. Henry Farber wasn't going anywhere. Schoeppe was.

But I decided not to. It was as if, by putting Schoeppe off, I could discount Gina's theory. I'd show her. I'd stick with Farber.

On the way to UCLA I got an idea. When I reached the campus I made a quick stop and had a brief conversation. Then I looked up Farber.

The history department is headquartered in Bunche Hall. Like the U.N. guy, as Iris had said, and entering the building made me think of her and her bucket of seaweed. I found my quarry lounging around his cramped, cluttered office. More than lounging; he was fast asleep. He slumped in a wheeled wooden chair with his feet up on his desk beside a stack of blue exam books. One arm dangled; the other lay protectively atop his crotch. He wore a pair of gray slacks, a button-down blue oxford, and a hideous tie with a fox-hunting theme. Soft snores emerged from his nostrils. In between the snores he was mumbling something about Annabella.

I walked in, sat on the desk, and shoved his feet off it. They clonked onto the floor. This jerked the rest of him out of his seat. His butt crashed to the carpet. His arms went every which way. "Annabella," he wailed.

His eyes opened, shut a second later, popped open again. After several tries they focused on his desk. He saw my legs. He moved his view up, up, until he was staring idiotically at my face.

I grinned down at him. "Does Maria know about Annabella?"

"Shit," he said.

"And does Annabella know about Maria? Important questions, these."

I reached down a hand to help him up. He looked it over, tilting his head to view its other side as if expecting to find a joy buzzer hidden there.

"It won't bite," I said.

He took my hand and I hauled him up, then pushed him back down into his seat.

"Do the Regents of the State of California know you take little nappies on their time?" I said.

"I don't have a class."

"Oh, that makes it okay." I dragged over a side chair and sat nice and civilly, with my legs crossed. "I thought we'd better have a chat under slightly less chaotic circumstances. By the way, how was the game Saturday?"

"I didn't see a lot of it. I was out on deck with Maria."

"Making all better, I suppose. How come a jerk like you does so well with women?"

"I don't have to answer that. In fact, I don't even have to talk to you, so why don't you just—"

I jumped up and swept my hand into the pile of blue books. They soared through the air and arranged themselves all over the floor. I snatched a framed certificate from the Organization of American Historians off the wall and held it high above my head. "Why don't I just wreck your office?"

"I'll call security."

"I'll call Maria and tell her about Annabella."

He chewed on his lip. "What do you want?"

"I want to know why you killed Brenda."

"You think if I killed Brenda the police wouldn't have figured it out by now?"

"It was worth a try. Look, she was a real good friend of mine and—"

"Yeah." A carnal smile. "A *real* good friend."

I bit my tongue. "What I was getting at is, I want her killer caught, and I thought even a jerk like you might have had a slight amount of feeling for her and want him caught too."

He shrugged. "At this point it's better for me that she's out of the way."

"You creep," said a voice from the doorway.

Farber turned to see who it was. I already knew, since I was the one who'd asked him to drop by.

"You utter creep," Eugene Rand went on. He stormed up to Farber, wearing his work gloves and carrying a fresh piece of *Euphorbia ammak*. Not something I'd foreseen. "How can you speak about her like that? That woman was the embodiment of everything good. You treated her like a toy and then you killed her, and you regard the whole thing like tiddlywinks. I was wrong about you. You are not a nice fellow."

"Who the hell are you?"

"You know who I am. You met me at the Botany department's spring social. I saw you there, fondling Brenda's buttocks when you didn't think anyone was looking. Well, Mr. Henry Farber, you won't be fondling anyone's buttocks anymore."

He drew back the ammak, preparatory to one of his barndoor swings. Farber hopped up, vaulted the desk, and cowered behind it. The cowering I expected; the vaulting was something of a surprise. "Jesus," he said. "You're a maniac. I didn't kill your damned Brenda." His eyes flashed toward me. "Tell him, would you? I didn't kill anybody. Shit, she was a great lay. I had everything I wanted. Why would I want her—"

Rand wailed, uttering an animal sound I'd have thought that soft man incapable of, fearful and lonely and hurt. "You just said you were glad she was dead."

"That was just macho bullshit," Farber said. Back to me. "Tell him, Portugal. Tell him it was macho bullshit."

"You're all macho bullshit, Henry." To Rand: "Put the plant away."

"I will not."

"You will."

"Not." He waved it at Farber again. "I'm going to kill you."

"Eugene, I'm going to tell you one more time: Put the euphorbia away."

He waved his club in my direction. "Don't try to stop me, or I'll have to use it on you."

I took a step toward him. "Eugene, Eugene. Who bathed your eyes when you euphorbiated yourself?" Another half step. "Who listened while you poured out your heart?" A baby step. "She was my friend too, Eugene, and—"

I leapt. He dodged, found the range on Farber, and hurled the euphorbia at him. He threw like a girl, but the Dodgers could have used a girl with control like he had. The branch end-over-ended across the room and clobbered Henry Farber directly in the left temple, breaking in half and splattering sap all over the place. Farber collapsed like a burst balloon.

"Oh," said Rand, all meek all of a sudden. "Oh. I think I've hurt him."

"And I can't think of anyone who deserves it more." I

went around the desk and found Farber sprawled on his back, with his hand clapped to his forehead and little streams of blood dribbling out between his fingers. He moaned, tried to get up, and failed. He groaned and tried again, and I took pity and helped him to a sitting position. "I'm ruined," he said.

"Hardly," I said. "Move your hand."

He didn't want to, but I finally got him to display his wound, a nice cut about an inch long surrounded by globules of latex. "Doesn't look that serious, Henry," I said. "But we don't want to get that sap in it. Here, use this." I pulled his ghastly tie up to the damaged area, pressed it down, laid his hand over it. "There. Now you'll be fine." I picked up the halves of Rand's weapon.

"What are you doing?" Farber asked. "That's evidence."

"Evidence of what?"

"That he assaulted me. And he probably killed Brenda too."

I shook my head. "No assault took place here today. Did it, Eugene?" The little guy shook his head too. "You see?"

"What do you mean?" Farber whined. "He threatened me with a spiny club. Then he threw the damned thing at me. If that's not an assault I don't know—"

"Shut up, Henry," I said.

"Huh?"

"I said keep your big yap shut. Nobody was in any danger here today. A little bump on the head? You could do worse getting on your boat. Now, if I hear about anybody filing any assault charges as a result of our little encounter here, I swear to God I will track down every last one of your girlfriends and tell them about the others. Maria. Annabella."

"Even Phoebe?"

"Even Phoebe. I mean it, Hank. So just keep your cool, such as it is."

"But he probably killed Brenda."

"I doubt it. And you probably didn't either, because you're all bluster, Hank, and if you tried to hurt Brenda, she would have made mincemeat out of you."

I left Farber on the floor, led Rand out of the office, and closed the door behind us. I threw the euphorbia pieces in a trash can and escorted Rand back to the conservatory. I made him promise to behave himself. What else could I do? Bind and gag him?

I went over to the Loews to try to track down Schoeppe. But he wasn't in his room, nor in the lobby or any of the eateries. I considered leaving him a message but thought that might put him on his guard, if he had anything to be on his guard about.

Another look at the sheet of paper Gina had given me told me nothing. It still could have been him and could have been not him. And even if she were right, what could I do about it if I couldn't find him?

I went back out and stood at the curb like a fool, not knowing what to do next, feeling sad and realizing it was a delayed reaction to my argument with Gina. A red Chevy Malibu drove by. It passed right in front of me, heading south on Ocean. I could see the driver's face clearly. When he realized I'd spotted him, he got a weird expression I couldn't quite place, and he stomped on the gas and zoomed away. Something nibbled at my mind. I was supposed to do something.

Right. The license plate. I squinted and I had it. It was an old blue one with orange letters. 555xyy. Did that mean anything, or was it just a random assignment from the Department of Motor Vehicles? xyy. Wasn't that the weird combination of chromosomes sex offenders had?

Okay. I had a license number. Now all I had to do was call the DMV to find out if it was registered to the LAPD or not.

I grabbed a phone inside and waited on hold for fifteen minutes before getting through to a supercilious young man who informed me that such information was *confidential* and that no one but the *forces of law* were entitled to obtain it. They did not want *stalkers* or other *undesirables* to use the data for their *depraved purposes*. His tone clearly said he thought I was one of those very *undesirables*.

Forces of law, huh? I pried Burns's card from my wallet and dialed. "Can you run a plate for me?"

" 'Run a plate'? You been watching *NYPD Blue*?"

"Can you?"

"This is not standard procedure."

"I know it's not standard procedure, damn it. But the number goes with the guy who's been following me. If, as you say, he's not one of you guys, then the number should tell you who it is. Why would you not want to find that out, unless you're lying to me and he really is a cop?"

"Makes sense. But I still can't give out information about plate numbers to any Tom, Dick, or Harry who calls up and asks me to. Besides, the computer's down."

"How convenient. Tell you what. I'll give you the number. You do what you want with it. If I don't hear anything back, I'll assume you and Casillas were lying. That work for you?"

"Yes."

"Good." I recited the number.

"Where will you be?" she asked. "Just in case?"

"Try me at home first, but my machine's broken, so try these next." I gave her Gina's cell phone, home, and business numbers.

As I walked out of the hotel, I placed the expression the guy in the Malibu had been wearing. It was embarrassment. Like I'd caught him with his hand in the cookie jar.

It was past four, and I hadn't had anything to eat since morning. My stomach had gnawed me into irritability. My brain needed sustenance. I drove west on Pico to a frankfurter-and-bun-shape hut called the Puppy Tale, a near-clone of a landmark called Tail o' the Pup near Beverly Center. Ripping off the name and ambience of well-known establishments is a long and honorable Los Angeles tradition.

I ordered a hot dog with mustard and sauerkraut, some fries, and an orange soda. I took them to the truck and threw Jefferson Airplane's *Crown of Creation* into the player.

I downed my dog, savoring the sourness of the kraut, barely tasting the meat, which was probably a good thing. When I was done eating I didn't go anywhere, because I had no idea where to go. I noticed the pile of *Euphorbia Journals* on the floor. Maybe I'd see something significant in one of them. I grabbed the top one, Volume Five. I leafed through half a dozen articles on euphorbia habitats, euphorbia culture, euphorbia lore. I stopped briefly to read a one-pager illustrated with a photo of two laughing African despots. They were equal-opportunity despots, one black, one white.

I turned the page and ran across an article by Sam, complete with a photograph of the author. He was holding up some euphorbia or other with a fierce botanical gleam in his eye.

"I am such a moron," I said.

The book had a cumulative index to the first eight volumes. I scanned it and found the entry I needed. I shuffled through the books until I found the one I sought. A frenzy of page-turning brought me to an article entitled "Euphorbias of the Madagascar Thorn Forest." It was rife with photos of its author, a German fellow by the name of Willy Schoeppe. One showed him standing in front of a Mahafaly tomb. I realized what had been bothering me when I looked at the Rauh books at Austin and Vicki's. On Saturday evening Schoeppe, supposedly an expert on such things, had called Brenda's tomb "a fine example of the Merina tradition." Not Mahafaly. Right island, wrong people.

But that hardly mattered in light of what else the photo, and the others, revealed. The gentleman in the article looked like he'd never smiled in his life. Gina had been right. He was not the man who'd shown up on my doorstep the previous Thursday night calling himself Willy Schoeppe.

23

He'd already checked out. Just fifteen minutes before, according to the chipper young man behind the desk, who believed Mr. Schoeppe had taken a shuttle to the airport but wasn't sure.

I ran back out. A flock of parking attendants surrounded my truck where I'd left it in the circular drive. I asked when the shuttle left, and one of them said five minutes or so ago.

How would they have gone? You could take the freeway, but that meant picking up the 405, and at that time of day that was chancy at best. I took Ocean south to Abbot Kinney to Washington, cut through a car wash, and hit Lincoln running. A couple of minutes later I was chugging up the hill into Westchester.

A little past the Furama Hotel and its KARAOKE EVERY NITE, Lincoln swells into a six-lane divided highway and remains one until it spills into Sepulveda right before the airport. As I pulled onto that stretch, I spotted something blue up ahead that looked like it might be a shuttle. I floored the accelerator. The truck backfired nastily before responding to my call. Sixty. Seventy. Eighty, ninety, and there I was on the shuttle's tail. I drew even and waved frantically to get the driver's attention. He was Indian or Pakistani, and his eyes bulged. When I got him to notice me, I pointed at his left front tire. "Flat," I hollered. "Danger. Better stop."

His mouth opened wide. He nodded quickly and guided the shuttle to the shoulder. I pulled over in front of him.

The driver hopped out and inspected the tire. As I reached him he said, "There is no problem with this tire." His nameplate identified him as A. Telang.

"It's the other one," I said. "The right front. Go look at it; it's flat, I promise."

A. Telang went off to check, and I hauled open the sliding passenger door. "All right, folks, just stay calm," I said. "Immigration and Naturalization Service. Border check." A couple of businessmen acted miffed at this delay to their very important business flights. A Hispanic woman crossed herself and tried to blend into the upholstery. "Willy Schoeppe" simply nodded and said, "Well done, Mr. Portugal."

"You'll have to get off, sir," I said.

"And if I choose not to?"

"I'd hate to create an incident, sir."

A. Telang returned to the scene. "I have thoroughly checked the tire you have mentioned, and it does not seem to have any injury."

"It doesn't? My mistake." To "Schoeppe": "Please, sir."

He sighed dramatically and said, "Very well, then. I suppose I owe you an explanation." He hopped out of the shuttle.

"I have a very important flight to Cincinnati," said one of the businessmen, a florid fellow threatening to burst his pukey-green suit.

"Yes," said the other, equally overweight but slightly better dressed. "And I have to be in Minneapolis to close a very important deal."

I fixed him with a steely glare. "Is any mere business dealing more important than protecting our country's borders from the assault of the unworthy?" The Hispanic lady melted further. Poor woman. I said to A. Telang, "Would you please pass his baggage out as well, sir? You may then proceed to your destination."

It's amazing what the mere hint of authority will do to some people. In seconds a familiar suitcase clomped to the pavement. In a few more the shuttle peeled away. Overhead, a 747 marked JAL CARGO screamed in for a landing.

"Get in the truck," I told my Teutonic friend.

He shrugged. "Certainly." He climbed in.

I went around to my side and did the same. "Okay, Mr. Schoeppe," I said. "You mind telling me what this is all about? But that's not your name, is it?"

"It certainly is, Mr. Portugal."

I grabbed the incriminating book, opened it to where I'd slid the dust jacket in to mark the place. "This isn't you."

He shook his head. "It is not. But my name is indeed Schoeppe."

"Meaning?"

"The man in the photo is my brother, Willy. I am Hermann Schoeppe."

He let me digest that for a second or three, then put his habitual smile back in place. "Poor Mr. Portugal. I feel sad to have misled you. But only about my identity, I assure you. No one in our organization would ever think about murdering anyone."

"What about that ranger in Madagascar?"

"The incident never happened. It is a story advanced by those who would have us end our business. I suspect your friend Sam Oliver invented it." Another giant airplane swooshed above our heads. Schoeppe consulted his watch.

"Don't worry about your flight," I said. "You have bigger problems right now."

"Oh?" He reached in his pocket, took out a tube of lip balm, touched himself up. "It is so dry here in Los Angeles. I will be glad to leave."

"You're not leaving anywhere."

"I believe I am."

"You've been impersonating your brother. The police would be very interested in that."

"Would they? I am not certain they would care. Although they might be curious about your ever-so-clever impersonation of an officer of the Immigration Service."

"You wouldn't."

"Ah, but I might. So. Allow me to finish my explanation. You will then please drive me to the airport."

"We'll see," I said.

He cleared his throat. "It was natural for you and all your friends here to assume those in my trade had something to do with Miss Belinski's death. After all, we have been painted as despoilers of nature, as a bête noire for you all to fear and rail against. But we are honorable businessmen. We exist to provide a product to those who want it."

"You rip up habitats and kill off species," I said, a bit sanctimoniously.

A small shrug. "Yes, in some instances. It cannot be helped. But we bring tremendous joy to those who desire our product." He waved a hand dismissively. "But enough of this philosophical argument. The simple fact of the matter is, I chose to come here after Miss Belinski's murder to make certain no residue of suspicion hung over my associates and myself. But now a new species of *Pseudolithos* in Namibia requires my attention."

"You're scum."

"Please, must we engage in pejoratives? We were getting along so well."

"*Pseudolithos* or no, you and your 'associates' are still under suspicion."

"Perhaps, but not for long. I have great faith in you."

"I don't follow."

"I have studied you. I have no doubt you, in cooperation with the authorities, will track down the actual murderer."

"Studied me? You didn't hire a big Italian guy to follow me around, did you?"

"No. I am here alone."

I watched his face. He still wore that ever-present smile, but now it seemed a bit deeper, as if he were pleased with me. The awful thing was, no matter what kind of creepy business he was engaged in, no matter that half a minute ago I'd called him scum, I liked the guy.

He gestured at his watch. "I am afraid I do not have the time to discuss this further."

What could I do? He had me over a barrel with my "ever-so-clever impersonation," and what was the point in keeping him there? I hopped out and threw his bag in the truck bed, and we got going. "But why impersonate your brother?" I asked.

"Would you have been as cooperative had you known my true identity?"

"Of course not."

"There is your answer. There were only two possible difficulties with this tactic. One is that your friend Sam Oliver knows my brother well. It is fortunate that he is away from Los Angeles."

"How did you know that?"

"At the risk of seeming clichéd, we have ways. The other possible problem is a gentleman named Lyle Tillis, whom I met in South Africa. Were I to run into him, I would have been unmasked. Fortunately, I have managed to steer clear of his path. Ah, the international terminal approaches. You will please drop me off there."

Which I did. I helped the plant smuggler with his bags, and I shook his hand, and I watched him walk off into the terminal.

At seven-ten I stood outside Gina's condo carrying a peace offering in a Baskin-Robbins bag. I hesitated before ringing, said the hell with it, and pressed her button. Our relationship had weathered bigger storms than an argument over a web page.

The speaker squawked. "Yes, Mr. Portugal?"

"How'd you know it was me?"

"I saw you out the window. Your truck needs a bath."

"You want to let me in?"

"Why should I?"

"Because I have many exciting adventures to recount."

"That all?"

"Because I've got a hot fudge—"

The buzzer buzzed and I went up. She was waiting with the door open, holding a big paperback entitled *Fix Your Files!* She snatched the bag and looked inside. "What kind of ice cream's under all this sauce?"

"Mint chocolate chip and jamoca almond fudge."

"You know me so well. Come on in."

Two steps inside the door I casually said, "You were right, you know."

"About . . . ?"

"Willy Schoeppe. He wasn't. Wasn't Willy, that is. He *was* Schoeppe."

While she demolished her sundae I filled her in on my encounter with the German, following that with Farber and

Rand and the airborne euphorbia. When I was done I said I was sorry for disbelieving her, and she pooh-poohed it, and we gave each other a hug, and everything was all right in the world of Joe and Gina.

I remembered something else. "I saw the guy who's been following me again. I got his—"

She clonked her palm to her forehead. "I'm such an idiot. I got a call from your friend Detective Burns. She tracked down that plate for you." She peeled a fluorescent green Post-it off her phone table. "How'd you get such pull with the cops?"

"Burns believes in community involvement."

She checked the note. "Do you know anyone named Salvatore Patronella?"

"I knew it. Vicki was right. The Mafia's after me."

"Not everyone named Salvatore's in the Mafia."

"No, only the hulking ones who wear sunglasses and follow people around. What did I do to piss off the Mob?"

"You horn in on any vending machines lately?"

"This is serious."

"Call your friend Burns back if you're worried."

"Good idea."

But Burns was out apprehending killers. I left a message, stealthily checked out the window for suspicious characters, and dropped onto the couch. I drummed my fingers. I scratched my leg. "Now what?"

"Right about now we're supposed to get a call from one of our informants."

"We don't have any informants."

"We'll have to cultivate some."

"You been keeping up with e-mail?"

"Yeah. Nothing interesting. And no more word from Succuman."

"I wish we could look at some of Brenda's older e-mail.

But I don't relish the thought of breaking into her house again. We'd end up in jail for sure."

She smirked. It was a hell of a smirk. "There might be another option."

"What's that?"

"We could dig through the garbage."

"You expect to find her secret e-mails in her garbage?"

"Not her garbage. My garbage."

"For what?"

"For the diskette."

"But it's bad."

"The file is bad. The other ones on the diskette may not be." She snatched up *Fix Your Files!* and shook it at me. "According to this, just because we can't read one file on a disk doesn't mean we can't read the others. As long as the fat's okay—"

"Disks have fat? Do they have bones too?"

"You're a riot. It's an acronym. It means file allocation table. If that's not damaged we may be able to read the other files."

"And to think I discouraged your computing education. Go dig out the diskette."

"That's your job. Why do you think I let you in?"

"Dig it out" turned out to be more than just an expression. The garbage can overflowed with a variety of trash in various stages of decomposition, all exuding a vaguely unsavory aroma. I gingerly removed a coffee filter full of grounds and an old Häagen-Dazs container dripping brown goo. Several balled-up tissues and half a head of wilted lettuce later, the disk turned up. A glob of something red decorated its surface. I held it by two fingers, grabbed a paper towel, and wiped it off as best I could. Gina took it and jiggled the little metal door. "Seems okay." She started up her computer and stuck the disk in. Up came a file.

"Which year is this?" I asked.

"Year before last. Right before the one we've already seen. Almost seen."

We paged down through the file but didn't find anything of interest. Gina went for the one before that. Nothing there either. Soon only the earliest—six years old—remained.

Pay dirt.

The last e-mail in the file, dated December 27, was addressed to dickmca@aol.com and went like this:

> *I've been thinking over your proposal from the Christmas party, and I must say it has some merit. But it would entail a lot of long, hard work, and frankly, I would be doing most of it, at least in the early stages. The whole thing wouldn't exactly be kosher either. Using the university's facilities for private gain. We might have to cut them in. None of this is a huge problem, but I have to take a hard look at what I have planned over the next few years and see if this fits in. As you know, I'm leaving for Madagascar next Thursday. Why don't I think it over while I'm overseas and give you an answer when I return?*

I looked up. "The Christmas party? The only Christmas party she and Dick were likely to have been to together was the CCCC one."

"I didn't know he had e-mail. Maybe we can go through his and discover something."

I shook my head. "Nah. Hope told me he just had it for a little while."

She popped the disk out. "So now that we have this fascinating disclosure, what does it do for us?"

"I don't know."

I got up and paced around, trying to decide what to do next. My pacing took me to the window, and I stopped there, gazing out on West Hollywood as the light diminished and the nightlife began. Two couples strolled by hand-in-hand across the street. One was an old man and woman, Russian immigrants perhaps; the other consisted of two shirtless young men.

My vision shifted downward, to our side of Havenhurst. I could see my truck parked out front. Gina was right. It did need a bath. But I didn't think the guy peeking into the cab was there to give it one. It was Salvatore Patronella.

"Get me your gun," I said.

"What in God's name for?"

"Mafia Man is outside."

"I'm not getting you the gun. If I get you the gun, he'll get hold of it in the struggle and shoot you."

"How do you know there'll be a struggle?"

"There's always a struggle. You're out of your mind, Joe. Call the police. Call your friend Burns."

"No. I want to deal with this myself."

"Call—the—fucking—police." She stood with her hands on her hips, glaring at me.

"Gi," I said. "I promise if it looks like there'll be a struggle, I'll back off. I'll just feel better if I have it in my pocket." I ran into the bedroom with Gina at my heels and went to the closet. "You said it was in here, didn't you?"

She interposed herself between the closet and me, pressing her arms back across the door like Scarlett O'Hara repelling the Yankees. I grabbed her shoulders, gently shoved her out of the way, opened the door, and reached up on tiptoe to explore the top shelf. "This bastard may have killed Brenda and Dick. I've got to get him now." I spied a Ferragamo box way in the back and slid it forward. If it held a pair of shoes, they were for the Tin Man.

"Fine," Gina said. "Just don't expect me to arrange your funeral."

"Deal." I lugged the box down, dropped it on her bed, and took off the top. A gun and a couple of metal cases were inside. It wasn't a very big gun, but it still seemed like it could seriously damage someone's anatomy. I hoped it wouldn't be mine.

Gina elbowed me aside. "If you're going to do this, you might as well do it right. Here." She grabbed one of the metal cases. "This is the magazine." She jiggled a little doohickey on the gun. "This is the safety. If it's on, like this, the gun won't shoot."

"Which way is that again?"

"Like—" She threw me an exasperated look. "You're going to get yourself killed." A giant sigh of resignation. "I'll take the gun." She did some stuff to it, and suddenly she was at the front door. "Come on, let's go."

We tiptoed down the two flights of stairs to the lobby, though why we tiptoed I don't know, since our adversary was outside and couldn't hear us. Gina held the gun straight down by her side like La Femme Nikita. I didn't think they'd taught her that at the Beverly Hills Gun Club.

I peered outside. Our quarry was diddling with the driver's side door. Great. He'd was going to plant a bomb. Pieces of Joe Portugal would litter the sky from Melrose to Sunset.

I smelled something and decided it was me. The scent of raw fear, or maybe I'd just gone too long without a shower. "I'm going out there," I whispered, and before Gina could object I did just that. I snuck right up behind the big guy. He didn't know I was there, or didn't care. I looked back at where Gina still lurked inside the doorway. She shrugged.

Bold action was needed. I tapped him on the shoulder. "Excuse me, Salvatore," I said. "Is there something I can do for you?"

He jumped about a foot and let out a sound like Chewbacca hacking phlegm. He pirouetted and stumbled back simultaneously, leaving him sprawled against the truck's cab. "Jesus Christ," he said. "You scared the shit outta me." Another weird wheeze emerged, not quite the strength of its predecessor. His face took on a slight purple cast. "Nobody calls me Salvatore."

"Sal, then. Why'd you do it?"

"The name's Sonny."

"Why'd you kill Brenda and Dick?"

"Huh? You think I—" He began breathing in little short pants. He flung open his jacket with his right hand and reached in with his left. I blundered backward and fell flat on my ass.

"Freeze, sucker." It was Gina. She stood three steps outside the doorway with her legs spread and the gun stuck out in front of her with both hands.

Sonny continued poking around inside his jacket.

"This is your last warning," Gina said.

"Stop with the warnings," he said. "I'm not even carrying a piece. I'm just trying to find my inhaler."

"Inhaler?" I said, rubbing my injured butt. "What inhaler?"

"My asthma inhaler. Where the hell—there it is." Out came his hand, holding a little metal canister in a plastic shell. He exhaled noisily, stuck it in his mouth, breathed in.

We maintained our ridiculous tableau until Sonny's breathing attained some semblance of normalcy. Gina came closer, gun still at the ready. She kept throwing sidelong glances, as if afraid the neighbors would see she was a pistol-packer.

There wasn't any reason to stay on the ground, so I got up. "Okay," I said, "why don't you tell us why you've been following me around."

"I can't," he said.

"If you don't I'm going to have Gina fill you full of lead."

"Jeez." He took a look at her and evidently thought she might do just that. "All right, I'll tell you. But he's gonna be pissed off."

"He who? Who sent you to follow me? Was it Schoeppe? Farber? Eugene Rand, for God's sake?"

Sonny stared at me. He took a look at his inhaler, deciding if this latest turn of events required another hit, before stuffing it back in his pocket. "He's gonna be *real* pissed off," he said. "He was pretty mad when you told him you'd seen me, and I think I did a pretty good job since then staying hid. Until now."

"He who?" Gina said. "*Who* was pretty mad?"

He took off his sunglasses and looked into my eyes. "Harold the Horse," he said. "Your father. That's who sent me."

24

SONNY WALKED INTO GINA'S CONDO AND HEADED FOR THE sofa. "Nice place you got here, lady."

"Thanks, I think." She went into the kitchen and stuck the gun in the refrigerator. "Can I get you anything? Coffee? Tea? Oxygen tent?"

"Nah, I'm okay."

She joined him on the sofa, while I grabbed a dining room chair and sat catty-corner to him at the end of the coffee table. He sat there telling us how wonderful his asthma medicine was. He didn't look all that threatening anymore, but an undercurrent of menace remained. Twenty, thirty years earlier he would have given me the absolute shakes.

"I was thinking," he said, "maybe we could make a deal so Harold wouldn't find out you got the drop on me."

"It's not going to happen, Sonny."

"How come you know my name?"

I told him about catching his plate number. He shook his head. "When I was younger I coulda trailed you for days without you knowing. Now my eyes aren't so good; I gotta stay closer."

"You trail many people lately?"

"To tell the truth, you're the first one since I got out of the slam."

"Which was?"

"In '75. I've sorta gone straight. I've been working at House of Suits for the last twelve years or so. But you know how it is. You always want to keep a finger in. Hey!"

"What?" I said.

"You want a nice suit? You don't tell Harold about this, I'll get you a—"

"Why'd he send you?"

He shrugged his massive shoulders. "He was worried about you. He read about you in the paper after the Belinski woman was knocked off. He thought you needed protection."

"Some protection." I smiled at him. "You didn't even have a piece."

He smiled back. I saw the flash of gold I'd noticed at Brenda's service. "Yeah, but I could still smack some heads."

"Why'd you let me see you at the funeral?"

Another shrug. "I figured if you saw me once it wouldn't be any big deal. If you saw me again you might think something was up."

"Sonny," Gina said, offering her most charming smile. "It's sweet that you've been taking care of Joe like this, but he really doesn't need it." She gestured toward the refrigerator and the firearm within. "We can take care of ourselves."

"You can, lady, that's for sure. Him I'm not so sure of."

"Thank you very much," I said.

They both looked at me. "Don't worry about Joe," Gina said. "I'll take care of him."

"Yeah," Sonny said. "I think you will."

After Sonny left I found Gina in the kitchen, staring at her empty sundae cup. "I need another," she said.

With Quicksilver Messenger Service in the tape player, we drove down Crescent Heights and turned left on Melrose. Our destination was the Baskin-Robbins near the Groundlings Theater. Our route took us through L.A.'s erstwhile center of cool. Wacko and the Soap Plant were gone. The trendy boutiques looked sparse and sad. A guy with a purple mohawk slouched by, a dispirited punk relic.

On the side streets off Melrose, though, things went on as always. Turn up Sierra Bonita or Gardner or Vista and you'd find Orthodox Jews raising bumper crops of girls in long dresses and pint-size rabbis-to-be. Down Martel or Fuller or Poinsettia, senior citizens sat on their porches, not caring that Melrose had indeed been terminally hip.

It hit me three blocks later, as I pulled into Baskin-Robbins's lot. The guy inside was just locking the door, but Gina dashed out, banged on it, and convinced him to let her in. When she realized I wasn't with her, she looked out at me. I waved the back of my hand and she returned to getting her fix.

I sat in the truck and thought. The more I thought about it, the more sense it made. When Gina got back in I said, "The street sign. Poinsettia Place."

"What about it?"

"It clued me in."

"You've lost it, Portugal, you've really lost it this time."

"The connection between Brenda and Dick. It's got something to do with poinsettias."

"It does?"

"They're all over the place. I saw some at the Kawamura, right before Rand tried to brain me. Why would they have poinsettias in a greenhouse full of succulents? And Dick was the poinsettia king of Los Angeles, yet Hope said Brenda brought him one around Christmas a couple of years ago. Now, why would anyone bring the poinsettia king of Los Angeles a poinsettia?"

"I don't know."

"I don't either, but I intend to find out. Give me your phone."

She pulled it out and I called Hope McAfee. "I've had an idea, and I need to follow up on it."

"What is it?"

"You know how you said Brenda brought Dick a poinsettia the one time she came over that wasn't for a board meeting?"

"Yes."

"Didn't that strike you as odd? I mean, Dick ran a nursery that sold probably thousands of poinsettias every year. Wouldn't that be a funny thing for her to bring?"

"I guess. I didn't really think about it. Everybody brings everybody a poinsettia around Christmas. It's the social thing to do. Dick knew that, that's why he stocked up so much, why we did so well with them. For all I know, Brenda bought it at McAfee's."

"Did you see it clearly? I'm sorry to put you through this, but—"

"Ssh. Let me try." She was silent half a minute. "I'm sorry. All I remember is a poinsettia."

"That's okay. Where did Dick get his poinsettias from?"

"A place called Paul's Poinsettia Plantation, down in Encinitas. He was their biggest retail customer. He used to go down there once or twice a year to look at new varieties."

"Do you have their number?"

"Let me go look in his book."

She got me the number and we signed off. I called Paul's and got a machine.

I drove Gina, then myself home. I thought about things

for a while and went to bed. In the morning my worst nightmare came true.

I'd set the clock for seven but woke up before it went off. I lay there, letting my day sort itself out in my head, then got up, made the bed, went through my bathroom routine.

I padded into the kitchen in my robe and karate slippers, made a cup of a nice Darjeeling, went out the back door and into the yard. It was cool, around sixty. The June gloom had taken a hiatus; we had a clear sky but for a few high clouds and a rapidly fading moon. I stared up at it, thinking how weird it was that thirty years ago men had walked there, odder still that we'd given up on it so soon after.

I tossed the tea bag in the trash bin and approached the greenhouse. I pulled the U-bolt, undid the latch, put the bolt back through, opened the door. I took a step inside. I saw wasps.

Just two at first, a yellow jacket and a golden polistes. Sometimes it's hard to tell them apart when they're aloft, but the polistes have an odd way of letting their legs drag down behind them that's usually a tip-off. Both of them were buzzing around near the top of the A-shaped roof.

I sensed rapid movement over to my left. Another yellow jacket was examining a pachypodium.

A flash of gold and black to my right. A polistes cruised over some cacti. A few feet beyond it, a mud dauber was smashing itself against the wall.

I shifted to a wide-angle view. At least a dozen wasps occupied the greenhouse. Panic froze me in place.

I heard footsteps outside. "Help!" I yelled as I turned, just in time to see the door slam closed. I could see someone's outline through the translucent fiberglass. Somebody not too big, maybe Gina's size. I heard the clank of metal against metal. Then nothing but receding steps.

"What the hell?" I said, pushing on the door. It didn't budge.

Another yellow jacket appeared from under a bench. I smashed my shoulder into the door. The greenhouse shook, but the latch held. "Who's out there?" I said. No one was, not anymore.

Another shot at the door. Nothing doing.

I turned and surveyed the greenhouse. Wasps filled the airspace. Perhaps a score of the black-and-yellow guys—the yellow jackets and golden polistes—as well as a half dozen mud daubers. And somewhere off at the edge of my vision, I caught a glimpse of something bigger. Something that was black and orange and altogether too frightening to focus on.

Buzzing came from overhead. A yellow jacket hovered not two feet above my scalp. I pulled my robe up over my head. The belt came undone and the robe drew open. I felt as if someone had drawn a bull's-eye on my penis. I jerked the robe closed, held it with one hand, turned back to the door. It had two fiberglass panels separated by a horizontal two-by-four. I could probably kick right through the bottom one. But then I'd have to crawl out through the opening, and that seemed a perfect opportunity for some gung-ho wasp to sting my ass.

My right hand tickled. I looked down. A golden polistes rested atop my knuckle. Its hind end bounced up and down a sixteenth of an inch from my skin. I flailed. This had the desired effect on the polistes, which went up, up, and away. It had the opposite effect on the other wasps. They all came over to see what the fuss was about.

I dropped to the floor and rolled under a bench. For a

moment I was alone down there. Then one of the mud daubers joined me. It hung out across the aisle, secure in the knowledge it could have me any time it wanted me.

I thrust at the walls with my feet. But the angle was lousy, and the large fiberglass panels had a lot of give, and I succeeded only in shaking the bench enough to tip something over. I mistook the dribbles of potting mix on the back of my neck for the wanderings of a wasp, and I drew away violently, smashing my head against the bottom of the bench. I cursed and yowled and vigorously rubbed the back of my head until I realized this behavior was an excellent wasp attractant and got myself under some semblance of control.

I felt a sort of nauseated dizziness from my head way down to my bowels. My breathing was quick and shallow. I thought I would hyperventilate. I tried to force myself to take deep, even breaths. I got *deep* right, but *even* escaped me.

One thing seemed apparent to my addled mind: Someone was unhappy with me. Knowing my overwhelming fear of wasps, they'd introduced a nice assortment into my greenhouse, then lurked in my yard, waiting to lock me in with them, knowing that in my frenzy I would smash into a wall and knock myself unconscious, after which the wasps could sting me at will. Maybe somebody *was* methodically killing off CCCC's leadership. Unable to come up with an appropriately brilliant way of offing me with a euphorbia, they'd switched to the animal kingdom.

But for the moment I was safe, I thought. Most of the wasps didn't know I was down there. As far as they could tell, I'd just disappeared. Their pinhead-size brains weren't capable of anything more.

The simultaneous appearance of three yellow jackets under the bench proved that brilliant theory wrong. I had to get out of there soon. It was only a matter of time until the big stingfest.

I tried another kick at the walls, drew the attention of a golden polistes, retreated into the corner. Up above, through the gaps in the bench, I could see the big black and orange thing, could hear the hum of its wings as it searched for a fat, tasty mammal to sting.

The gravel beneath me was making my ass sore. Sweat ran down from my hair into my eyes.

Suddenly, as if at a signal from the barely seen black and orange giant, half a dozen winged creatures surrounded me. Everywhere I looked, wasps gazed back at me through faceted eyes.

Ten times. In the same place. Without dying.

I pulled the robe over my head again and rolled out into the aisle. I vaulted onto the center bench, knocking over half a dozen plants. Across the aisle a spot amidst a batch of cacti looked big enough for my foot. I took a flying leap.

I looped over the aisle, brought my right foot down right on target. I willed it to contribute just the extra bit of momentum I needed and pushed off on it, plunging forward, directing my shoulder at the corrugated fiberglass wall, hoping that I wouldn't just bounce back, fall on the bench among the cacti, and become lunch for the wasps.

As I hit the wall I was virtually certain that was exactly what was happening. I felt resistance, tensed for the bounce-back—

—and crashed through the wall.

I heard the crack and felt the shudder. Ragged edges scraped my skin. Suddenly the balding lawn was rushing up at my head. As was a rather large lava-rock planter, filled with dudleyas, a gift from Sam Oliver.

I twisted in midair like a Flying Wallenda and managed to miss the planter. Almost. My head grazed the rock, then hit the dirt. The rest of me followed shortly thereafter.

I lay there for several seconds, idiotically worried about the plants I'd knocked over during my escape. I threw a look at the greenhouse. A tear in one fiberglass panel followed a corrugation from the top of the bench to the roofline. The gap was only a couple of inches. I didn't see how anything as big as me had gone through such a small opening. While I was trying to figure this out, a mud dauber peeked out of the crack, decided freedom was a good idea, and flew off.

"They're getting out," I said.

The dual blows my head had taken were affecting my thinking. I thought if the wasps escaped into the outside world, they'd all show up to harass me again. So I hopped up and grabbed some duct tape from the garage and gingerly fastened the edges of the crack back together. The vents remained stuck closed, and the metal flaps on the outside of the fan enclosure sealed that portal.

Finally, all was quiet. No wasp-waisted fiend buzzed anywhere in my vicinity. Just a normal Tuesday morning in Culver City.

Until, as the adrenaline drained, I realized I'd been stung.

It started as a pinprick in my right side, near my waistline. Just enough to notice, to reach for, to begin to scratch. Suddenly it flared into its full painful glory. Like someone had stuck a hot wire a quarter inch into my skin and wiggled it around. I clapped my hand to the area just as the pain spread, flaring through my entire right side. A wave of nausea passed through me. Then dizziness. Next thing I knew I was lying facedown on the lawn.

I got to my feet and bumbled inside and into the bathroom, ran cold water on a washcloth, slapped it to my side. For an instant the pain brightened, then the agony began to recede. My breathing approached normal. The nausea ebbed to a dull rumbling in my gut.

When I dared to pull the cloth away, I discovered a red welt decorating my waistline, three, maybe four inches in diameter. At its center a tiny, redder spot, the assumed point of attack. I rewet the cloth, plastered it to my side, and went into the bedroom to use the phone.

The woman at the exterminators' said they could come Thursday. I told her it was an emergency. She said Wednesday. I said, "There's a million wasps in my fucking greenhouse, lady," and she hung up on me.

I'd show her. I found a bug bomb in the garage left over from one of my biennial ant invasions. I pulled on long rubber gloves and brought the bomb over to the greenhouse. I jerked the U-bolt from the latch, got down on my knees, opened the door just enough to slip the bomb in with my gloved hands, activated it, and shut the door.

The pain in my side had lessened to a dull roar. The welt was bigger now, six or seven inches, and a lovely rose pink.

I went inside, considered phoning Burns, decided against it. What would she do, send the police entomologist? Instead, I called Gina. But she was with the city council lady and couldn't talk. She said she'd come over around dinnertime and hung up on me.

I got in the shower and let cold water beat down upon my sting. By the time I emerged I was functioning more or less normally. I dried off and applied some witch hazel. That helped some, though now an element of itchiness had joined the discomfort parade. I found some shorts whose waistband fell below the distressed area and went out to the Jungle to think.

Who knew about my aversion to wasps? The sad answer was, just about everyone I knew. The insects were common in L.A., and anyone who'd spent any time with me outdoors had been subjected to my insane behavior when one showed up. Sam, for instance. *"Nothing to worry about, my boy."*

I wondered if he was right. Now that I'd actually been

stung and lived to tell the tale, maybe my relentless fear over the last thirty-five or so years had been a gigantic waste of energy.

But I'd only been stung once. What if it had been more? What if it had been ten times in the same place?

I phoned Paul's Poinsettia Plantation. "May I speak to Paul, please?"

"Which one?" said the woman who'd answered.

"How many are there?"

"Four. Bill Paul Senior, Bill Paul Junior, Tommy Paul, Annie Paul."

"Oh. I thought Paul was a first name."

"Everyone does."

"Sorry. I'm with McAfee's up in L.A. We've had a little change of management here, and I need to go over a few things."

"McAfee's?"

"Yes."

"I see." Silence for several seconds. "This is Annie Paul. I handle the account. I was so sorry to hear about Dick. What did you say your name was?"

I told her, then thought the hell with it and said, "Look, Mrs. Paul—"

"Ms. I'm Bill Senior's daughter."

"Ms. Paul, then. I don't work for the nursery. The truth is, I'm a friend of Dick's, and I'm trying to figure out who killed him. And I've developed a suspicion the whole thing is somehow related to poinsettias."

"That sounds ridiculous."

"Yes, I know. And I don't have any real evidence, but—"

"It sounded ridiculous when I thought of it too."

Had I heard her right? "You thought of the same thing?"

"I did. Thought of it right off. I just didn't know what to do about it, and the more time that passed, the easier it was to think it was a silly idea."

"Can you be a little more specific?"

Not quite yet she couldn't. "Are you really a friend of Dick's?" she asked.

"Yes. And Brenda Belinski's. The woman who was killed first."

"I knew her as well."

So Brenda had known a poinsettia person. I had to be on the right track.

Annie Paul said, "You're not the killer, are you?"

"No."

She was silent for ten or fifteen seconds. I let her consider whatever she was considering. Finally she said, "Can you come down here?"

"Is there something you can't tell me on the phone? Is someone listening?"

"Don't be paranoid, Mr. Portugal. It's just that the whole thing will be so much easier if you can see rather than just hear."

"See what, Ms. Paul?"

"The plants, Mr. Portugal. I want you to see the plants."

25

I GRABBED THE WITCH HAZEL AND A BOTTLE OF DRINKING water and was on the 405 south in ten minutes. An hour and three quarters later, I exited the freeway at the Encinitas exit, where a sign told me I was in the POINSETTIA CAPITAL OF THE WORLD. I pulled into Paul's Poinsettia Plantation's parking lot at the stroke of twelve.

I renewed the witch hazel on my sting. The welt had ceased growing, and the itch threatened to surpass the pain in terms of irritation. When I'd finished nursing myself I stepped down from the truck and took stock. It was a bit warmer than it had been in L.A. The sky was cloud- and smog-free. Dozens of huge greenhouses lined up along a gentle slope to my right, filling an area equal to several football fields.

I walked toward the only building that didn't seem to be a growing area, a long, low structure that had been added onto several times with little regard for architectural consistency. As I approached, a woman emerged from one of the stucco sections. She appeared to be about my age, with broad shoulders and hips and a well-tanned face. Her eyes were brown, her hair on a swift slide from brown into gray. She wore khaki shorts and a long-sleeved denim shirt with the sleeves rolled up, and carried a black three-ring binder.

She walked swiftly toward me. "Mr. Portugal, I presume," she said, offering a firm handshake.

"Call me Joe. Quite a layout you've got here."

"And I'm Annie. Yes. It does spread, doesn't it? Please come this way."

She took me on the grand tour, showing me the various greenhouses, reciting the names of the plants within. She showed me the complicated arrangement of shades that enabled the plants to receive the six weeks of fourteen-hour "nights" they needed in order to bloom for the holiday season.

We stopped at a greenhouse way on the other side of the property, much smaller than the others, newer as well. She asked me to tell her what I knew. When I finished she undid a big padlock and slid the door open. "I wish I'd done something when Dick was still alive," she said. "If I had, we might not have lost him as well."

"What would you have done?"

"I don't know, called someone. But it seemed so tenuous. Just an offhand remark Brenda made."

"You're being too vague for me."

She shook her head. "Sorry. Let me show you. Then we'll talk about what it all means." We went in. Hundreds, perhaps thousands of bloomless poinsettias lined the benches. She led me to a corner where a single tray of three-inch plastic pots sat alone. "Here they are."

"They?"

She stood next to me and opened her binder. "Look."

It was an eight-by-ten color photo in a plastic sleeve, showing a small poinsettia. It looked like any other poinsettia, except for one thing. The bracts, instead of being red or whitish or some mottled salmon color, bore chevrons of alternating red and white. Just like the red and green ones on the mysterious *Euphorbia milii*.

"We wanted to call it Candy Cane," Annie said. "But Dick insisted on Sweet Hope, and Brenda went along with him. They wouldn't let us have the propagation rights unless we named it that. It was to have been a surprise for Dick's wife on their fortieth anniversary."

"When did you get these?"

"Last winter. But we'd been talking about it for five years. Dick dropped by one spring and asked if we'd be interested in a poinsettia with striped bracts. Of course we said yes. We have our own genetic-research staff, look at thousands of new plants, and usually aren't interested in cultivars from outside sources. But how could we turn this down? The market will be huge."

"And Brenda cooked it up."

"Yes. Something to do with gene-splicing, although where the gene came from I have no idea."

I did, but didn't see any point in telling her. "What happens next?"

"We propagate them. We'll take cuttings, and in a year or two we'll license them, on a limited basis at first. It'll be several years before the public sees even the smallest amount. But a couple of Christmases after that you'll be seeing it all over the country." She turned the page, showed me another photo. A few more. They all looked pretty much the same.

"That offhand remark you mentioned. What was that all about?"

"When Brenda and Dick were down here last December, we were talking about the difficulties of developing new varieties. Brenda said she never wanted to go through that kind of thing again. It was too time-consuming. It took her away from her conservation efforts and all."

"About that offhand remark . . ."

"I'm coming to it. It was one of the difficulties she was referring to. Evidently someone else was involved in Sweet Hope's development. Brenda said that 'a certain party'—and those were her exact words—was being a bit uppity. Dick agreed but said he was sure it was all bluster."

All bluster. The exact words I'd used to describe Henry Farber.

"Have you considered the possibility that you and the rest of your family might be in danger?"

She nodded. "It has crossed my mind. But after the initial shock I began to think Brenda and Dick probably had a lot more in common than our business venture. If there was a connection it could have nothing to do with poinsettias. I understand they were both officers in some cactus club up in L.A. Maybe that's the connection."

We left the greenhouse behind and walked back to where my pickup was parked. I shook hands and climbed in. "What do you intend to do now?" Annie asked.

"Figure out who this mystery person is, I guess."

I waited for her to say, "Find the bastard." She didn't. I fired up the truck and started back for L.A.

🌵

Catherine answered the door and ushered me into the living room, where Dad and Leonard were watching a *Wiseguy* rerun. Leonard looked up. "Hello, *boychik*," he said.

"Hello, Leonard."

"Hello, Joseph," said my father. He had the remains of a cigar in his mouth, unlit, for all I knew the same one he'd had when I'd seen him last. His eyes were wary. He could tell by the look on my face that I'd sussed out his little surveillance scheme. Or Sonny had called him.

"Hi, Dad. We need to discuss something. Can we go out back?"

He tucked the cigar butt in his shirt pocket. "Sure, Joseph."

When we sat down outside he saw me scratching my side. I told him I'd been stung. He said see, it wasn't so bad. I told him yeah, once wasn't so bad. But ten times in the same place would be bad.

He hesitated, then did something he'd never done in all the years since he'd gotten out of prison. He reached across the table and took my hand, pulled it toward him, wrapped it in both of his. "I was worried about you, Joseph."

I wanted to pull away, tell him I was a big boy. I was forty-four years old, for God's sake, and I didn't need a Mafia nanny to keep me out of trouble. But, sitting there with my hand enclosed in his warm, gnarled ones, all the anger drained. "I appreciate that, Dad."

"With your mother gone you're all I have left. I didn't want some cockamamy killer sticking a posy up your ass."

"I can watch my own ass, Dad."

He watched my face, then nodded slowly. "Sonny agrees."

"Dad, about Sonny, he was doing a hell of a job; it was only by accident I got—"

He shook his head. "Don't worry about Sonny. That old wop and me go back a long way."

"Dad!"

He held up a hand. "Don't start with that politically correct stuff. Sonny and me are old friends. I call him a wop, he calls me a kike. It's no big deal."

"Old friends or no, how'd you manage to talk him into trailing me for you?"

Dad patted my hand with one of his and pulled both of his back. I felt like someone had ripped a cozy blanket off me on a winter morning.

Slowly the feeling receded. My father still hadn't answered. "How, Dad?"

"We go back a long way—"

"I know that, Dad, get to the point."

"Sonny owed me a favor, that's all. Now we're even."

"What—"

"Joseph." With that one word I was eight years old again. "It's nothing you should know about."

"Okay," said eight-year-old Joseph.

"Good. So tell me, how are you doing with your investigation?"

I returned to adulthood and briefed him on the high points.

"So now you'll find this mystery man," he said.

"Or mystery woman."

He shook his head. "This is a man. Trust me. A woman would have slipped a letter opener into their hearts."

"That's awfully sexist, Dad."

"Again with the politically correct. If this is a woman I'll eat my hat."

"You do that, Dad. Look, I've got to go. Gina's coming over, and I don't want her to have to wait for me."

"Call her up; bring her over here. They had some nice chicken at Ralphs. Leonard and me bought plenty."

"Another time. I promise. As soon as this murder stuff is over, I'll bring Gina over and the five of us will have a nice evening together."

"That would be good. I like Gina. Even if she is a little crazy with this lesbian stuff."

🌵

I stuck my head in the greenhouse and sniffed. A vague chemical smell remained, but the air seemed healthful enough. As the day heated up the fan would have come on and drawn the toxic fumes out.

I stood in the entrance and scanned the premises. Nothing moved. A couple of feet down the center bench, an inch from the edge, a yellow jacket lay motionless. I went over and hesitantly poked it with a plant label. It didn't respond. It was, I decided, dead.

A cautious inspection revealed several other dead wasps, along with an assortment of other insects who'd been caught in the crossfire. I felt a twinge of guilt. Now, with most of my mental capacity in place, I knew it would have been all right to simply leave the greenhouse door open and let the wasps find their way out. They may have been frightful, but they weren't evil, and I'd mercilessly bug-bombed the life out of them.

All such thoughts evaporated when I came across the giant invader I'd merely caught glimpses of in the morning. It lay at the base of my white-haired *Cephalocereus senilis*, a.k.a. Mexican old man cactus. The wasp, even in death, was the scariest thing I'd seen since the original *Alien*. It was two inches long, with substantial red-orange wings. The body was a nasty blue-black, with a delicate wasp waist and a huge stinger at its nether end. Even in death it gave me the shivers.

I suspected it was a tarantula hawk. I bent in for a closer look.

"Joe? You in there?"

I screamed like the heroine in a Wes Craven movie, sprang back, nearly fell on my ass.

"This has got to do with wasps, I just know it," Gina said. She stood just outside the greenhouse, wearing a polo shirt and jeans and carrying a weird flower arrangement.

"How'd you guess?" I tried and failed to regain a smidgen of composure. "Someone tried to do me in with them."

I was expecting a wisecrack, but I guess the look on

my face told her this wasn't your everyday wasp panic. She came in and put down her flowers and wrapped her arms around me.

After she got me calmed down, I told her about my wonderful day, starting with the ordeal in the greenhouse. When we finished trying to decide who'd locked me in, I reported on my pilgrimage to the poinsettia capital of the world. We kicked around the identity of the mysterious third party before moving on to my tête-à-tête with Harold the Horse.

I concluded with the discovery of the outsize insect corpse. "I have a book inside I want to check it against."

"Go get it," she said. "I'll bag the wasp."

I went in and pulled Hogue's *Insects of the Los Angeles Basin* from its shelf. By the time I came back outside, Gina had retrieved the dead tarantula hawk. She had it in the palm of her hand.

"Put that down," I said.

"Why?" she said. "It's dead. It's harmless. Just ID it so we can get rid of it."

A quick review of Hogue determined I was right. "It says that people who've been stung by one describe it as extraordinarily painful. Are you sure it's dead?"

She deposited the wasp on the bench and poked it with her finger. "Deader than a doorknob."

"I think that's 'doornail.' "

"It's deader than that too."

I consulted the book again. It said tarantula hawks were uncommon in our area, although they were occasionally seen out in the hills. "Kind of out of its element," I said. "Somebody went to a lot of trouble to capture this. This and all the other ones."

"I suppose so."

"Why would anyone go to all that trouble? Not to kill me. When I was in there with them, I thought that was what was going on, but I was temporarily insane. If someone is trying to do away with me, there are better ways."

"Maybe they just wanted to scare you."

"Why?"

"Because you're getting too close."

"Too close to whom? If I'm getting close to somebody, I sure as hell don't know who it is."

"They think you do."

I sighed. "This is starting to get to me."

"Starting?"

I pointed at the wasp. "What do you think we ought to do with that?"

"Stuff it and mount it over your mantel."

"I'm serious."

"Throw it in the garbage. What else would you do with it?"

"I don't know, dust it for fingerprints maybe."

She rolled her eyes at me.

"Okay, let's toss it. And the others too."

When we were done dumping the casualties in the trash, I picked up the flowers Gina had been carrying, a ridiculous arrangement in a bulky vase shaped like the Venus de Milo. Half a dozen beautiful red roses poked out of it, but that was where normalcy ended. The stargazers had little bows on them, and the anthuriums had been painted silver, and the whole thing was rife with long skinny leaves stapled into loops. "Hey, what's this all about?"

"Oh, that. Carlos made it for me. A sign of his affection, as he put it."

"He actually gets paid for this kind of stuff?"

"Big bucks."

"And you thought you could fob it off on me."

"That wasn't my intention, but now that you mention it . . . no, I just thought you could use a laugh."

"You dragged it over here to give me a laugh?"

"Yeah. You've been kind of sour lately."

"I guess I have." I checked out the flowers again. "This thing is a crack-up. It ought to be in the Smithsonian."

"You should have seen me trying to keep a straight face when he brought it over. I mean, the roses are sweet, but the rest of it . . ."

I pictured her at her front door, biting her cheeks, shifting her weight from foot to foot like she does when she's trying to get rid of somebody, and suddenly I was giggling. Then I was into a big, full-bodied chortle, and before long I was cackling my head off. Gina started in too, and soon the two of us were in conniptions. Somewhere in there I dropped the vase and the flowers went all over the place and Venus was missing more than just her arms, and that got us started all over again. Every time I thought I was calming down, I'd catch a glimpse of her hysterics, and that would set me off anew.

Finally the laugh level diminished, and as I began to catch my breath, I began to appreciate what she'd done, lugging that thing over just to cheer me up. For the millionth time I realized just how much having a friend like Gina meant to me. Someone who would put up with my plant mania and my wasp phobia, who would bare-handedly pick up a winged invader from the hills so I could ID it. Someone with whom I could share anything, no matter how stupid, no matter how small. Someone who—

Time compressed. I went from point A to point M for murder in two or three seconds. And I wasn't even stoned.

I stopped laughing. A second or two later Gina realized I'd quieted down and her giggles petered out too, although she was still snickering when she asked, "What happened? Is something wrong?"

"No," I said. "Nothing's wrong."

"You stopped so suddenly, I thought you hurt yourself. Are you sure everything's okay?"

"Everything's okay. Everything's more than okay. Want to know why?"

"Sure."

"It's simple," I said. "I figured out who did it. I know who killed Brenda and Dick."

26

WE DROVE EAST ON CULVER UNTIL IT MERGED WITH Venice, then north on La Cienega. I think Gina knew I was headed to her place, and I think she knew why, but she didn't say anything about it. When we got there I made a couple of calls and we got what we needed from the kitchen.

We headed west on Santa Monica Boulevard. I pulled to the curb in front of A Different Light, the gay bookstore, where once I'd helped Gina search the stacks for something to explain why she couldn't decide on girls or boys. Across the street was the West Hollywood sheriff's station. Part of me wanted to run in there and say, phone your friends in the LAPD, tell them what I found out.

Instead, I rejoined the flow of traffic, cut north to Sunset, and drove through the glare of the Strip. We passed the Roxy, which, Annie Paul had told me, had once been a poinsettia packinghouse. On around the curve where the lights ended, and through the mansions of Beverly Hills, before turning left onto the UCLA campus.

We threaded our way around Circle Drive until the bulk of Pauley Pavilion blotted out the night, and drove into the tiny lot at the Kawamura Conservatory. I turned off the engine, pocketed the key, and turned to Gina. "You don't have to do this, you know."

"Of course I do."

We sat for ten minutes. My sting itched like crazy. A car clattered up. The engine cut out, and the vehicle settled on creaking springs. The driver got out and walked silently to my window. "Hello," said Eugene Rand.

"Hi, Eugene," I said. "I'm glad you could make it."

"Of course I made it. I would do anything to catch Brenda's killer. You know that."

I introduced him to Gina. He hardly took notice. He walked toward the conservatory's front door, but I jumped out of the truck and asked him to stop. "Does the back entrance open from the outside?"

He turned. In the dim light filtering in from the road, I thought his expression had turned peevish. "Yes."

"Let's go in that way. I'd like to keep this door locked."

He shrugged and disappeared around the side of the building. Gina exited the truck and followed. I grabbed my flashlight and brought up the rear. A couple of big eucalyptus overhung the conservatory's side. I could barely make out Gina's outline in that stretch. I snapped on the flashlight and pointed it at the ground in front of her.

Gina reached the end and disappeared around the corner. I anticipated a crash, a scream, some out-of-the-ordinary sensory event that would tell me I didn't know what the hell I was doing. None came. Seconds later I, too, rounded the corner. Gina stood in the glimmer of the one dim floodlight back there, while Rand sorted through a ringful of keys. He opened the padlock on the gate. We passed through the supply area. The *Aeonium lindleyi* no longer sat in the dimness atop the first-aid kit but had a new place in a new pot out where it would get its full complement of sun.

Rand unlocked the back door and we went in. I directed

the flashlight beam down the entry corridor. A dozen large white flowers reflected it back at me. One was a foot or more across. *Selenicereus macdonaldiae*, I guessed; it had the biggest flower of all the cacti. A strong floral scent filled the air, pleasant if a bit cloying.

"These are amazing," Gina said.

"They'll all be dead by morning."

She glanced back over her shoulder.

"Don't say it," I told her.

I gave Rand the flash, and Gina and I followed him to the light switch. He'd obviously watered that day; the air was humid and had that peculiar musty smell greenhouses get, and a few puddles remained on the ground. He clicked the switch, and a couple of fluorescent fixtures, four bulbs in all, lit up over to our left where the potting bench was. One of the bulbs buzzed and blinked and decided to go back to sleep.

"It's kind of spooky, don't you think?" Rand said.

I looked at the poor schlub standing there, wondering about what I was doing. What right did I have, taking the law into my own hands like this? I looked at my watch. Nine-twenty.

I got my flashlight back and promptly dropped it. Twenty seconds of switch-pressing convinced me I'd blown out the bulb. I put the flash on a bench and began to sort through the upright Madagascar euphorbias sprinkled about. Gina and Rand stood awkwardly by. "Nice euphorbia," Gina said, fingering the small oval leaves on a two-foot cylinder of spines.

"That's an alluaudia," Rand said.

"So it is. Light's not too good."

I looked up from where I was poking around under a bench. "It does kind of look like some of the Madagascar euphorbs. It's a good example of convergent evolu—"

"Spare me the botany lesson," Gina said. She opened her purse, checked its contents, snapped it shut.

Five minutes later I had what I was looking for. It was way at the back of a bench; a fockea's vining stems had draped themselves around it, nearly covering it. It only had a few leaves, and of those only one was striped.

I disengaged it and brought it over to Gina and Rand just as a vehicle pulled up. The driver gunned the engine and shut it off. "He's here," I said.

Footfalls sounded on gravel. "Anybody there?" said a voice outside.

"Around back," I shouted. "To your right."

His appearance took longer than expected; I worried he'd taken a wrong turn, would keep going until he reached Sunset Boulevard. But then we heard footsteps in the entry corridor and he appeared. "Hello?"

"Over here, Lyle," I said.

He saw us and came closer. "Haven't been here at night before. Spooky."

"That seems to be the general consensus. Lyle, have you met Eugene Rand?"

He glanced over at Rand. "Yeah. At Dick's. How are you?" No one made any move to shake hands.

"Fine, I guess."

"Good, good." He saw the plant I still had in my hand. "What are we, giving out door prizes?" No one responded. "So, Joe, what's so damned important we had to come out here this time of night?"

I looked at each of them in turn. Rand. Lyle. Finally Gina, who'd sidled a few steps away. "I've solved Brenda's and Dick's murders. I need your help in apprehending the killer."

A silly little grin grew around Lyle's mouth. "You devil. You figured it out."

I nodded, put down the plant, leaned against a bench. "Once upon a time a plant called *Euphorbia milii* grew in Madagascar. Then one day explorers came along and saw its vibrant red flowers and said, We have to have this. So they took some away and spread it throughout the world, and they called it crown of thorns because they thought it looked like what Christ wore on his head when he was crucified. It probably wasn't, given that the Romans never heard of Madagascar."

"What did they know?" Gina said.

"That plant became very popular among succulent collectors, even though it's not really very succulent, and—"

"Excuse me, Joe," Lyle said. "I know all this, and I'm betting Rand here does too, and you can tell your girlfriend on your own time. It's kind of late."

I held my hands up in front of me. "Forgive me. I was just trying to set the scene." I pushed myself away from the bench. "One day a milii seedling appeared unlike any other. Instead of the normal, green leaves, this one had leaves like a sergeant's stripes. Alternating red and green. An interesting curiosity, to say the least." I picked up the milii again. "Like this one." I brought it over to Rand. "Somehow Brenda got hold of this unique plant. One day she showed it to Dick McAfee. And Dick got an idea. What if Brenda could isolate the gene that caused the stripes? And what if that gene could be transferred to that other well-known euphorbia, the poinsettia? Dick relished his position as the poinsettia king of Los Angeles and thought a plant like that would be a sensation."

"I don't like poinsettias," Rand said.

"Nor do I. But a whole lot of people do. Lots of money to be made there."

"You think?" Lyle said.

I nodded. "Lots. Enough to set somebody up for life

maybe. Or several somebodies." I caught Gina's eye. "Maybe enough to be a motive for murder."

"That seems silly," Rand said.

"The way I figure it, somebody else was involved in the discovery. They wanted a cut. Brenda said no. Dick said no. So this somebody whacked both of them." I looked at Gina. Her purse sat on a bench. Her hands were behind her back.

I twirled dramatically and spoke directly to Eugene Rand. "You gave yourself away, Eugene, by showing up at Dick's house. Why would you do that, and lie about being a member of the club, unless you wanted to check up and see if anyone suspected you?"

"I came because I thought I might get a clue about Brenda's murderer. If you can play detective, why can't I?"

I unleashed an accusatory finger. "You were the one who discovered the plant with the strange leaves, right here in this very conservatory. And you, loyal employee that you are, ran right to Brenda with it."

"That's not true," Rand said.

"And Brenda said, thanks, Eugene, that's a good boy, now go back to your watering. And then she went ahead and took the plant you'd shown her and tried to make a whole lot of money off it. You felt betrayed, didn't you, Eugene? Here the woman you'd been so loyal to was totally blowing you off. Not to mention that you had lust in your heart for her."

"You're making this up." He looked frantically over at Lyle. "He's making this up, honest. I never saw the plant until much later."

"You little shit," Lyle said. "You killed my buddy Dick." He bounded over to Rand, grabbed each of his shoulders in a meaty paw, and squeezed.

"Ow," Rand whined. "You're *hurting* me."

"Lyle, please," I said. "I did ask you to come here so we

could apprehend the killer, but let's not be violent. There's been enough violence." Lyle stopped squeezing but maintained his grip. "So then, Eugene," I went on, "you bided your time. You waited until the proper psychological moment, until the new poinsettia with the spliced-in gene from the plant *you* discovered had been delivered to the propagator. You waited until Brenda was just about to go back to Madagascar, the land she loved, the land where the plant originated, and it all fell together for you in a murderous epiphany, and you accosted her in her own home and forced a *Euphorbia abdelkuri* down her throat. For years you'd pined for her, and now, in a last symbolic act, you plunged—"

"No, no, none of this happened. I loved her, I never would have wanted anything to—"

"And after you were done you left the remains of the murder weapon at my house and called the police to tell them it was there, and then a couple of days later you offed Dick too, most imaginatively, I might add, and—"

"No, no. You're wrong. I wouldn't hurt anyone. Anyway, I never even heard of you until you came up here to the conservatory, and by that time they'd already found the plant at your place. You told me that yourself. You called it the death plant."

"I did?" I shut up and made myself look confused. "Hmm. I guess you're right." I turned to Gina. "And it sounded so good." Back to the others. "Okay, plan B."

"What the fuck?" Lyle said.

"What the fuck indeed," I said. "You did it, Lyle."

27

LYLE STARED AT ME LIKE I'D JUST GROWN AN EXTRA NOStril. "That's bullshit and you know it."

"I think not," I replied. "Most of what I said was true. Except that it was you who wanted a cut, and that Brenda didn't show the plant to Dick. He showed it to her. He got it from you. You're always giving away plants, Lyle. But when you found out they were going to make money off this one, you wanted a cut."

"I don't have to stand here and listen to—"

"How come you told me you'd never seen a striped milii?"

"What? I never—"

"Sure you did, and that was your big mistake. It just seemed a little funny to me. Austin and Sam each had one, so it couldn't have been that much of a secret. But you said you'd never heard of it." I threw Gina a little smile. "Best friends share everything, Lyle. So why wouldn't Dick have shared his nifty find with you?"

Eugene Rand was trying to extricate himself from Lyle's grasp. Lyle held on, casually, with just enough grip on Rand's shirt to keep the little man from escaping. "I must have misunderstood. Yeah, Dick showed me—"

"Just shut up a minute. You might as well shut up, because too much points at you for it to be anyone else."

"Like what? Not that it matters, since I didn't do it."

Rand squirmed. His eyes darted around, looking for an escape route. Another fluorescent was blinking, throwing fleeting shadows across his face.

"Let him go, Lyle," I said.

He glanced down at Rand, seemed unaware he'd been holding him. He didn't let go though. "Fuck a duck, Joe, I don't know what's gotten into you."

"How long did it take you to collect the wasps? Everyone knows how afraid of them I am. But you live out there in the boonies. Tarantula hawk country."

"What wasps?"

"Although that part I think I understand. I was poking around, I could have found something out, you wanted to scare me. The thing I don't get is, why pick on me earlier on? Why plant the abdelkuri at my place? And the roll of plant ties in my gym bag. You slipped that in at Brenda's funeral, right?"

His denial surprised me. It surprised me because it wasn't a denial at all. "You were handy," he said quietly. "You lived near her. It wasn't anything personal. Had to get the cops interested in someone else."

Nobody spoke. I'd suddenly gotten what I was looking for, and I didn't know what to do with it. Finally I found my voice. "Those little abdelkuris you showed me the other day. That obviously wasn't the first batch you grew. What happened to the others from the bunch the death plant came from? You couldn't leave them lying around where the cops could find them."

"I put them in a Dumpster in North Hollywood. Really hurt to do that." He seemed deep in thought. Now was the time when he was supposed to break down sobbing, babbling something about having a right to the money, explaining how he'd hatched his plan, et cetera, et cetera.

Instead, Lyle snatched up Eugene Rand and threw him at me.

Rand tumbled through the air like a rag doll, yelling at the top of his lungs, while I marveled at the casual manner in which Lyle had tossed him. He rotated in midair and smashed into me at right angles. I fell backward. A bench hit just below my butt and I landed in a cactus patch, with Rand atop me. Spines made themselves at home in my back, my legs, my arms. My head crashed into the bench top. I saw stars. My vision blurred. I heard one, two heavy footsteps.

Atop me, Rand swept his limbs wildly. "Get off," I said. The footsteps abruptly stopped.

Rand continued his scrabbling. I pushed him off me. Off the bench too. He grunted when he hit the ground. I sat up and scanned the area, which wouldn't stay still long enough to be scanned.

Eugene Rand, the poor little guy I'd gotten involved in this charade to get Lyle off his guard, lay on his stomach amidst the gravel covering the ground.

Lyle loomed over Gina, his huge arms over his head, like a Kodiak bear on *Wild Kingdom* preparing to do something dreadful. "No!" I yelled.

My vision snapped back to focus, my heart back to its usual location in my chest. Lyle's arms were indeed up in the air, but as a reaction to the gun Gina had pointed at him.

"Time to call the cops," she said.

I checked on Rand. He'd sat up and his back was pressed against a vertical two-by-four holding up a sagging piece of bench. A small trickle of blood decorated his head, partially obscuring the map of Argentina, but other than that he seemed okay.

I extracted the two longest cactus spines from my left

forearm and moved over next to Gina. "You brought the plant with you to Brenda's, didn't you, Lyle? You went over there to ask one more time for a cut of the poinsettia money, and you brought her the abdelkuri as a little bribe. Did you know Brenda hated getting gifts?"

His eyes darted toward the entryway as if gauging his chances of escaping through it. "Everybody likes a freebie now and then."

"You killed her because she turned down a plant? Seems a little excessive."

Another glance at the entrance. "She said she couldn't be bribed and she had one that was ten times bigger anyway. When I asked for a cut of the poinsettia, she picked up the abdelkuri and threw it at me. I just lost it. I smacked her, and then I saw the piece lying there and—"

"And Dick figured out you did it. That's what he was going to tell me when I came over after Brenda's funeral."

"I asked him not to."

"And when he said he would anyway, you dropped by and hit him on the head and nailed him up to make it look like some crazy was on the loose. Your own best friend."

"It was kind of Magda's idea."

"Then you acted all upset about Dick."

"I *was* upset. My best buddy dead and everything."

Gina broke in. "Can't we talk about all this later? I think it's time to call the cops."

"Good idea," I said.

I picked up her purse and reached in for the phone. Magda Tillis strolled out of the entryway with a double-barreled shotgun pointed our way. I froze.

Gina's back was to her. "Come on, Joe, I know you hate cell phones, but make an exception."

"Uh."

"I'm not going to like this, am I?"

"No."

"Please place your pistol on the ground," Magda said.

"That would be Lyle's wife, wouldn't it?" Gina said.

"Yup," I said.

"My guess is she has something that shoots pointed at me."

"Right again. You'd better do what she says."

Gina knelt and carefully complied. She placed the gun on the ground. Right in the middle of one of the puddles left over from Rand's watering.

"What the hell'd you do that for?" Lyle said.

"If we can't have it, neither can you," Gina said.

"Fuck a duck." He glanced longingly at the puddle before moving over to stand next to his wife.

"You're making a big mistake, Magda," I said. "So far you're not guilty of anything other than protecting your husband, just like any wife would do. Oh, and locking me in the greenhouse. That was kind of bad. At least I assume it was you. The person I saw running away was way too small to be Lyle. But this gun stuff, this puts it into the realm of . . . the realm of . . . help me out here, Gi."

"Aiding and abetting," Gina said. "There's a definite aid and abetment going on here."

"Quiet, you!" Magda said. "I should have listened to my husband. I should have just let him kill you. But I thought there had been enough killing. I thought we could scare you away. This was incorrect. Lyle!"

"Yes, hon?"

"What should we do with this interloper?"

"I guess we're gonna have to kill him after all. And his girlfriend too."

Whoa. "Kill him"? A day or two back I'd thought maybe I was next in line, but that was all kind of nebulous. Now someone with a shotgun was talking about using it. Where was Sonny when I needed him?

"Yes, you are correct," Magda said. "But this will be the end of the killing. For when it is done we will flee. Is now the time, my dearest?"

"It's as good a time as any," Lyle replied. He reached for the shotgun.

Someone else came barreling into view. Someone with a map of Argentina on his head. "Murderers!" Eugene Rand wailed, a millisecond before crashing into the Tillises.

If he hadn't had the element of surprise, if he hadn't seemed such an inconsequential little man, Lyle probably would have knocked him away with one swat of his beefy arm. But Lyle had clearly forgotten about him and tumbled backward, falling heavily on top of Magda. She screamed. The shotgun went off, more loudly than I could have imagined, and flew from her grip. Glass shattered above and rained down upon us.

The trained commando team of Joe and Gina jumped into action. So did the homicidal duo. Everyone but Eugene Rand dived for the shotgun. He was laid out on the ground with his now-much-bloodier head up against a cinder block.

Legs and arms and bodies. English, Spanish, and Hungarian expletives. Another shotgun blast, and shredded succulents sailing through the air. Magda fleeing into the entry corridor, with Gina nipping at her heels.

Suddenly there was no one between me and the shotgun. I vaguely recalled that shotguns tended to have two shells, which would mean this one had shot its wad, but it still seemed like a good idea to grab it. Holding tight to the barrel end, I rolled to my feet, leaving Lyle lying on the ground in a patch of weeds.

I leapt to where I could guard the way out and held on to

the shotgun like a baseball bat. My stance was better than Eugene Rand's had been with the euphorbia the other day, but not much. I waved the weapon back and forth, daring him to challenge me.

He came to his knees, then his feet. He rushed me. I swung for the seats and connected with his left kidney.

He roared in pain, jumped back, and clutched his battered side. From outside came the sounds of a scuffle.

Lyle regarded me with murder in his eyes, which I thought was fair since he had it everywhere else in his body. He came at me again. I took a left-handed stance. Big swing and a miss. But close.

He abruptly turned and ran toward the front door. I knew it was locked, and if he thought about it he'd realize the same, since I'd made him go around back when he arrived. But he didn't think about it, or he didn't care, and for all I knew the door would open from the inside. I took off after him, into the dim light farthest from the fluorescents.

He had five paces on me when his mighty shoulder crashed into the front door. It bowed but remained shut. "Damn it to hell," he muttered, staring at the door like it had personally insulted him. He turned, snatched an eight-inch pot that was home to some nondescript cactus, and hurled it at the wall. Glass splintered. Chain-link fence confronted him. He made an animal noise.

I almost had him then, but he saw me coming and took off. He ended up in the same blind alley in which Eugene Rand had taken a poke at me with a euphorbia.

I wondered if maybe this particular shotgun could handle more than two shells. But, given what I knew about guns, I'd probably blow myself up trying to find out, and I didn't think Lyle would tell me if I asked. "Give it up, Lyle," I said. "It'll make it easier for you if you give up now."

"No," he said. "It'll make it easier for *you*." He picked up a gorgeous crested golden barrel cactus, with inch-long yellow spines and a body twisted into a beautiful otherworldly brain shape. It was the biggest crest of that species I'd ever seen. At least it was until he threw it at me and I ducked and it crashed into a saguaro and broke into a half dozen pieces.

It was quickly followed by a *Stapelianthus neronis* in a six-inch pot, a lumpish yet desirable succulent milkweed. This missile disintegrated on the bench top, generating enough cuttings to supply the entire CCCC. "Lyle, you're ruining some amazing plants," I said, always careful to keep things in perspective.

"What do I care? I can't have any plants in the big house." A stunning *Pachypodium brevicaule* whooshed at me. Picture a potato with big yellow flowers. I batted it aside with the shotgun.

I had to end it. Not only was he decimating the collection, but one of these times he was going to connect, and I would be picking spines from my eyes and not just my forearms. I took a step toward him. "Na-na-na-na-na," I said in a voice that would have infuriated any eight-year-old.

Lyle was considerably older than that. "What the hell are you doing?" he asked, launching a volley of hooked-spined mammillaria.

Another two steps. "Magda wears army boots," I said.

His face turned vicious and he came at me. I ducked his outstretched hands, extended my arm to its limit, and swept the shotgun into a mighty arc. I caught the hanger of the pot containing the giant *Euphorbia antisyphilitica* that Rand had almost sent down upon us. It teetered once, twice, and, just as Lyle's hands encircled my throat, it slipped off its water pipe and descended onto his head.

Something made a cracking noise—bone or plastic, I

wasn't sure which. Lyle's hands dropped from my neck. He said, "Oof," or something similar, and collapsed unconscious at my feet.

I ran outside. Gina had Magda in a pretty damned good full nelson. "Lyle?" she asked.

"He was tired," I said. "He's taking a nap."

28

I RUSHED BACK INSIDE TO CHECK ON RAND. AS I KNELT AT his side he sat up and took a swing at me. I caught his fist in my hand. "Eugene," I said. "It's me. Joe."

He slowly focused. "Did we get 'em?"

"We got 'em. I'm sorry I acted like I thought you did it. I'm sorry I put you through that."

"Doesn't matter. We got 'em."

I helped him up, pointed him at the first-aid kit, and called the police. They said they'd send somebody and page Burns at home. While they were at it, I said, could they send some paramedics for Rand? He'd patched himself up and was wandering around, righting overturned pots, but I couldn't tell if the daze he was in was any different from his normal one.

As I waited for reinforcements I stood over Lyle with the shotgun at the ready. Merlin the mule popped into my mind. I wondered who would take care of him now, with his owners in, as Lyle had called it, "the big house."

Ten minutes after I called, two officers arrived and took the Tillises into custody. The paramedics were next. They checked Rand over and said he probably had a concussion and just to be on the safe side they ought to take him to the hospital. They loaded him on a gurney. One tucked him in while the other went to check Lyle's head.

Burns showed up. Casillas too. Burns told the paramedics to hold on a minute, asked Rand a couple of questions, and said he could go, that she'd catch up with him at the hospital.

He was rather pleased about all the attention he was getting. "This is the most excitement I've ever had," he told me as they wheeled him into the ambulance. "I'm certainly glad I sent you that e-mail. Although at the time I didn't know it was you."

"You're Succuman?"

"Yes. I'm rather proud of that ID."

"As well you should be. But why'd you deny you'd ever seen a striped milii when I came to see you? The day you attacked me."

"I thought you might be the killer."

"So you told some total stranger on the Internet, who you hadn't an inkling the identity of, to go looking for this big clue."

"I liked the tone of the request. Clever and to the point."

"Gina wrote it."

He nodded. "I liked that it came from a woman. Designwoman, you know? No one who could ever, you know, have relations with Brenda."

Best not to show him the light. "How'd you know the plant had something to do with the murders?"

"I didn't, for sure. But it seemed so important to Brenda, I just had a hunch."

After the paramedics drove Rand off, Gina and I answered some questions for the two detectives. Burns said we'd have to come down the next day and make a statement. We said okay and turned to go, but I stopped and walked back up to Casillas. He was wiping his forehead with a tissue. "You owe me an apology," I said.

"For what?"

"For dragging me down to the station not once, but twice, and generally treating me like a criminal."

"That's what I get paid for. So I was wrong. Big deal."

"That's it?"

"That's it." He turned his back on me and went to talk to one of the officers.

"Maybe I can apologize for him." It was Burns, in a snug black T-shirt and jeans, looking a lot more attractive than she usually did in her cop suits.

I shook my head. "Not necessary. He's probably right."

"He's a hell of a cop."

"As are you, Detective Burns."

We eyed each other for a second or three. "We'll see you tomorrow," I said, and gathered up Gina. We rode home in silence and pulled into my driveway in the wee hours of Wednesday morning.

🌵

We sat on the couch, spooning rocky road from a container of Dreyer's I found in the back of the freezer. An empty bottle of witch hazel sat on the table before us, its contents spent on my sting and spine punctures. We talked about Brenda, and my father, and Eugene Rand, and everybody else we'd encountered since stumbling upon Brenda's body. Everyone except Carlos and Amanda. Somehow we skipped around them.

My eyes kept slipping closed. Gina's as well. I said, "It's bedtime," and Gina nodded sleepily.

We stood up and she began removing cushions from the

couch. I put a hand on her arm, turned her around to face me. "Gi?"

"Yes?"

"How would you feel about sleeping together?"

Her eyes searched my face. "I'm not sure that would be a good idea."

I shook my head. "I mean just sleeping. In the same bed."

"Oh. Didn't I suggest that just the other day?"

"It was a good suggestion."

I let her use the bathroom first. When she was done I went in. I brushed my teeth and stripped to my Jockeys. Put my T-shirt back on. Took it off again and came out. When I looked at the bed, I cleared my throat.

"Something wrong?" she asked.

"You're on my side."

She grinned. "It's my side too."

"At your house it's your side. At my house it's mine. When we do this at your house, you can sleep on that side."

"When we do it at my house? Is this going to become a habit?"

"I don't know. It might. Let's see how it works out tonight."

She laughed and shoved over. I turned off the light and slid in beside her. We lay there, a foot or two apart. I reached out and took her hand in my own. I listened to her breathing, slow and regular. "Gi?"

"Hmm?"

"Tonight, when Lyle threw Rand at me, and you got the drop on him with the gun. I couldn't really tell what was going on, and for a second it looked like Lyle was going to do something really awful to you." I squeezed her fingertips. "That was one of the worst moments of my life. The thought of losing you—"

She reached over and placed a finger on my lips. "Let's not talk about it, okay? We're safe now. Go to sleep, baby."

We moved a bit closer and slipped off into dreamland.

The first thing I saw when I awoke was Gina's face. After all that fuss we'd both ended up on my side of the bed. The two of us were entangled there, wrapped up like a couple of kittens.

She had a bit of sleep stuff in the corner of one eye. Her breath eased in, out, in, out; her lips were ever so slightly parted. Her black hair fell effortlessly over the side of her face. I wrapped a bit around my fingers, moved it aside.

She woke up. I watched the split second of disorientation, then she smiled as she realized where she was. It would have been the easiest thing in the world to move my head just a few inches, lay my lips upon hers. I'm pretty sure I know what would have happened.

And after that, what? Things were safe the way they were. So instead of traveling those few inches, I disengaged myself. I rolled out of bed and went into the bathroom. If she'd asked me to come back, I would have. But she didn't.

By the time I finished showering, she was dressed. We went back up to her place so she could clean up and change and took separate vehicles to see Burns and Casillas. We didn't talk about that morning for a long time.

I adopted Brenda's birds. She'd entrusted them to my care while she was gone, and now that she was gone forever I felt it appropriate to take them under my wing. I built a big floor-to-ceiling enclosure for them in my parents' bedroom, where they get plenty of air and light and seed and everything else canaries like. I threw Muck and Mire in with the Marx Brothers contingent, and they all get along famously.

I called Iris Bunche. We met for iced tea at Jimmy's on the UCLA campus and convinced ourselves that something was going on, so we went out on a real date. Then several more, but after a few weeks the relationship was called off due to mutual lack of interest.

In early July I got a letter from Amanda Belinski, thanking me for bringing her sister's murderer to justice. On a muggy Sunday evening a month later, I picked up the phone and gave her a call. Her machine answered. I didn't leave a message.

The Joe Portugal Guide to Botanical Nomenclature

EVERYONE'S ALWAYS ASKING ME THE DIFFERENCE BETWEEN a succulent and a cactus. It's pretty simple. A succulent is any plant with leaves, stems, or roots containing water-storing tissue. A cactus is a member of a particular family of stem succulents, Cactaceae, defined by flower characteristics and the presence of areoles, special spots on the stem from which spines, flowers, and new branches grow. (More about plant families a bit later.)

Nearly all cacti are succulent, but not all succulents are cacti. When you hear someone talking about "cacti and succulents," it's kind of like saying "pizza and food." It really should be "cacti and other succulents," but if you start insisting on stuff like that, people think you're a pain in the neck.

I've been using "cacti" as the plural of "cactus," which is the most common usage. But you'll also hear people refer to their collections as "my cactus," or even "my cactuses," and nobody harangues them about it.

Cacti are native to the New World, with a couple of dubious exceptions found in Madagascar and Sri Lanka. The other succulents occur all over the world but are especially prevalent in Africa.

Okay. On to plant families. All plants in each family have certain characteristics in common, sometimes things like the structure of the flower and fruit, sometimes esoteric stuff understood only by botanists. Let's consider Rosaceae, the rose family. Besides roses it includes many common fruits, ranging from apples to strawberries. To a botanist all these plants are cousins.

Families are broken up into genera, one of which is a genus. The plants in each of these have more in common with each other than with others in their family. Back to Rosaceae: within it, apples are in the genus *Malus* and strawberries in *Fragaria*. But all the stone fruits, like peaches and plums and almonds, are in *Prunus*. Why? Similarities in their seeds, among other things.

Next we come to the species. The word is both singular and plural, although occasionally you'll hear somebody talking about a "specie." Try not to make fun of them. A species is one particular type of plant, like a white oak or a golden barrel cactus or a daffodil. The scientific name for a species consists of two words, the genus and the specific name. So the peach is *Prunus persica*, and the plum is *P. salicina* or *P. domestica*, depending on whether it's Japanese or European. (When it's clear which genus you're dealing with, you can reduce its name to the initial letter, as I did here.)

Just one more level, I promise: the variety. It's a further subdivision of a species. For example, the nectarine, *Prunus persica nucipersica*, is, to a botanist, a variety of the peach.

Family names (which always end in -aceae) are capitalized. So are genus names, when they refer to the genus as a whole or are part of the scientific name. Genera and scientific names are printed in italics. Thus, "I collect the genus *Euphorbia*. My favorite is *Euphorbia milii*." But when a genus or species name is used because a plant lacks a common name, it's neither capitalized nor italicized. "I have a lot of euphorbias. The miliis are my favorites."

Now on to the plants mentioned in *The Cactus Club Killings*, alphabetized for your convenience:

Aeonium lindleyi is a leaf succulent native to the Canary Islands. It forms small green rosettes and is a remedy for contact with euphorbia sap.

Agave is a genus of leaf succulents, mostly from Mexico. It's where tequila comes from. A lot of people see the spines on its leaves and call it a cactus. It's not.

Alluaudia is covered under Didieriaceae.

Boweia volubilis, known as the "climbing onion," isn't really a succulent, but its weird behavior appeals to collectors. It's a member of the lily family and sends out long leafless stems from onionlike bulbs.

Cephalocereus senilis, from Mexico, is one of several plants known as the "old man cactus," due to its blanket of long white hair.

Ceropegia is a genus in the milkweed family, mostly from the Old World, which indulges in all sorts of weird growth forms. Its flowers resemble miniature parachutes.

Cyphostemma comes from Africa and is a member of the grape family. It forms a fat caudex—a water-storing central stem—and has peeling bark and red fruits similar to grapes. But don't eat them.

Didieriaceae is a small family of plants with marginally succulent stems that inhabit the thorn forest of Madagascar. It includes the genera *Alluaudia* and *Didieria*.

Dracaena draco, known as the dragon tree, is native to the Canary Islands. It grows to twenty feet high and wide and has dagger-shape leaves. Not really a succulent, but spectacular.

Dudleya is a genus of leaf succulents from Mexico and the west coast of the U.S. Its leaves are usually pale green.

Epiphyllum refers to two groups of plants. The first is a genus of jungle cacti with flat, leaflike stems. Their white flowers appear in the evening and last only one night. The name is also used for the thousands of hybrids of this genus with other cactus genera, with spectacular flowers in every color but blue.

Euphorbia contains thousands of species, some succulent and some not, ranging from tiny garden spurges to huge trees. Its growth forms vary wildly, but all euphorbias share a very simple flower type, known as a cyathium. The white (occasionally yellow) sap that seeps from wounded euphorbias is always an irritant and in some species is quite caustic. In the tale related here, we encounter: *Euphorbia abdelkuri*, a strange gray stem succulent from the island of Socotra; *E. ammak*, a strongly spined African species; *E. antisyphilitica*, a spindly stemmed plant from Mexico, named for its supposed medicinal properties; *E. flanaganii*, one of the medusa-head species from Africa, with a spherical central stem sprouting dozens of thin green arms; *E. francoisii*, a dwarf from Madagascar, with leaves in shades of green, pink, and silver; *E. grandicornis*, another African species, this one with long, vicious spines; *E. milii*, the "crown of thorns," with semisucculent stems and blood-red flowers, native to Madagascar; *E. obesa*, aptly described by its common name "baseball plant," yet another African species; *E. pachypodioides*, a spindle-shaped Madagascan plant topped by a crown of oval leaves; *E. pulcherrima*, originally from Mexico, the poinsettia; *E. restricta*, a small South African species with lots of spiny arms; *E. tirucalli*, from Africa, misleadingly known as the "pencil cactus," with particularly nasty sap; and *E. viguieri*, a spiny Madagascan species with red or orange flowers.

Ferocactus is a genus of strongly spined barrel cacti from Mexico and the southwest U.S.

Fockea is an African genus in the milkweed family, characterized by a fat, water-storing caudex from which vinelike stems grow.

Hoya is popularly known as the "wax plant." Members of this Asian genus in the milkweed family are often grown as house plants because of their weird leaf forms and clusters of fragrant flowers.

Mammillaria is the second-biggest cactus genus. Its two-hundred-plus species range from the U.S. to Venezuela but are highly concentrated in Mexico. It's known as the "nipple cactus" because its areoles are perched on conelike tubercles instead of along ribs as in most cacti.

Pachypodium is a popular genus in the oleander family. Species include *P. brevicaule*, which resembles a well-aged cow pie in habitat; *P. decaryi*, with a stem shaped like a football; and *P. horombense*, whose caudex can reach the size of a watermelon. These are all native to Madagascar; other pachypodiums come from South Africa.

Pelargonium, the genus that includes the garden geranium, also contains African species with succulent stems or tuberous roots. They're winter growers and die in warm weather.

Pereskia is the exception to the rule that all cacti are succulent. They're leafy, woody plants that can form trees or gigantic vines. What makes them cacti? Flower characteristics and areoles.

Portulacaceae is the purslane family. It includes one of the few annual succulents, *Portulaca grandiflora*, known as "rose moss" or "moss rose," depending on which book you read. It's related to neither moss nor roses. You wouldn't guess it to look at its members, but botanically this is the family closest to the cacti.

Pseudolithos is a rare genus in the milkweed family. They're stem succulents from Africa.

Rhipsalis are jungle cacti with pencillike or flattened, barely succulent stems. Their small white flowers give rise to berrylike fruits, often white; thus the common name "mistletoe cactus."

Sansevieria is a genus of borderline leaf succulents, including the "mother-in-law's tongue" often found in homes and shopping malls. It's been placed in various families by different authorities. Sansevierias come from Africa.

Sarcocaulon is similar to the succulent pelargoniums, but its species have spines and somewhat different flowers. They, too, are winter growers.

Selenicereus macdonaldiae comes from Central America. It's a vining cactus whose white flowers last one night and are the largest among all the cacti, giving rise to the common name "queen of the night."

Stapelianthus neronis is an exceedingly rare Madagascan stem succulent in the milkweed family.

Of course, it's difficult to visualize a plant from a couple of lines of description. If you'd like to see photos of some of the types mentioned in this book, and you've been seduced by the Internet, point your web browser to http://walpow.com, a site belonging to one of the other guys in the Culver City Cactus Club. Gina designed it, by the way. Part of her recent alarming streak of computer geekdom.